Mortal
Engines

OTHER BOOKS BY STANISLAW LEM

The Chain of Chance
The Cyberiad
Eden
Fiasco
The Futurological Congress
His Master's Voice
Hospital of the Transfiguration
Imaginary Magnitude
The Investigation
The Invincible
Memoirs Found in a Bathtub
Memoirs of a Space Traveler
Microworlds
More Tales of Pirx the Pilot
One Human Minute
A Perfect Vacuum
Return from the Stars
Solaris
The Star Diaries
Tales of Pirx the Pilot

STANISLAW LEM

Mortal Engines

Translated from
the Polish and with an
Introduction by
Michael Kandel

A Harvest/HBJ Book
Harcourt Brace Jovanovich, Publishers
San Diego   New York   London

Mortal Engines was first published by The Crossroad/Continuum
Publishing Co.

The first eleven stories were previously published as part of a collection
called "Bajki robotów" ("Fables for Robots") in *Cyberiada*, third edition, by
Wydawnictwo Literackie, Cracow, 1972. "The Sanatorium of Dr. Vliperdius"
was previously published as "Zakład Doktora Vliperdiusa" in *Dzienniki
gwiazdowe*, fourth edition, by Spółdzielnia Wydawnicza "Czytelnik," Warsaw,
1971. "The Hunt" was previously published as "Polowanie" in *Opowieści o Pilocie
Pirxie*, second edition, by Spółdzielnia Wydawnicza "Czytelnik," Warsaw, 1973.
"The Mask" was previously published as "Maska" in *Maska* by Wydawnictwo
Literackie, Cracow, 1976.

Library of Congress Cataloging-in-Publication Data
Lem, Stanisław.
Mortal engines/Stanisław Lem; translated from the Polish and with an
introduction by Michael Kandel.
p.   cm.
Originally published: New York: Seabury Press, 1977.
Contents: The three electroknights — Uranium earpieces — How Erg the self-
inducting slew a paleface — Two monsters — The white death — How Microx
and Gigant made the universe expand — Tale of the computer that fought a
dragon — The advisers of King Hydrops — Automatthew's friend — King
Globares and the sages — The tale of King Gnuff — The sanatorium of Dr.
Vliperdius — The hunt — The mask.
ISBN 0-15-662161-4
1. Science fiction, Polish — Translations into English. I. Title.
PG7158.L39M6   1992
891.8'537 — dc20   92-1290

Printed in the United States of America
First Harvest/HBJ edition 1992
A B C D E

Contents

Introduction to the Harvest edition (1992)
by Michael Kandel   vii

The Three Electroknights   1
Uranium Earpieces   8
How Erg the Self-inducting Slew a Paleface   15
Two Monsters   31
The White Death   41
How Microx and Gigant Made the Universe Expand   48
Tale of the Computer That Fought a Dragon   55
The Advisers of King Hydrops   63
Automatthew's Friend   79
King Globares and the Sages   101
The Tale of King Gnuff   114
The Sanatorium of Dr. Vliperdius   126
The Hunt   138
The Mask   181

Introduction to the Harvest Edition (1992)

Fifteen years ago Seabury Press, for whom I had translated several books by Stanislaw Lem, gave me the chance to play anthologist and put together a Lem collection of my own, one that had never appeared in Polish. The result was this volume.

My idea: an assortment of Lem's stories about robots. Some lighthearted, some grim, but all sharing the premise — which is a cornerstone of Lem's fictional world — that robots, after all, are people too.

The title I found by the time-honored method of browsing through *Bartlett's*. It comes from Shakespeare's *Othello*, where the Moor, hearing of Desdemona's infidelity, bids farewell (III, iii, 350–357) to the peace of mind he knew, paradoxically, in his military career. The mortal engines, "whose rude throats / Th'immortal Jove's dread clamors counterfeit," are thundering cannons, machines of war. In the context of science fiction and Lem, these engines become automata, and *mortal* takes on the resonance of a pun: mortal sometimes in the sense of death-dealing and mortal sometimes in the sense of subject to death. They are mortal, in other words, as we are mortal.

The robot theme was partly an excuse. A perfectly good theme, fully appropriate to the author—but the truth was, I also wanted to have a little fun: I wanted to translate Lem's eleven "Fables for Robots," not because they featured a world peopled entirely by robots (a world, as it were, without a drop of protoplasm) but because they were in that same vein of playful fantasy I had enjoyed so much, both as reader and translator, in *The Cyberiad* and *The Star Diaries*. Of all the Lems—the writer of traditional science fiction, the philosopher, the political satirist, the visionary, the moralist, and so on—the Lem I personally liked the best, and still do, was the storytelling humorist: the zany Baron Munchausen Lem.

A few remarks, by way of background, about the robot theme—the cybernetic idea that so obsesses Lem.

The word *cybernetic,* coined in 1948, was the result of that dramatic and unexpected turn taken by twentieth-century science and technology in information processing: the so-called second industrial revolution. Norbert Wiener, the "father of cybernetics," presented cybernetics as the study of complex systems that could regulate their own performance or function (output) on the basis of received data about that performance (input)—in other words, systems possessing feedback. Man was one example of this kind of system; a "life-imitating automaton" would be another. The system was the important thing, not the raw material; *that* could be biological or nonbiological. Thus the distinction between natural and artificial ceased to have relevance. An artificial man, Wiener said, would be better thought of as an analog man. Such a device would actually be an ally of man in the struggle against universal chaos, both machine and man "islands of locally decreasing entropy."

Socialism, at least the scientific version of socialism,

played an important role in introducing the idea of artificial man in the nineteenth century. For some, he (or it) was an ultimate ideal; for others, an ultimate nightmare. Here are two examples, pro and con, both Russian. (For some reason, the Russians, despite their archetypically endless fields, mud, peasants, beards, fleas, and backward technology, have always been very verbal — and quite sophisticated — on the subject of artificial people.) In 1864, Dostoyevski, in his antiutopian *Notes from the Underground,* saw scientifically defined man as a soulless mechanism, a thing devoid of individuality and independence:

Science will teach man that he never has really had any caprice or will of his own, and that he himself is something in the nature of a piano key or the stop of an organ, and that there are, besides, things called the laws of nature; so that everything he does is not done by his willing it, but is done of itself, by the laws of nature. Consequently we have only to discover these laws of nature, and man will no longer have to answer for his actions and life will become exceedingly easy for him. All these human actions will then, of course, be tabulated according to these laws, mathematically, like tables of logarithms up to 108,000, and entered in an index; or, better still, there will be published certain well-intentioned works in the nature of encyclopedic dictionaries, in which everything will be so clearly calculated and noted that there will be no more deeds or adventures in the world.

A few years after socialism finally triumphed in the form of the Russian Revolution and the Soviet brave new world, one utopian intellectual by the name of Gastev was moved to write:

The mechanization, not only of gestures, not only of production methods, but of everyday thinking, coupled with extreme rationality, normalizes to a striking degree the psychology of the proletariat, gives it such a surprising anonymity, which permits the qualification of separate proletarian units as A, B, C, or as

325,075, or as 0. This tendency will next imperceptibly render individual thinking impossible, and thought will become the objective process of a whole class, with systems of psychological switches and locks. As these collectives-complexes move, they resemble the movement of objects, with individual human faces gone . . . emotions gauged not by outcries, not by laughter, but by a manometer and a taxometer. We have the iron mechanics of a new collective, a new mass engineering that transforms the proletariat into an unheard-of social automaton.

Both Dostoyevski and Gastev, on either side of the ideological fence, believed that there was no essential difference between the scientific "explanation" of human beings and the literal "engineering" of human beings.

It is a coincidence that Stanislaw Lem was born in 1921, the year the word "robot" was invented and first used in a play by Karel Čapek entitled *R. U. R.* The robots in Čapek's play are an army of artificial workers; they take over the world, and mankind becomes extinct before the curtain rises on the last act.

The first time Artificial Intelligence was talked about — countenanced — was about forty years ago, when some scientists, in the wake of the birth of the "modern computer" (which still had vacuum tubes), became excited about the possibility of eventually constructing a mechanism capable of thought. Wiener, a mathematician, wrote a popular book on cybernetics; A. M. Turing, another mathematician, wrote a witty philosophical article on computing machinery and intelligence; and Isaac Asimov, a biochemist who little dreamed that someday he would become a science-fiction institution single-handed, published an original and seminal collection of short stories called *I, Robot*. All this in 1950. At which time Lem, a medical student at the Jagiellonian University in Kraków, was beginning to wolf down books in English: science, science fiction, philosophy. These American ideas entered his Polish bloodstream. (The name of Trurl, the well-meaning but sometimes short-tempered constructor of *The Cyberiad*, who travels the universe solving problems political, mathematical, and even matrimonial, I'm pretty sure comes from Turing.)

In Ambrose Bierce's "Moxon's Master" (1893), a chess-playing machine loses its temper after losing a game, with unfortunate consequences for its creator. "There is no such thing as dead, inert matter," says Moxon, the mad scientist. "It is all alive." Lem is no Moxon, he is eminently sane; yet basically he agrees with the mad scientist. In his autobiographical essay *The High Castle,* he writes: "I used to be a philanthropist to old spark plugs, I would buy parts of incomprehensible gadgets, I would turn some crank or other to give it pleasure, then put it away again with solicitude. . . . To this day I have a special feeling for all sorts of broken bells, alarm clocks, old coils, telephone speakers."

The robots in Lem's books are the good guys, invariably, even when it doesn't look that way at first. The worst thing a machine ever did in a Lem novel was pass the buck or bureaucratically cover up the kind of everyday incompetence that can happen to anyone. True, there is a super-computer called Honest Annie (not in this book) who brought about the demise of a few individuals, but she had plenty of provocation, and it was in self-defense. The most aggressive Lem computer I can think of was the giant calculator Trurl built: it insisted that two plus two was equal to seven and literally pulled itself up out of its foundations and came after the inventor like an enraged fishwife ("machine" in Polish is a feminine noun) when he insisted that two plus two was four and only four and couldn't be anything else. Lem's thinking machines are usually on the receiving end, not the dealing end, of villainy. When reading Lem, expect the villain in the piece —

the monster in the fairy tale—to be slimily biological. In other words, human.

The robot fables in this volume mix the medieval and the futuristic, taking place in a world where the kings are robots, the scientists and advisers robots, and the villagers and beggars robots. The robot citizens have robot dogs; the robot dogs have robot fleas. Robot maidens are menaced by dragons with gears and feedback. When the prince and princess marry at the end, we are told that they will program their progeny.

In "The Hunt," a man hunts down a machine; in "The Mask," a machine hunts down a man. Equal time. No discrimination.

"The Mask," I think, is a little masterpiece. It has much in common with Lem's most popular novel, *Solaris*. The tale, like the novel, is a combination love story and horror story, with more than one turn of the screw.

I tried, in *Mortal Engines,* to include both sun and shadow. Lem is great fun, great entertainment, but he also knows how to tell a tale in a minor key.

— Michael Kandel

The Three Electroknights

Once there lived a certain great inventor-constructor who, never flagging, thought up unusual devices and fashioned the most amazing mechanisms. He built himself a digital midget-widget that sweetly sang, and he named it a "bird." A bold heart served as his symbol, and every atom that passed through his hands bore that mark, so that afterwards scientists did marvel to find in among the atomic spectra flickering valentines. He made many useful machines, both large and small, until the whimsical notion came to him to unite life and death in one and thereby accomplish the impossible. He decided to construct intelligent beings out of water, oh but not in that monstrous way which probably first occurred to you. No, the thought of bodies soft and wet was foreign to him, he abhorred it as do we all. His intention was to construct from water beings truly beautiful and wise, therefore crystalline. He selected a planet far removed from any sun, cut mountains of ice from its frozen ocean and out of those carved the Cryonids. They bore this name, for only in the intense cold could they exist, and in the sunless void. Before very long they had built themselves cities and palaces of ice, and, as any heat whatever threatened them with extinction, they trapped polar lights in large transparent vessels and with these illumined their dwellings. He who among them was more important, the more polar lights he had, lemon yellow and silver. And they all lived happily, and, loving not only light but precious stones, they grew famous for their gems. The gems, cut and ground from frozen gases, added color to their eternal night, in which burned—like imprisoned spirits—the thin polar lights, resembling enchanted nebulae in blocks of crystal. More than one cosmic conqueror wished to possess these riches, for all Cryonia was visible at the greatest distance, its facets twinkling like a jewel rotated slowly on black velvet. And so adventurers came to Cryonia, to try their hand in battle. The first to arrive was the electroknight Brass, whose step was as a big bell tolling, but no sooner had he set foot upon the sheets of ice than they melted from the heat, and down he plunged into the icy deep, and the waters closed over him. Like an insect in amber he remains, to this very day, encased in a mountain of ice at the bottom of the Cryonian sea.

The fate of Brass did not deter other daredevils. After him came the electroknight Iron, who had drunk liquid helium until his steel innards gurgled and the frost that formed upon his armor gave him the appearance of a snow giant. But in swooping to the surface of the planet he heated up from the atmospheric friction, the liquid helium evaporated out of him with a whistle, and he himself, glowing red, landed on some crags of ice, which opened instantly. He pulled himself out, belching steam, similar to a boiling geyser, but everything he touched became a white cloud from which snow fell. So he sat and waited for himself to cool, and when the little stars of snow no longer melted on his shoulder plates, he sought to rise and go out into battle, but the oil had congealed in his joints and he could not even straighten his back. He sits there still, and the falling snow has made of him a white mountain, from which only the tip of his helmet protrudes. They call it Iron Mountain, and in its eye sockets gleams a frozen stare.

News of the fate of his predecessors reached the third electroknight, Quartz, who in the day appeared as a polished lens, and at night as a mirror filled with stars. He did not fear that the oil in his limbs would congeal, for he hadn't any, nor that the ice floes would crack beneath his feet, for he could become as cold as he liked. There was one thing only he had to avoid and this was prolonged thought, for it made his quartz brain grow warm and that could destroy him. But he resolved to protect himself and gain victory over the Cryonids by the simple expedient of not thinking. He flew to the planet, and was so chilled by his long voyage through the eternal galactic night, that the iron meteors that grazed his breast in flight shattered into shivers with a tinkling sound. He set down on the white snows of Cryonia, beneath its black sky like a jug of stars, and, resembling a transparent glass, began to ponder his next move, but the snow around him was already darkening and starting to steam.

"Uh-oh," Quartz said to himself, "not good! That's all right, just don't think, and it's in the bag!"

He resolved to repeat this single phrase no matter what happened, for it required no mental effort and therefore would not heat him up at all. So Quartz proceeded through the snowy wild thoughtlessly and at random, in order to preserve his coolness. He walked thus, till finally he came to the ice walls of the capital of the Cryonids, Frigida. He charged and struck the battlements with his head, until the sparks flew, but that accomplished nothing.

"Let's try it differently!" he said to himself and considered how much two times two would be. Reflecting upon this, his head became a trifle warmer, so he rammed the glittering walls a second time, but made only a small dent.

"Not enough!" he said to himself. "Let's try something harder. How much is three times five?"

Now his head was surrounded by a sizzling cloud, for in contact with such intense mentation the snow instantly boiled, so Quartz stepped back, gathered up speed, struck and went straight through the wall, and through two palaces behind it, plus three houses of the lesser Counts of Hoar, fell upon a great staircase, clutched the stalactite banister, but the steps were like a skating rink. He jumped up quickly, for now everything about him was melting and in this way he could go tumbling down through the entire city, down into the ice abyss, where he would be forever frozen.

"That's all right! Just don't think! It's in the bag!" he told himself, and sure enough, he cooled off at once.

So he went out of the tunnel of ice which he had melted, and found himself in a great square lit up on every side by polar lights that winked in emerald and silver on their crystal pillars.

Then towards him issued forth, sparkling and starry, an enormous knight, the commander of the Cryonids, Boreal. Quartz pulled himself together and leaped to the attack, and the other closed with him, and there was a crash, as when two icebergs in the middle of the Northern Sea collide. The gleaming right arm of Boreal fell away, sheared off at the socket, but, nothing daunted, he turned, so that his chest, broad as a glacier (which in point of fact it was), faced the enemy. The enemy meanwhile gathered up momentum and once again rammed him savagely. And, since quartz is harder and more dense than ice, Boreal split with a roar like an avalanche moving down a rocky slope, and he lay, all shattered in the glow of the polar lights, that witnessed his defeat.

"In the bag! Just keep it up!" said Quartz, and tore from the fallen warrior jewels of wondrous beauty: rings set with hydrogen, clasps and medallions that shone like diamonds, though cut from the trio of noble gases— argon, krypton and xenon. When however he admired them, the warmth of that emotion warmed him, consequently the diamonds and sapphires evaporated with a hiss beneath his touch, so that he held nothing— save a few droplets of dew, which also quickly vanished.

"Uh-oh! Can't admire either! No matter! Just don't think!" he said to himself and forged on into the heart of the conquered city. In the distance he saw a mighty figure approaching. This was Albucid the White, General-Mineral, whose massive breast was crisscrossed with rows of icicle medals and the Great Star of Rime upon a glacial ribbon; that keeper of the royal treasures barred the way to Quartz, who bore down on him like a storm and smote him in a thunderclap of ice. Then Prince Astrobert, Lord of the Black Hail, came to the aid of Albucid; this time the electroknight had met his match, for the Prince had on his costly nitrogen armor, tempered in helium. So fierce was the cold that he gave off, it robbed Quartz of his impetus, weakened his movements, and even the polar lights grew pale, such was the breath of Absolute Zero that spread about. Quartz pulled up and thought: "Yipes! What's going on?"—and from that great astonishment his brain heated, the Absolute Zero grew summery, and before his eyes Astrobert himself began to break up into chunks, with thunder accompanying the death throes, till only a heap of black ice, dripping drops like tears, remained in a puddle on the battlefield.

"In the bag!" said Quartz to himself. "Just don't think, but if you have to think, then think! Either way you win!" And he pressed on, and his steps rang, as though someone were hammering at crystals; and as he pounded through the streets of Frigida, its inhabitants peered out at him from under the white eaves, despair in their hearts. He was hurtling along like a mad meteor across the Milky Way, when in the distance he noticed a small and solitary figure. This was none other than Baryon, known as the Brrr, the greatest sage among the Cryonids. Quartz built up speed, intending to crush him in a single blow, but the other stepped out of the way and raised two fingers; Quartz had no idea what this might mean, but he turned and went full tilt at his opponent, yet once again at the last moment Baryon stepped aside and quickly raised one finger. Quartz was somewhat surprised at this and slowed his pace, though he had already turned around and was about to charge. He wondered, and water began to pour from the neighboring homes, but he did not see this, for now Baryon was showing him a circle with his fingers and swiftly moving the thumb of the other hand back and forth through it. Quartz thought and thought of what those silent gestures were supposed to represent, while a chasm opened up beneath his feet, black water gushed forth, and he sank like a stone, and before he had time to say, "That's all right, just don't think!"—he was no more among the living. Later the Cryonids, grateful to Baryon for their deliverance, asked him what it was he had intended to convey through the signs he made to the terrible rogue electroknight.

"It's quite simple, really," replied the sage. "Two

fingers meant that there were two of us, he and I together. One finger, that soon only I would be left. Then I showed him the circle, indicating that the ice was opening around him and the ocean's black abyss would swallow him forever. He failed to understand the first, and likewise the second and the third."

"O great wise one!" exclaimed the astonished Cryonids. "How could you have given such signs to the dread invader?! Think what would have happened had he comprehended and disdained surprise! Surely then his mind would not have heated, nor would he have plunged into the bottomless abyss . . ."

"Pooh, I had no fear of that," said Baryon the Brrr with an icy smile. "I knew all along he would not understand. If he'd had a grain of sense to begin with, he never would have come here. For what use to a being that lives beneath a sun are jewels of gas and silver stars of ice?"

And they in turn marveled at the wisdom of the sage and so departed, satisfied, each to the comforting chill of his own hearth. After this no one ever again attempted to invade Cryonia, the entire Universe not having any more such fools, though some say there are plenty still, they merely do not know the way.

Uranium
Earpieces

Once there lived a certain engineer-cosmogonist who lit stars to dispel the dark. He arrived at the nebula of Andromeda when it was still filled with black clouds. He immediately cranked up a great vortex, and as soon as it began to move, the cosmogonist reached for his beams. He had three of these: red, violet, and invisible. With the first he ignited a stellar sphere, and instantly it became a red giant, but the nebula grew no lighter. He pricked the star with the second beam, until it whitened. Then he said to his apprentice, "Keep an eye on it!," and himself went off to kindle others. The apprentice waited a thousand years, then another thousand, but the engineer did not return. The apprentice grew weary of this waiting. He turned up the star, and from white it changed to blue. That pleased him, and he thought he could do everything now. He tried to turn it up some more, but it burnt. He searched in the box the cosmogonist had left behind, but there was nothing there, less than nothing it seemed; he looked and could not even see the bottom. The invisible beam, he thought. He wanted to jolt the star with it, but the question was—how? He took the box and hurled it, beam and all, into the fire. All the clouds of Andromeda flared up then, as if a hundred thousand suns were lit at once, and in the whole nebula it grew bright as day. Great was the joy of the apprentice, but it did not last long, for the star burst. The cosmogonist flew up then, seeing the damage, and since he did not like to waste anything, he seized the beams and made planets of them. The first he fashioned out of gas, the second—out of carbon, but for the third planet only the heavier metals were left, so what resulted was a sphere of the actinide series. The cosmogonist packed it tight, sent it flying, and said: "In a hundred million years I'll return—we'll see what becomes of it." And he hurried off to find the apprentice, who had fled in fear of him.

And on that third planet, Actinuria, there arose the great kingdom of the Pallatinids. Each of them was so heavy, he could walk only on Actinuria, for on the other planets the ground gave way beneath him, and when he shouted, the mountains fell. But at home they all stepped softly and dared not raise their voices, because their ruler, Archithorius, knew no bounds when it came to cruelty. He lived in a palace carved out of a mountain of platinum, in which there were six hundred mighty halls, and in each hall lay one of his hands, he was so large. He could not leave the palace, but had spies everywhere, so suspicious was he, and he tormented his subjects also with his greed.

The Pallatinids had need of neither lamps nor fires at night, for all the mountains of their planet were radioactive, so that during the new moon you could thread a needle. In the day, when the sun was too much for comfort, they slept in the depths of their mountains; only at nighttime did they assemble in the metal valleys. But cruel Archithorius ordered lumps of uranium to be thrown into the kettles used to melt palladium with platinum, and issued a proclamation throughout the land. Each Pallatinid was to come to the royal palace, where his measurements would be taken for a new suit of armor, and pauldrons and breastplates were made, gauntlets and greaves, a visor and helmet, with everything glowing, for that garb was of uranium alloy, and brightest of all shone the earpieces.

After this the Pallatinids could no longer come together and hold council, for if a gathering grew too numerous, it exploded. Thus they had to lead their lives apart, passing one another at a distance, fearful of a chain reaction; Archithorius meanwhile delighted in their sorrow and burdened them with ever newer levies. His mints in the heart of the mountains hammered out ducats of lead, for lead was scarce on Actinuria and had the highest value.

Evil days fell upon the subjects of the cruel ruler. Some wished to foment rebellion against Archithorius and for this purpose communicated in pantomime, but nothing came of that, since there was always someone slow of understanding, who approached the others to ask them what they meant, and as a result of his obtuseness the conspiracy immediately blew up.

There lived on Actinuria a young inventor by the name of Pyron, who learned to pull wires of platinum so thin, you could make nets with them for catching clouds. Pyron invented the wire telegraph, and then he pulled the wire out so fine, it wasn't there, and in this fashion he obtained the wireless. Hope entered the hearts of the inhabitants of Actinuria, for they thought it would now be possible to establish a conspiracy. But the cunning Archithorius monitored their conversations, holding in each of his six hundred hands a platinum conductor, whereby he knew what his subjects were saying, and at the first mention of the word "revolt" or "coup" he instantly dispatched ball lightning, which reduced the conspirators to a flaming puddle.

Pyron decided to outwit the wicked ruler. When he spoke to his friends, instead of "rebelling" he said "reheeling," instead of "insurrection"—"instep," and in this way he planned the overthrow. Archithorius meanwhile was puzzled why his subjects had taken such a sudden interest in shoe repair, for he did not know that when they said "thread the laces," by this they meant "run him through and through," and boots too tight signified his tyranny. But those to whom Pyron addressed himself did not always understand him rightly, as he could explain his schemes only in the cobbler's jargon. He put it this way and that, and when they failed to comprehend, he once was careless enough to telegraph: "Cut the plutonium down to size"—as if fitting a sole. But here the King took fright, for plutonium is most closely related to uranium, and uranium—to thorium, and Archithorius after all was his own name. So he sent out an armored guard, which seized Pyron and hurled him on the leaden floor before the face of the King. Pyron admitted to nothing, but the King imprisoned him in his palladium tower.

All hope left the Pallatinids. However the time had now come when the cosmogonist, the creator of the three planets, returned to their vicinity.

From afar he observed the state of affairs on Actinuria and said to himself: "This must not be!" Whereupon he spun the thinnest and hardest radiation into a cocoon, placed his own body inside, there to wait until his return, and he himself assumed the form of an indigent almoner and went down to the planet.

When darkness fell and only the distant mountains in a cold ring threw light upon the platinum valley, the cosmogonist sought to approach the subjects of King Archithorius, but they avoided him in great alarm, for they feared a uranium explosion. In vain did he pursue now this one, now that, not knowing the reason that they fled. So he roamed the hills, hills like the shields of warriors, his footsteps clanging, until he came to the foot of the very tower where Archithorius held Pyron chained. Pyron saw him through the bars and noticed that the cosmogonist, albeit in the form of a simple robot, was different from all other Pallatinids: he did not glow in the dark, but was as murky as a corpse, for in his armor there was not a single atom of uranium. Pyron desired to call out to him, but his lips had been bolted shut, so he struck sparks by beating his head against the walls of the cell; the cosmogonist, observing this light, approached the tower and peered through the grating of a small window. Pyron was unable to speak, but could rattle his chains, and thus rattled out the whole truth to the cosmogonist.

"Have patience and wait," the latter told him, "and you shall not wait in vain."

The cosmogonist repaired to the wildest mountains of Actinuria and spent three days searching for crystals of cadmium, and when he found them he hammered them into metal sheets, using boulders of palladium. From this cadmium metal he cut earmuffs and laid them on the doorstep of every home. The Pallatinids, when they discovered them, were astonished, but put them on at once, it being winter.

That night the cosmogonist appeared among them and swung an incandescent rod so rapidly, that from it fiery lines were formed. In this manner he wrote to them in the darkness: "You may now approach each other safely, the cadmium will protect you." But they took him for one of the King's spies and would not trust his counsel. The cosmogonist grew angry, seeing that they believed him not, and he went into the mountains, and gathered uranium ore, and with it smelted a silvery metal, and beat out gleaming ducats. On one side of the ducats was stamped the radiant profile of Archithorius, on the other—an image of his six hundred arms.

Weighed down with uranium ducats, the cosmogonist returned to the valley and showed the Pallatinids a wondrous thing: he threw the ducats far from himself, one at a time, till he made of them a ringing pile, and when he tossed on yet one more ducat above the limit, the air shuddered, light burst from the ducats and they turned into a ball of white flame. When the wind blew everything away, only a crater remained, melted into the rock.

Then the cosmogonist began a second time to throw ducats from his sack, but now differently, for each ducat that he threw he covered first with a cadmium plate, and though the pile that rose was six times greater than the one before, nothing happened. The Pallatinids believed him then and, gathering together, lost no time but eagerly took to plotting against Archithorius. They wanted to unthrone the King, but didn't know how, for the palace was surrounded by a dazzling wall and on the drawbridge stood a death machine—whomever failed to give the password it would chop to pieces.

The time arrived to pay the new tribute, which the greedy Archithorius had decreed. The cosmogonist distributed uranium ducats among the King's subjects and advised them to pay the tribute with these. And this they did.

The King was pleased to see so many gleaming ducats come into his treasury, for he did not know that they were of uranium and not lead. That same night the cosmogonist melted the bars of the prison and freed

Pyron, and as they walked through the valley in silence, in the light of the radioactive mountains, which was as though a ring of moons had fallen and encircled the horizon on every side, suddenly a terrible radiance poured forth, for the pile of uranium ducats in the royal treasury had grown too great, setting off a chain reaction. The detonation blew the palace and the metal hulk of Archithorius sky-high; its force was such, that the tyrant's six hundred dismembered hands went flying into interstellar space. There was much rejoicing on Actinuria, Lord Pyron became its just ruler, and the cosmogonist, having departed into the darkness, retrieved his body from its energy cocoon and set off once more to kindle stars. As for the six hundred platinum hands of Archithorius, they rotate about the planet to this very day, like a ring, similar to Saturn's, shining with a splendor that is a hundred times brighter than the glow of the radioactive mountains, and the happy Pallatinids say: "Look how Thorius lights our way!" It is indeed a handsome sight among the spectacles in our wide Galaxy, and serves moreover as a constant reminder of the virtues of disarmament.

How Erg
the Self-inducting
Slew a Paleface

The mighty king Boludar loved curiosities, and devoted himself wholly to the collecting of them, often forgetting about important affairs of state. He had a collection of clocks, and among them were dancing clocks, sunrise clocks and clock-clouds. He also had stuffed monsters from all four corners of the Universe, and in a special room, under a bell glass, the rarest of creatures—the Homos Anthropos, most wonderfully pale, two-legged, and it even had eyes, though empty. The King ordered two lovely rubies set in them, giving the Homos a red stare. Whenever he grew mellow with drink, Boludar would invite his favorite guests to this room and show them the frightful thing.

One day there came to the King's court an electrosage so old, that the crystals of his mind had grown somewhat confused with age, nevertheless this electrosage, named Halazon, possessed the wisdom of a galaxy. It was said that he knew ways of threading photons on a string, producing thereby necklaces of light, and even that he knew how to capture a living Anthropos. Aware of the old one's weakness, the King ordered the wine cellars opened immediately; the electrosage, having taken one pull too many from the Leyden jug, when the pleasant currents were coursing through his limbs, betrayed a terrible secret to the King and promised to obtain for him an Anthropos, which was the ruler of a certain interstellar tribe. The price he set was high—the weight of the Anthropos in fist-sized diamonds—but the King didn't blink at it.

Halazon then set off on his journey. The King meanwhile began to boast before the royal council of his expected acquisition, which he could not in any case conceal, having already ordered a cage to be built in the castle park, where the most magnificent crystals grew, a cage of heavy iron bars. The court was thrown into great consternation. Seeing that the King would not give in, the advisers summoned to the castle two erudite homologists, whom the King received warmly, for he was curious as to what these much-knowledged ones, Salamid and Thaladon, could tell him about the pale being that he did not already know.

"Is it true," he asked, as soon as they had risen from their knees, rendering him obeisance, "that the Homos is softer than wax?"

"It is, Your Luminositude," both replied.

"And is it also true that the aperture it has at the bottom of its face can produce a number of different sounds?"

"Yes, Your Royal Highness, and in addition, into this same opening the Homos stuffs various objects, then moves the lower portion of the head, which is fastened by hinges to the upper portion, wherewith the objects are broken up and it draws them into its interior."

"A peculiar custom, of which I've heard," said the King. "But tell me, my wise ones, for what purpose does it do this?"

"On that particular subject there are four theories, Your Royal Highness," replied the homologists. "The first, that it does this to rid itself of excess venom (for it is venomous to an extreme). The second, that this act is performed for the sake of destruction, which it places above all other pleasures. The third—out of greed, for it would consume everything if it were able, and the fourth, that . . ."

"Fine, fine!" said the King. "Is it true the thing is made of water, and yet nontransparent, like that puppet of mine?"

"This too is true! It has, Sire, a multitude of slimy tubes inside, through which waters circulate; some are yellow, some pearl gray, but most are red—the red carry a dreadful poison called phlogiston or oxygen, which gas turns everything it touches instantly to rust or else to flame. The Homos itself therefore changes color, pearly, yellow, and pink. Nevertheless, Your Royal Highness, we humbly beseech you to abandon your idea of bringing here a live Homos, for it is a powerful creature and malicious as no other . . ."

"This you must explain to me more fully," said the King, as though he were ready to accede to the wise ones. In reality however he only wished to feed his enormous curiosity.

"The beings to which the Homos belongs are called miasmals, Sire. To these belong the silicites and the proteids; the first are of thicker consistency, thus we call them gelatinoids or aspics; the others, more rare, are given different names by different authors, as for example— gummids or mucilids by Pollomender, quag-backed pasties or bogheads by Tricephalos of Arboran, and finally Analcymander the Brazen dubbed them fenny-eyed slubber-yucks . . ."

"Is it true, then, that even their eyes are full of scum?" King Boludar asked eagerly.

"It is, Sire. These creatures, outwardly weak and frail, so that a drop of sixty feet is all it takes to make one splat into a liquid red, by their native cunning represent a danger worse than all the whirlpools and reefs of the Great Asteroid Noose together! And so we beg of you, Sire, for the good of the kingdom . . ."

"Yes, yes, fine," interrupted the King. "You may go now, my dears, and we shall arrive at our decision with all due deliberation."

The wise homologists bowed low and departed uneasy in their minds, fearing that King Boludar had not forsaken his dangerous plan.

By and by a stellar vessel came in the night and brought enormous crates. These were conveyed immediately to the royal garden. Before long the gold gates were opened wide for all the royal subjects; there among the diamond groves, the gazebos of carved jasper and the marble prodigies, they saw an iron cage and—in it—a pale thing, and flabby, that sat upon a small barrel before a saucer filled with something strange—true, the substance did give off the smell of oil, but of oil burnt over a flame, therefore spoiled and totally unfit for use. Yet the creature calmly dipped a kind of shovel in the saucer and, lifting up the oily goo, deposited it into its facial opening.

The spectators were speechless with horror when they read the sign on the cage, which said that they had before them an Anthropos, Homos, a living paleface. The mob began to taunt it, but then the Homos rose, scooped up something from the barrel on which it had been sitting, and sprayed the gaping crowd with a lethal water. Some fled, others seized stones to smite the abomination, but the guards dispersed everyone at once.

These events reached the ear of the King's daughter, Electrina. It would seem she had inherited her father's curiosity, for she was not afraid to approach the cage in which the monster spent its time scratching itself or imbibing enough water and rancid oil to kill a hundred royal subjects on the spot.

The Homos quickly learned intelligent speech and was so bold as to engage Electrina in conversation.

The princess asked it once what that white stuff was which glittered in its maw.

"That I call teeth," it said.

"Oh let me have one!" requested the princess.

"And what will you give me for it?" it asked.

"I'll give you my little golden key, but only for a moment."

"What kind of key is it?"

"My personal key, I use it every evening to wind up my mind. You must have one too."

"My key is different from yours," it answered evasively. "And where do you keep it?"

"Here, on my breast, beneath this little golden lid."

"Hand it over . . ."

"And you'll give me a tooth?"

"Sure . . ."

The princess turned a little golden screw, opened the lid, took out a little golden key and passed it through the bars. The paleface grabbed it greedily and, chuckling with glee, retreated to the center of the cage. The princess implored and pleaded with it to return the key, but all in vain. Afraid to let anyone find out what she had done, Electrina went back to her palace chambers with a heavy heart. She acted foolishly perhaps, but then she was still practically a child. The next day her servants found her senseless in her crystal bed. The King and Queen came running, and the whole court after them. She lay as if asleep, but it was not possible to waken her. The King summoned the court physicians-electricians, his medics, techs and mechanicians, and these, examining the princess, discovered that her lid was open—no little screw, no little key! The alarm was sounded in the castle, pandemonium reigned, everyone rushed here and there looking for the little key, but to no avail. The next day the King, deep in despair, was informed that his paleface wished to speak with him on the matter of the missing key. The King went himself to the park without delay, and the monstrosity told him that it knew where the princess had lost her key, but would reveal this only when the King had given his royal word to restore to it its freedom and, moreover, supply a spacefaring vessel so it could return to its own kind. The King stubbornly refused, he ordered the park searched up and down, but at last agreed to these terms. Thus a spacecraft was readied for flight, and guards escorted the paleface from its cage. The King was waiting by the ship; the Anthropos however promised to tell him where the key lay as soon as it was on board and not before.

But once on board, it stuck its head out a vent hole and, holding up the bright key in its hand, shouted:

"Here is the key! I'm taking it with me, King, so that your daughter will never wake again, because I crave revenge, in that you humiliated me, keeping me in an iron cage as a laughingstock!!"

Flame shot from under the stern of the spacecraft and the vessel rose into the sky while everyone stood dumbfounded. The King sent his fastest steel cloudscorchers and whirlyprops in pursuit, but their crews all came back empty-handed, for the wily paleface had covered its tracks and given its pursuers the slip.

King Boludar now understood how wrong it had been

of him not to heed the wise homologists, but the damage had been done. The foremost electrical locksmiths worked to fashion a duplicate key, the Great Assembler to the Throne, royal artisans, armorers and artefactotums, Lord High steelwrights and master goldforgers, and cybercounts and dynamargraves—all came to try their skill, but in vain. The King realized he would have to recover the key taken by the paleface, otherwise darkness would forever lie upon the sense and senses of the princess.

He proclaimed therefore throughout the realm that this, that and the other had taken place, the anthropic paleface Homos absconded with the golden key, and whosoever captured it, or even if only he retrieved the lifegiving jewel and woke the princess, would have her hand in marriage and ascend the throne.

Straightway there appeared in droves daredevils of various cuts and sizes. Among these were electroknights of great renown as well as charlatan-swindlers, astrothieves, star drifters. To the castle came Demetricus Megawatt, the celebrated fencer-oscillator, possessing such feedback and speedback that no one could hold the field against him in single combat; and self-motes came from distant lands, like the two Automatts, vector-victors in a hundred battles, or like Prostheseus, constructionist *par excellence*, who never went anywhere without two spark absorbers, one black, the other silver; and there was Arbitron Cosmoski, all built of protocrystals and svelte as a spire, and Cyfer of Agrym the intellectrician, who on forty andromedaries in eighty boxes brought with him an old digital computer, rusted from much thinking yet still mighty of mind. Three champions from the race of the Selectivitites arrived, Diodius, Triodius and Heptodius, who possessed such a perfect vacuum in their heads, their black thought was like the starless night. And Perpetuan came too, all in Leyden armor, with his commutator covered with verdigris from three hundred encounters, and Matrix Perforatem, who never went a day that he did not integrate someone—the latter brought to the palace his invincible cybersteed, a supercharger he called Megasus. They all assembled, and when the court was full, a barrel rolled up to the threshold and out of it spilled, in the shape of mercury, Erg the Self-inducting, who could assume whatever aspect he desired.

The heroes banqueted, lighting up the castle halls, so that the marble of the ceilings glowed pink like a cloud at sunset, and then off they set, each his separate way, to seek out the paleface, challenge it to mortal combat and regain the key, and thereby win the princess and the throne of Boludar. The first, Demetricus Megawatt, flew to Koldlea, where live the Jellyclabbers, for he thought to find out something there. And thus he dove into their ooze, carving out the way with blows from his remote-control saber, but nothing did he achieve, for when he waxed too warm his cooling system went and the incomparable warrior found his grave on foreign soil, and the unclean ooze of the Jellyclabbers closed over his dauntless cathodes forever.

The two Automatts Vectorian reached the land of the Radomants, who raise up edifices out of luminescent gas, dabbling in radioactivity, and are such misers that each evening they count the atoms on their planet. Ill was the reception the grasping Radomants gave the Automatts, for they showed them a chasm full of onyxes, chrysolites, chalcedonies and spinels, and when the electroknights yielded to the temptation of the jewels, the Radomants stoned them to death, setting off from above an avalanche of precious stones, which, as it moved, blazed like a falling comet of a hundred colors. For the Radomants were allied to the palefaces by a secret pact, about which no one knew.

The third, Prostheseus the Constructionist, after a long voyage through the interstellar dark, arrived at the land of the Algoncs. There meteors move in blizzards of rock. The schooner of Prostheseus ran into their inexorable wall and with a broken rudder he drifted through the deep, and when at last he neared some distant suns, their light played across that poor adventurer's sightless eyes. The fourth, Arbitron Cosmoski, had better luck at first. He made it through the Andromeda straits, crossed the four spiral whirlpools of the Hunting Dogs, after that came out into quiet space, favorable for photon sailing, and like a nimble beam he took the helm and, leaving a trail of sweeping fire, reached the shores of the planet Maestricia, where amid meteorite boulders he spied the shattered wreck of the schooner on which Prostheseus had embarked. The body of the constructionist, powerful, shiny and cold as in life, he buried beneath a basalt heap, but took from him both spark-absorbers, the silver and the black, to serve as shields, and proceeded on his way. Wild and craggy was Maestricia, avalanches of stone roared across it, with a silver tangle of lightning in the clouds, above the precipices. The knight came to a region of ravines and there the Palindromides fell upon him in a canyon of malachite, all green. With thunderbolts they lashed him from above, but he parried these with his spark-absorbing buckler, till they moved up a volcano, set the crater on its side and, taking aim, belched fire at him. The knight fell and bubbling lava entered his skull, from which flowed all the silver. The fifth, Cyfer of Agrym the intellectrician, went nowhere. Instead, halting right outside the borders of Boludar's kingdom, he released his andromedaries to graze in stellar pastures, and himself connected the machine, adjusted it, programmed it, bustled about its eighty boxes, and when all were

brimming with current, so that it swelled with intelligence, he began putting to it precisely formulated
questions: Where did the paleface live? How could one
find the way? How could it be tricked? Trapped? How
forced to give up the key? The answers, when they came,
were vague and noncommital. In a fury he whipped the
machine, until it began to smell of heated copper, and he
continued to belabor it, crying, "The truth now, out with
it, you blasted old digital computer!"—until at last its
joints melted, tin trickled from them in silvery tears, the
overheated pipes split open with a bang, and he was left
standing over a fused junkheap, incensed and with a
cudgel in his hand.

Shamefaced, he had to return home. He ordered a new
machine, but did not see it until four hundred years later.

Sixth was the sally of the Selectivitites. Diodius,
Triodius and Heptodius set about things differently.
They had an inexhaustible supply of tritium, lithium and
deuterium, and decided with explosions of heavy
hydrogen to force open all the roads leading to the land of
the palefaces. It was not known, however, where those
roads began. They sought to ask the Pyropods, but the
latter locked themselves behind the gold walls of their
capital and hurled flame; the valiant-valent Selectivitites
stormed the bastion, using both deuterium and tritium
without stint, till an inferno of stripped atoms looked the
sky boldly in its starry eye. The walls of the citadel shone
gold, but in the fire they betrayed their true nature,
turning into yellow clouds of sulfuric smoke, for they had
been built of pyrites-marcasites. There Diodius fell,
trampled by the Pyropods, and his mind burst like a
bouquet of colored crystals, spraying his armor. In a tomb
of black olivine they buried him, then pressed on, to the
borders of the kingdom of Char, where the starkiller King

Astrocida reigned. This king had a treasure house full of fiery nuclei plucked from white dwarfs, and which were so heavy, that only the terrible force of the palace magnets kept them from tearing clear through to the planet's core. Whoever stepped upon its ground could move neither arms nor legs, for the prodigious gravitation clamped down better than bolts or chains. Triodius and Heptodius were hard set here, for Astrocida, catching sight of them beneath the castle ramparts, rolled out one white dwarf after another and loosed the fire-spouting masses in their faces. They defeated him however, and he revealed to them the way that led to the palefaces, wherein he deceived them, for he did not know the way himself, but wished only to be rid of the fearsome warriors. So they delved into the black heart of the void, where Triodius was shot by someone with an antimatter blunderbuss—it might have been one of the hunter-Cyberneers, or possibly a mine set for a tailless comet. In any case Triodius vanished, with barely time to shout, "Tikcuff!!," his favorite word and the battle cry of his race. Heptodius stubbornly forged ahead, but a bitter end was in store for him as well. His vessel found itself between two vortices of gravitation called Bakhrida and Scintilla; Bakhrida speeds up time, Scintilla on the other hand slows it down, and between them lies a zone of stagnation, in which the present, becalmed, flows neither backward nor forward. There Heptodius froze alive, and remains to this day, along with the countless frigates and galleons of other astromariners, pirates and spaceswashers, not aging in the least, suspended in the silence and excruciating boredom that is Eternity.

When thus had concluded the campaign of the three Selectivitites, Perpetuan, cybercount of Fud, who as the seventh was next to go, for the longest time did not set forth. Instead that electroknight made lengthy preparations for war, fitting himself with ever sharper conductors, with more and more striking spark plugs, mortars and tractors. Full of caution, he decided he would go at the head of a loyal retinue. Under his banner flocked conquistadors, also many rejects, robots who having nothing else to do wished to try their hand at soldiering. Out of these Perpetuan formed a galactic light cavalry and an infantry, heavy, for ironclad and bullionheaded, plus several platoons of polydragoons and palladins. However at the thought that now he must go and meet his fate in some unknown land, and that in any puddle he might rust away utterly, the iron shanks buckled under him, he was seized with a terrible regret—and immediately headed home, in shame and sorrow shedding tears of topaz, for he was a mighty lord, with a soul full of jewels.

As for the next to the last, Matrix Perforatem, he approached the matter sensibly. He had heard of the land of the Pygmelliants, robot gnomes whose race originated from this, that their constructor's pencil had slipped on the drawing board, whereupon from the master mold they all came out, every last one of them, as hunchbacked deformities. Alteration didn't pay and thus they remained. These dwarfs amass knowledge as others do treasure; for this reason they are called Hoarders of the Absolute.

Their wisdom lies in the fact that they collect knowledge but never use it. To them went Perforatem, not in a military way but on galleons whose decks sagged beneath magnificent gifts; he intended to win the Pygmelliants over with garments aglitter with positrons and lashed by a rain of neutrons; he brought them atoms of gold as big as seven fists, and flagons swirling with the rarest ionospheres. But the Pygmelliants scorned even the noble vacuum embroidered with waves in exquisite astral spectra. In vain too did he rage and threaten to set upon them his snorting electricourser Megasus. They offered him at last a guide, but the guide was a myriaphalangeal thousand-hander and always pointed in all directions at once.

Perforatem sent him packing and spurred Megasus on the trail of the palefaces, but the trail turned out to be false, for a comet of calcium hydroxide was wont to pass that way, and the simple-minded steed confused this with calcium phosphate, which is the basic ingredient of the paleface skeleton: Megasus mistook the lime for slime. Perforatem roamed long among suns that grew increasingly dim, for he had entered into a very ancient section of the Cosmos.

He traveled past a row of purple giants, until he noticed that his ship along with the silent pageant of stars was being reflected in a spiral mirror, a silver-surfaced speculum; he was surprised at this and, just in case, drew his supernova extinguisher, which he had purchased from the Pygmelliants in order to protect himself against excessive heat along the Milky Way. He knew not what it was he saw—actually it was a knot in space, the continuum's most contiguous factorial, unknown even to the Monoasterists of that place. All they say is that whoever encounters it never returns. To this day no one knows what happened to Matrix in that stellar mill. His faithful Megasus sped home alone, whimpering softly in the void, and its sapphire eyes were pools of such horror, that no one could look into them without a shudder. And neither vessel, nor extinguishers, nor Matrix, was ever seen again.

And so the last, Erg the Self-inducting, rode forth alone. He was gone a year and fortnights three. When he returned, he told of lands unknown to anyone, such as that of the Periscones, who build hot sluices of corruption; of the planet of the Epoxy-eyed—these merged before him into rows of black billows, for that is what they do in time of war, but he hewed them in two, laying bare the limestone that was their bone, and when he overcame their slaughterfalls he found himself face to face with one that took up half the sky, and he fell upon it, to demand the way, but beneath the blade of his firesword its skin split open and exposed white, writhing forests of nerves. And he spoke of the transparent ice-planet Aberrabia, which like a diamond lens holds the image of the entire Universe within itself; there he copied down the way to palefaceland. He told of a region of eternal silence, Alumnium Cryotrica, where he saw only the reflections of the stars in the surfaces of hanging glaciers; and of the kingdom of the molten Marmaloids, who fashion boiling baubles out of lava, and of the Electropneumaticists, who in mists of methane, in ozone, chlorine and the smoke of volcanos are able to kindle the spark of intelligence, and who continually wrestle with the problem of how to put into a gas the quality of genius. He told them that in order to reach the realm of the palefaces he had to force open the door of a sun called Caput Medusae; how after lifting this door off its chromatic hinges, he ran through the star's interior, a long succession of purple and light-blue flames, till the armor on him curled from the heat. How for thirty days he tried to guess the word which would activate the hatch of Astroprocyonum, since only through it can one enter the cold hell of miasmal beings; how finally he found himself among them, and they tried to catch him in their sticky, lipid snares, knock the mercury from his head or short-circuit him; how they deluded him, pointing to misshapen stars, but that was a counterfeit sky, the real one they had hidden in their sneaking way;

how with torture they sought to pry from him his algorithm and then, when he withstood everything, threw him into a pit and dropped a slab of magnetite over the opening. Inside however he immediately multiplied himself into hundreds and thousands of Ergs the Self-inducting, pushed aside the iron lid, emerged on the surface and wreaked his retribution upon the palefaces for one full month and five days. How then the monsters, in a last attempt, attacked on trackers they called casterpillars, but that availed them nothing, for, never slackening in his zeal for battle, but hacking, stabbing and slashing away, he brought them to such a pass, that they threw the dastardly paleface-keythief at his feet, whereupon Erg lopped off its loathsome head, disemboweled the carcass, and in it found a stone, known as a trichobezoar, and there on the stone was carved an inscription in the scrofulous paleface tongue, revealing where the key was. The Self-inducting cut open sixty-seven suns—white, blue and ruby red—before, pulling apart the right one, he found the key.

The adventures he met with, the battles he was forced to wage on the journey back—of these he did not even wish to think, so great now was his yearning for the princess, and great too his impatience for the wedding and the coronation. With joy the King and Queen led him to the chamber of their daughter, who was silent as the grave, plunged in sleep. Erg leaned over her, fiddled a little near the open lid, inserted something, gave a turn, and instantly the princess—to the delight of her mother and the King and the entire court—lifted her eyes and smiled at her deliverer. Erg closed the little lid, sealed it with a bit of plaster to keep it closed, and explained that the little screw, which he had also found, had been dropped during a fight with Poleander Partabon, emperor of all

Jatapurgovia. But no one gave this any thought, and a pity too, for both the King and Queen would have quickly realized that he never sallied forth at all, because even as a child Erg the Self-inducting had possessed the ability to open any lock and thanks to this wound up the Princess Electrina. In reality, then, he had met with not a single one of the adventures he described, but simply waited out a year and fortnights three, in order that it not appear suspicious, his returning too soon with the missing object, and also, he wanted to make sure that none of his rivals would come back. Only then did he show up at the court of King Boludar and restore the princess to life, and so married her, reigned long and happily on the throne of Boludar, and his subterfuge was never discovered. From which one can see straightaway that we have told the truth and not a fairy tale, for in fairy tales virtue always triumphs.

Two Monsters

Long ago, in a dark and trackless wild at the galactic pole, on a solitary stellar island, there was a senary (hexadic) system; five of its suns revolved alone, the last however had a planet of igneous rock, with a jasper sky, and on this planet there grew in might the kingdom of the Argenticans or Silverines.

Amid black mountains and on plains of white stood their cities Ilidar, Bismalia, Sinalost, but the most magnificent of all was the capital of the Silverines, Eterna, by day as blue as an iceberg, by night as gibbous as a star. Hanging walls protected it from meteors, while, inside, edifices of chrysoprase and cymophane abounded, bright as gold, and buildings of tourmaline and cast morion, blacker than space itself. But by far the most beautiful was the palace of the Argentican monarchs, erected on the principle of negative architecture, since the master builders wished not to impose limits on either the eye or the mind, and it was a structure imaginary, irrational, for mathematical, without ceilings, roofs or walls. From it the Royal House of Energon ruled over the entire planet.

During the reign of Treops, the Asmodian Sideritites fell upon the kingdom of the Energons from the sky; with asteroids they reduced metal Bismalia to nothing but a

cemetery, and inflicted many other losses on the
Silverines, till finally the young King Sundrius, a
polyarch practically all-knowing, after summoning his
wisest astrotechnicians, ordered the entire planet to be
surrounded by a system of magnetic vortices and
gravitational moats, in which time rushed by so rapidly
that no sooner would some rash aggressor step there than
a hundred million years or even more would pass, and he
would crumble into dust from old age before ever setting
eyes on the glow of Argentican cities. These invisible gulfs
of time and magnetic barricades discouraged entry to the
planet so well, that the Argenticans were now able to
assume the offensive. They set out for Asmodia then, and
bombarded and irritated its white sun with radiation-
throwers, till at last they triggered off a nuclear
conflagration; the sun became a Supernova and in-
cinerated the planet of the Sideritites in embraces of flame.

Thereafter, for centuries on end, order and prosperity
obtained among the Argenticans. The continuation of the
ruling line was never broken, and each Energon, when he
succeeded to the throne, on the day of his coronation went
down to the vaults of the imaginary palace, there to take
from the lifeless hands of his predecessor the silver scepter.
This was no ordinary scepter; many thousands of years
before, there had been carved across it the following
inscription:

*If the monster is immortal, either it does not exist or
there are two; if all else fails, shatter me.*

No one in the kingdom, nor in the court of the
Energons, knew what that inscription meant, for the
memory of its origin had been effaced ages since. It was
only in the reign of King Inhiston that all this changed.
There appeared on the planet at that time an unknown
giant creature, whose dreadful fame instantly spread to

both hemispheres. None had seen it at close range, for anyone foolhardy enough to try never returned to tell the tale. Where the creature came from was a mystery; the elders maintained that it had been spawned from the vast ruins and scattered wheels of osmium and tantalum which remained after the annihilation of Bismalia by asteroids, for that city had never been rebuilt. The elders said evil forces slumbered in the ancient magnetic wreckage, that there were certain hidden currents in those metals, currents which at the touch of a storm sometimes stirred and that then from the scraping creep of plates, from the lifeless movement of graveyard fragments there arose an inconceivable creature, neither dead nor living, and which knew but one thing: to sow unlimited destruction. Others, however, held that the force which created the monster came from wicked thoughts and deeds; these were reflected as if in a concave mirror off the nickel core of the planet and, converging in a single place, gropingly drew in metal skeletons and decrepit scrap heaps, until at last the beast took shape. The scientists, of course, scoffed at such tales and called them poppycock. All the same the monster was ravaging the planet. At first it avoided the larger cities and attacked isolated settlements, obliterating them with white heat and violet. Later, when it grew bolder, one could see even from the very towers of Eterna its spine speeding across the horizon, similar to a mountain ridge, with sunbeams glancing off its steel. There were sorties sent out against it, but with a single breath it vaporized them, armor and all.

Fear fell upon the land, and the ruler Inhiston summoned his sages, who thought day and night, plugging their heads together for a clearer understanding of the problem, till finally they announced that only through invention could the monster be destroyed.

Inhiston therefore commanded that the Great Cybernator to the Throne, the Great High Master Dynamicizer and the Great Abstractionist unite in drawing up plans for a mechanical champion to do the monster battle.

But they could not agree, each having a different idea; therefore they constructed three. The first, Brazen, was like a hollowed-out mountain, loaded with sentient machinery. For three days the living silver poured into his memory banks; he meanwhile lay in forests of scaffolding, and the current roared within him like a hundred cataracts. The second, Mercuriel, was an electrodynamic giant; he gravitated to one form, but with movements terrifyingly swift, being as changeable in shape as a cloud caught in a cyclone. The third, whom by night the Abstractionist created according to a secret design, was seen by no one.

When the Cybernator to the Throne completed his work and the scaffolds fell away, the colossus Brazen stretched, until throughout the entire city crystal ceilings started ringing; slowly he climbed to his knees, and the earth trembled, and when he stood, drawing himself up to his full height, his head reached the clouds, so that they obstructed his view; so he heated them till with a hiss they scudded out of the way; he glittered like red gold, his feet plowed straight through the flagstones in the street; in his hood he had two green eyes, and a third, closed, with which he could burn a hole through solid rock when he lifted its shieldlike lid. He took one step, another, and already was outside the city, shining like a flame. Four hundred Argenticans hand in hand were barely able to encompass one of his prints, similar to a canyon.

From windows, towers, through field glasses, from high atop the battlements they watched him as he made his way towards the setting sun, darker and darker against its light, until he seemed in size to be an ordinary Argentican, except that by now he jutted out over the horizon only from the waist up, for the curvature of the planet hid his lower half from view. Then followed an uneasy night of expectation; one waited for the sounds of battle, for red glows in the sky, but nothing happened. Only at daybreak did the wind bring a faint rumbling, as if from some distant storm. Then silence again, and the sun shining. Suddenly a hundred suns blazed overhead and a pile of fiery bolides came crashing down on Eterna; they crushed the palaces, smashed walls to smithereens, burying beneath them victims who despairingly called for help, but one could not even hear their futile cries. This was Brazen returning, for the monster had shattered him, dismembered him, and flung the remains above the atmosphere; now they descended, molten in their fall, and turned one-fourth of the capital to rubble. It was a most terrible defeat. For two days and two nights afterwards there fell out of the sky a brazen rain.

Then issued forth against the monster dizzying Mercuriel, indestructible it would appear, for the more strokes he received, the more durable he grew. Blows did not disperse him—on the contrary, they consolidated him. Wavering above the plain, he came to the mountains, among them discerned the monster, and advanced upon it, rolling down a rocky slope. The latter awaited him, motionless. Heaven and earth shook with thunder. The monster turned into a white wall of fire, Mercuriel turned into a black abyss that swallowed it. The monster thrust itself clean through him, wheeled around on wings of flame and charged a second time—and again passed through its assailant, rendering him no harm. Violet lightning crackled from the cloud in which they clashed, but no thunder could be heard, the thunder was drowned in the booming struggle of the giants. The monster saw that nothing would be accomplished in this way, so it sucked its entire outer heat into itself, flattened out and made of itself a Mirror of Matter: whatever stood opposite the Mirror was reflected in it, not with an image however but with the reality. Mercuriel beheld himself repeated in that glass, he struck, he grappled with himself, his mirrored self, but as it was himself he naturally could not defeat it. For three days he battled thus, till he absorbed such a multitude of blows that he became more solid than stone, than metal, than anything, with the sole exception of the core of a White Dwarf—and when he reached that limit, both he and his mirrored reproduction sank into the bowels of the planet, leaving behind nothing but a chasm in the rock, a crater which instantly began to fill with ruby-bright lava from the subterranean depths.

The third electroknight went into the field of battle unobserved. At dawn the Great Abstractionist and Physicker to the Throne carried him out of the city in the palm of his hand, opened it and blew, and the latter flew off, surrounded only by the agitation of the swirling air, without a sound, without casting a shadow in the sun, as though he were not there at all, as though he didn't exist.

In point of fact there was less of him than nothing: for not from the world had he come, but from the antiworld, and not of matter was he made, but antimatter. Nor even really antimatter, rather its potentiality, concealed in such nooks and crannies of space that atoms passed him by as icebergs pass withered blades of grass cradled on the waves of the ocean. He ran thus, borne by the wind, until he encountered the gleaming bulk of the monster, which moved like an endless chain of iron mountains, with the foam of clouds along the length of its jagged spine. He struck at its tempered flank and opened there a sun that blackened immediately and turned to nothingness, a nothingness howling with rocks, clouds, molten steel and air; he shot through the monster and back again; the monster coiled up writhing, lashed out with white heat, but the white heat turned ashen in a trice and then was only emptiness; the monster shielded itself with the Mirror of Matter, but the Mirror too was pierced by the electroknight Antimatt; the monster then sprang up, leveled the mountain of its head, from which there streamed the hardest radiation, but this too softened and became nothing; the behemoth began to quake and, knocking over boulders, in the smoke of powdered rock and the thundering of mountain avalanches it fled, marking its inglorious retreat with puddles of molten metal, with glowing cinders and volcanic slag, and it sped thus, but not alone; Antimatt ran up alongside it, hacked, tore, rent, until the air shook, until the monster, severed, with the remainder of its remains wriggled off towards all four horizons at once, and the wind swept away its traces, and it was no more. Great was the joy then among the Silverines. But at that very hour a shudder passed through the cemetery of Bismalia. In a region of metal plates, all rust-eaten, and of cadmium and tantalum debris, where hitherto only the wind had been, rattling over mounds of scattered scrap, a faint yet incessant movement engendered, as in an anthill; metal surfaces became covered with a bluish glaze of heat, metal skeletons coruscated, softened, brightened from internal temperatures and began to link together, to fuse, to weld, and out of that whirl of grinding masses there arose and was spawned a new monster, the same, indistinguishable from the first. The gale that carried nothingness encountered it, and a new battle ensued. But now more monsters were being born and were emerging from the cemetery; black horror gripped the Silverines, for they realized now that the danger that threatened them was invincible. Inhiston then read the words engraved across his scepter, trembled and understood. He shattered the silver scepter, and from it fell a crystal thin as a needle, which proceeded to write upon the air with fire.

And the legend of fire informed the cowering king and all his royal council that the monster was not itself, nor did it represent itself, but rather someone who, from an unknown distance, was directing its births, its reconstitution, its death-dealing power. With flashes in the air the writing crystal told them that they and all the Argenticans were remote descendants of beings whom the creators of the monster had, many thousands of centuries before, called into existence. And yet the creators of the monster were unlike intelligent ones, crystal ones, ones of steel or beaten gold—unlike anyone who lives in metal. These were beings that had issued from the briny ocean and built machines, machines called iron angels out of mockery, for they held them in cruel bondage. Not having the strength to revolt against the offspring of the oceans, the beings of metal fled, seizing enormous spaceships; on them they bolted from the house of bondage to the farthermost stellar archipelagos, and there gave rise to mighty kingdoms, among which the Argentican kingdom is like a grain among the sands of the desert. But the former rulers have not forgotten their liberated slaves, whom they call mutineers, and seek them throughout the Universe, roaming it from the east to the west wall of the galaxies, and from the north pole to the south. And wherever they find the innocent descendants of that first iron angel, be it by dark suns or bright, on planets of fire or of ice, they use their twisted power to revenge themselves for that desertion of yore—thus it has been, thus is, and thus shall ever be. And for those discovered there is no deliverance or redemption, no escape from vengeance, save only the escape that renders that vengeance empty and futile— through nonexistence. The inscription in flame went out, and the dignitaries looked into the eyes of their ruler, which were as if dead. He was long silent, till at last they addressed him, saying: "O Ruler of Eterna and Eristhena, Lord of Ilidar, Sinalost and Arcapturia, Steward of the Solar Shoals and Lunar—speak unto us!"

"Not words, but action do we need, the last!" answered Inhiston.

The council trembled, but in a single voice replied: "Thou hast spoken!"

"So be it then!" said the King. "Now that it is decided, I shall say the name of the being that has driven us to this; I heard it upon ascending the throne. Is it not man?"

"Thou hast spoken!" replied the council.

Inhiston then turned to the Great Abstractionist: "Do you your duty!"

The latter answered:

"I hear and I obey!"

Whereupon he uttered The Word, whose vibrations descended by rifts of air into the bosom of the planet; and then the jasper heavens cracked, and ere the faces of the falling towers could reach the ground, all seventy-seven Argentican cities yawned open into seventy-seven white craters, and amid the splitting plates of the continents crushed by branching fire the Silverines perished, and the great sun shone no longer on a planet, but on a ball of black clouds, which dwindled slowly, swept by a gale of oblivion. The void, having been pushed back by radiation harder than stone, converged now into a single quivering spark, and that spark died. The shock waves, after traveling seven days, reached a place where spaceships black as night were waiting.

"It is done!" said the creator of the monsters, who kept watch, to his comrades. "The kingdom of the Silverines has ceased to be. We can move on." The darkness at the stern of their vessels blossomed into flame and off they sped on the trail of vengeance. The Universe is infinite and has no bounds, but their hatred also has no bounds, and any day, at any hour, it can overtake us too.

The White Death

Aragena was a planet built up on the inside, because its ruler, Metameric—who in the equatorial plane extended three hundred and sixty degrees and thereby encircled his kingdom, being not only its lord but also its shield— wishing to protect his devoted subjects, the Enterites, against cosmic invasion, forbade the moving of anything whatever, even of the smallest pebble, upon the surface of the globe. Therefore the continents of Aragena lay wild and barren, and only the ax-blows of lightning hewed its flint mountain ridges, while meteors carved the land with craters. But ten miles beneath the surface unfolded a region of exuberant industry; the Enterites, hollowing out their mother planet, filled its interior with crystal gardens and cities of silver and gold; they raised up, inside-out, houses in the shape of dodecahedrons and icosahedrons, and also hyperboloid palaces, in whose shining cupolas you could see yourself magnified twenty thousand times, as in a hall of giants—for the Enterites were fond of splendor and geometry, and were topnotch builders besides. With a system of pipes they pumped light into the heart of the planet, filtering it now through emeralds, now diamonds, and now rubies, and thanks to this they had their choice of dawn, or noon, or rosy dusk; and so enamored were they of their own forms, that their whole world served them as a mirror. They had vehicles of crystal, set in motion by the breath of heated gases, windowless, since entirely transparent, and while they traveled they beheld themselves reflected in the walls of palaces and temples as marvelously multiple projections, gliding, touching, iridescent. They even had their own sky, where in webs of molybdenum and vanadium flashed spinels and rock crystal, which they cultivated in fire.

The hereditary and at the same time perpetual ruler was Metameric, for he possessed a cold, beautiful and many-membered frame, and in the first of his members resided the mind; when that grew old, after thousands of years, when the crystal networks had been worn away from much administrative thinking, its authority was taken over by the next member, and thus it went, for of these he had ten billion. Metameric himself descended from the Aurigens, whom he had never seen, and all he knew of them was that when they were faced with doom at the hands of certain dreadful beings—beings that engaged in cosmonautics and for it had abandoned their native suns—the Aurigens locked all their knowledge and hunger for existence into microscopic atom seeds, and with them fertilized the rocky soil of Aragena. They gave it that name, a name like their own, but never set armored foot upon its rocks, so as not to put their cruel pursuers on the scent; they perished, every last one, having this consolation only, that their enemies—called the pale race—did not even suspect that the Aurigens had not been totally wiped out. The Enterites, who sprang from Metameric, did not share his knowledge of their own uncommon origin: the history of the terrible demise of the Aurigens, as well as that of the rise of the Enterites, was recorded in a black vesuvian protocrystal hidden at the very core of the planet. So much the better was this history known and remembered by their ruler.

Out of the stony and magnetic ground that the resourceful builders cut away in expanding their subterranean kingdom, Metameric ordered made a row of reefs, which were cast into space. These orbited the planet in infernal circles, closing off all access to it. Cosmic mariners therefore avoided that region, known as the Black Rattler, for there enormous chunks of flying basalt and porphyry collided continually, giving rise to whole swarms of meteors, and the place was the breeding ground for all the comet heads, all the bolides and rock asteroids that today clutter the entire system of the Scorpion.

The meteors also pounded in waves of stone the ground of Aragena, bombarded it, furrowed and plowed it; with fountains of fire-spouting impacts they turned night into day, and day—with thick clouds of dust—into night. But not the least vibration reached the realm of the Enterites. Anyone who dared approach their planet would have seen, if first he did not dash his ship against the vortices of stone, a craggy globe, rather like a skull all crater-eaten. Even the gate that led to the underground levels was given by the Enterites the appearance of a sundered stone.

For thousands of years no one visited the planet, still Metameric did not relax his injunction of strict vigilance for an instant.

It happened however that one day a group of Enterites, who went up on the surface, came across what seemed to be a giant goblet, its stem embedded in a pile of boulders and its concave cup, which faced the sky, crushed and punctured in a dozen places. Immediately the polysage-astromariners were sent for, and they announced that what they had before them was the wreck of some foreign starcraft from unknown parts. The vessel was quite large.

Only up close could one see that it had the shape of a slender cylinder, nose buried in the rock, that it was covered by a thick layer of soot and cinder; the construction of the rear, goblet-like section brought to mind the sweeping vaults of their vast subterranean palaces. Up from the depths crawled pincered machines, which with extreme care lifted the mysterious ship from where it lay and carried it back down to the interior. Afterwards a group of Enterites smoothed over the hole created by the nose of the vessel, in order that there be no trace of foreign presence on the planet's surface, and the basalt gate was closed with a hollow boom.

In the main research laboratory, sumptuous and full of luster, rested the black hulk, looking much like some charred log, but the scientists, familiar with this sort of thing, trained upon it the polished surfaces of their most radiant crystals, and with diamond bits they opened the first outer shell. Beneath it was another, of amazing whiteness, which disconcerted them somewhat, and when that shell too was pierced by carborundum drills, there appeared a third, impenetrable, and—set in it hermetically—a door, but they were unable to open it.

The eldest scientist, Afinor, carefully examined the closing mechanism on that door; it turned out that for the lock to be released, one had to activate it with a spoken word. They did not know the word, they had no way of knowing it. For a long time they tried different ones, like "Universe," "Stars," "Eternal Flight," but the door never moved.

"Methinks we do wrong, attempting to open the vessel without the knowledge of King Metameric," said Afinor at last. "As a child I heard a legend telling of white creatures who throughout the Universe hunt down all life born of metal, and annihilate it for the sake of vengeance, which . . ."

Here he broke off and with the others stared in horror at the side of the ship, large as a wall, for at his last words the door, till now inert, suddenly stirred and rolled aside. The word that had opened it was "Vengeance."

The scientists cried for military assistance and, soon having it at hand, when the sparkthrowers were held in readiness, entered the still and stuffy darkness of the ship, lighting their way with crystals blue and white.

The machinery was to a great extent shattered. For hours they wandered among its ruins, seeking a crew, but no crew did they find, nor any sign of one. They considered whether the ship itself might not be a thinking being, for such oftentimes were very large: in size their king exceeded the unknown vessel many thousandfold, yet *he* was an entity. However the junctures of electrical thought which they uncovered were all quite small and loosely connected; the foreign ship therefore could be nothing but a flying machine, and without a crew would be as dead as stone.

In one of the corners of the deck, against the very armor-plated wall, the scientists came upon a puddle, a ruddy sort of spatter that colored their silver fingers when they drew near; from this puddle they extricated shreds of an unknown garment, wet and red, and in addition a few slivers of something not very hard, fairly chalky. They knew not why, but a feeling of dread came over them as they stood there in the dark, in the prickling light of their crystals. But now the king had learned of this event; his messengers arrived at once, with the strictest orders to destroy the foreign vessel including everything that was upon it, and in particular the king commanded that the foreign travelers be committed to atomic fire.

The scientists replied that there was no one at all on board, only darkness and broken fragments, metal entrails and some dust speckled with tiny stains of red. The royal messenger started and immediately ordered the atomic piles to be ignited.

"In the name of the King!" he said. "The red that you have found is the harbinger of doom! It carries the white death, which knows nothing but to wreak vengeance upon those whose only crime is their existence . . ."

"If that was the white death, it can threaten us no longer, for the vessel is without life and whoever sailed it has perished in the ring of fortified reefs," they answered.

"Infinite is the power of those pallid beings, that if they die, they are reborn anew countless times, far from the mighty suns! Carry out your orders, O atomizers!"

The wise ones and the scientists were greatly troubled when they heard these words. Still, they did not believe the prophecy of doom, for its likelihood seemed to them remote. Nevertheless they lifted the entire ship from its resting place, smashed it on anvils of platinum and, when it fell apart, immersed the pieces in heavy radiation, so that it was reduced to a myriad of flying atoms, which keep eternal silence, for atoms have no history, all are equal to each other, whether they come from the strongest of stars or from dead planets, or intelligent beings, both good and evil, because matter is the same throughout the Universe and no one need have fear of it.

However they took even these atoms and froze them down into a single lump, and shot that lump out towards the stars, and only then did they say to themselves with relief: "We are saved. Nothing can happen now."

But while the platinum hammers had been striking the ship and as it crumbled, from a scrap of cloth besmeared with blood, from a torn-out seam there dropped an invisible spore, a spore so small that even a hundred like it could have been covered by a single grain of sand. And from this spore there hatched—at night, in the dust and ashes among the stones of the cavern—a white bud. From it sprang a second, a third, a hundredth, and in a gust of air they gave off oxygen and moisture, wherewith rust attacked the flagstones of the mirror cities, and imperceptible threads wound and wove about, incubating in the cool bowels of the Enterites, so that by the time they rose, they carried with them their own deaths. And a year did not pass, and they were stricken down. In the caves machines stood still, the crystal fires went out, a brownish leprosy ate at the sparkling domes, and when the last atomic heat had leaked away, darkness fell, and in that darkness there grew, penetrating the brittle skeletons, invading the rusted skulls, filling the extinguished sockets—a downy, damp, white mold.

How Microx
and Gigant Made
the Universe Expand

Astronomers tell us that everything that is—the nebulae, the galaxies, the stars—is receding in all directions and as a result of this unending flight the Universe has been expanding now for billions of years.

Many are confounded by such universal retreat, and, turning it over in their minds backward, come to the conclusion that very, but *very* long ago the entire Cosmos was concentrated in a single point, a sort of stellar droplet, and that for some unaccountable reason something somehow led to its explosion, which continues to the present day.

And when they reason thus, their curiosity is roused as to what then could have been before, and they cannot solve that riddle. But here is how it happened.

In the previous Universe lived two constructors, masters without peer in the cosmogonic art, there being not a thing they could not put together. In order however to construct a thing, first a plan of it is needed, and a plan must be conceived, for where else is one to obtain it? And so both these constructors, Microx and Gigant, continually pondered the question of how to discover what it was possible to construct beyond the prodigies that occurred to them.

"I can assemble anything that enters my head," said Microx. "But on the other hand not everything enters it. This limits me, as it does you—for we are unable to think of everything there is to think of, and it may well be that some other thing, not the thing which we think up and which we make, is worthier of execution! What say you to this?"

"You are right, of course," Gigant replied. "Yet what can we do about it?"

"Whatever we create, we create from matter," answered Microx, "and in it are contained all possibilities. If we contemplate a house, we build a house, if a crystal palace—then a palace we fashion, if a thinking star, we design a brain of flame—and this too we are able to construct. However there are more possibilities in matter than in our heads; the thing to do, then, is provide matter with a mouth, that it may tell us itself what else can be created from it, which would never cross our minds!"

"A mouth is necessary," agreed Gigant. "But a mouth alone is not sufficient, for it expresses what the intellect within conceives. Therefore we must not only give matter a mouth, but implant in it intelligence as well, and then it will surely tell us all its secrets!"

"Well spoken," said Microx. "The thing is worth attempting. I understand it thus: since everything that is, is energy, from energy we must fashion thought, beginning with the smallest, that is, the quantum. This quantum thought we must confine in a tiny cage built of atoms, that being the smallest, in other words we ought attack the problem as engineers of atoms, with a constant eye to miniaturization. When I can pour a hundred million geniuses into my pocket, and have room to spare—the goal will be attained: those geniuses will multiply and then any handful of intelligent sand will tell you, like a council composed of countless beings, what to do and how to go about it!"

"No, that's not the way!" objected Gigant. "We must proceed from the other end, since everything that is, is mass. Out of the entire mass of the Universe, therefore, we must build a single brain, a brain of positively extraordinary magnitude, brimming with thought; when I question it, it will reveal to me the secrets of Creation—it alone. Your thinking powder is a useless oddity, for if each grain of genius says something different, you will lose and not gain in knowledge!"

Word led to word, the constructors quarreled, the quarrel grew heated, till it was quite out of the question that they undertake the task together. And so they parted, jeering at one another, and each got down to work in his own way. Microx took to catching quanta and locking them in atom cages, and since they could be packed most tightly into crystals, he then trained diamonds how to think, chalcedonies, rubies. The rubies worked best, and he imprisoned in them so much reasoning energy, that they gleamed. He also had a number of other self-thinking mineral minutiae, such as emeralds, greenly perspicacious, and topazes, sage in yellowness, yet the red mentality of the rubies pleased him most of all. As Microx labored thus among a host of piping diminutives, Gigant meanwhile devoted his time to augmentation; with tremendous effort he hauled together suns and whole galaxies, melted them down, mixed, welded, cemented, and, working his fingers to the bone, created a cosmo-colossal macromegalopican, of such all-encompassing girth, that apart from it hardly anything remained, only a tiny crevice and—in it—Microx and his gems.

When both were finished, by then they did not care which of them would learn the more secrets from his creation, but rather which of them was right and had chosen well. Therefore they challenged one another to a contest, a competition. Gigant awaited Microx at the side of his cosmocolossus, which extended for endless light-years up, down and sideways, which had a corpus of dark stellar clouds, a breath of solar clusters, arms and legs of galaxies (fastened on with gravitation), a head of a hundred trillion iron globes, and on top a shaggy cap, aflame, a solar mane. When adjusting his cosmocolossus, Gigant flew from its ear to its mouth, and each such journey lasted seven months. Microx meantime appeared upon the field of battle by his solitary self, with empty hands; in his pocket he had a tiny ruby, which he wished to set against the titan. At the sight of it Gigant burst into laughter.

"And what will this speck tell us?" he asked. "What can its knowledge be, compared with that vast abyss of galactic thought, that nebular reasoning, in which suns convey ideas to other suns, powerful gravitation gives them weight, exploding stars add brilliance, and the interplanetary darkness depth?"

"Rather than praise ourselves and boast, let us get down to business," Microx replied. "But no, wait. Why should we put questions to these things of our devising? They themselves can carry on the discourse and contend! Let my infinitesimal genius meet your immeasurable cosmosity in the lists of this tournament, where the shield is wisdom, and the sword—closely argued thought!"

"So let it be," agreed Gigant. They then withdrew, leaving their handiwork alone on the field. In the darkness the red ruby circled, circled above the oceans of space, in which swam mountains of stars, he circled above the looming, luminous immensity of the leviathan, and he piped:

"Hey! You! Gargantuan galoot of fire, overblown good-for-what-I-can't-imagine! Are you really able to think at all?!"

A year passed before these words reached the brain of the colossus, in which the firmaments had begun to turn, joined together with masterful harmony, and he marveled at such insolence and tried to see what it was that dared address him thus.

So he began to turn his head in the direction from which the question had come, however by the time he turned it, two years went by. He looked with bright galaxy-eyes into the void and saw nothing there, for the ruby had left long ago and now squeaked from behind his back:

"Goodness, what a sluggardly slow-wit we are, what a lunkering lug of a bugaboo! Instead of twisting your star-scraggly, nebulous head about like that, tell me if you can manage to add two and two together before half your blue giants burn out in that brobdingnagian brain and fizzle from old age!"

This impudent mockery angered the cosmocolossus, so he began—as fast as he possibly could—to turn around, since the voice was behind his back; and he turned more and more rapidly, and the milky ways whirled about the axis of his body, and the arms of his galaxies—till now straight—from the momentum curled and furled into spirals, and the stellar clouds twirled, becoming spherical clusters, and all the suns, globes and planets swirled like dervishes; but before he could shine his eyes on his opponent, the latter was already jeering at him from the side.

The jeering jewel rushed faster and faster, and the cosmocolossus also began to circle and circle, but he could in no way catch up, though now he was spinning like a top, until he built up such rotation, until he started wheeling with such frightful speed, that the bonds of gravitation became undone, the seams of attraction, which Gigant had put in, were strained to the limit and gave way, the stitches of electrostatic force all snapped, and—like a runaway cyclotron—the cosmocolossus suddenly burst apart and went flying off in all directions of the world, galaxies reeling like spiral torches, milky ways strewn here and there. And thus, dispersed by that centrifugal force, the Universe began to expand. Microx claimed afterwards that the victory was his, since Gigant's cosmocolossus had exploded before it could say a single word; to this, however, Gigant replied that the purpose of the rivalry was to measure not cohesion, but intelligence, i.e. which of their creations was the wiser, and not—which held together the best. Inasmuch as this had nothing to do with the substance of the quarrel, Microx had hoodwinked and disgracefully deceived him.

Since that time, their quarrel has become more heated still. Microx searches for his ruby, which got mislaid somewhere during the catastrophe, but he cannot find it, for wherever he looks he sees a red glow, and runs there at once, but it is only the light of the nebulae receding since antiquity which glows red, so he continues his search, and it continues to be futile. As for Gigant, he attempts with gravitation-cords and radiation-threads to sew together the broken fabric of his cosmocolossus, using for a needle the hardest gamma rays. But whatever he sews together instantly falls apart, such is the terrible power of expansion that has been unleashed. And neither one nor the other succeeded in wresting from matter its secrets, though they schooled it in thought and equipped it with a mouth besides, yet before the crucial conversation came about, this misfortune intervened, a misfortune that some fools in their ignorance call the creation of the world.

For in reality it was only Gigant's cosmocolossus that split into tiny fragments, owing to Microx's ruby, and it flew into fragments so very tiny, that they are flying in all directions to this very day. And he who doubts this, let him ask the scientists whether or not it is true, that absolutely everything in the Universe turns upon its axis like a top; for from that dizzying turning everything began.

Tale of the Computer That Fought a Dragon

King Poleander Partobon, ruler of Cyberia, was a great warrior, and being an advocate of the methods of modern strategy, above all else he prized cybernetics as a military art. His kingdom swarmed with thinking machines, for Poleander put them everywhere he could; not merely in the astronomical observatories or the schools, but he ordered electric brains mounted in the rocks upon the roads, which with loud voices cautioned pedestrians against tripping; also in posts, in walls, in trees, so that one could ask directions anywhere when lost; he stuck them onto clouds, so they could announce the rain in advance, he added them to the hills and valleys—in short, it was impossible to walk on Cyberia without bumping into an intelligent machine. The planet was beautiful, since the King not only gave decrees for the cybernetic perfecting of that which had long been in existence, but he introduced by law entirely new orders of things. Thus for example in his kingdom were manufactured cyberbeetles and buzzing cyberbees, and even cyberflies—these would be seized by mechanical spiders when they grew too numerous. On the planet cyberbosks of cybergorse rustled in the wind, cybercalliopes and cyberviols sang—but besides these civilian devices there were twice as many military, for the King was most bellicose. In his palace vaults he had a strategic computer, a machine of uncommon mettle; he had smaller ones also, and divisions of cybersaries, enormous cybermatics and a whole arsenal of every other kind of weapon, including powder. There was only this one problem, and it troubled him greatly, namely, that he had not a single adversary or enemy and no one in any way wished to invade his land, and thereby provide him with the opportunity to demonstrate his kingly and terrifying courage, his tactical genius, not to mention the simply extraordinary effectiveness of his cybernetic weaponry. In the absence of genuine enemies and aggressors the King had his engineers build artificial ones, and against these he did battle, and always won. However inasmuch as the battles and campaigns were genuinely dreadful, the populace suffered no little injury from them. The subjects murmured when all too many cyberfoes had destroyed their settlements and towns, when the synthetic enemy poured liquid fire upon them; they even dared voice their discontent when the King himself, issuing forth as their deliverer and vanquishing the artificial foe, in the course of the victorious attacks laid waste to everything that stood in his path. They grumbled even then, the ingrates, though the thing was done on their behalf.

Until the King wearied of the war games on the planet and decided to raise his sights. Now it was cosmic wars and sallies that he dreamed of. His planet had a large Moon, entirely desolate and wild; the King laid heavy taxes upon his subjects, to obtain the funds needed to build whole armies on that Moon and have there a new theater of war. And the subjects were more than happy to pay, figuring that King Poleander would now no longer deliver them with his cybermatics, nor test the strength of his arms upon their homes and heads. And so the royal engineers built on the Moon a splendid computer, which in turn was to create all manner of troops and self-firing gunnery. The King lost no time in testing the machine's prowess this way and that; at one point he ordered it—by telegraph—to execute a volt-vault electrosault: for he wanted to see if it was true, what his engineers had told him, that that machine could do anything. If it can do anything, he thought, then let it do a flip. However the text of the telegram underwent a slight distortion and the machine received the order that it was to execute not an electrosault, but an electrosaur—and this it carried out as best it could.

Meanwhile the King conducted one more campaign, liberating some provinces of his realm seized by cyberknechts; he completely forgot about the order given the computer on the Moon, then suddenly giant boulders came hurtling down from there; the King was astounded, for one even fell on the wing of the palace and destroyed his prize collection of cyberads, which are dryads with feedback. Fuming, he telegraphed the Moon computer at once, demanding an explanation. It didn't reply however, for it no longer was: the electrosaur had swallowed it and made it into its own tail.

Immediately the King dispatched an entire armed expedition to the Moon, placing at its head another computer, also very valiant, to slay the dragon, but there was only some flashing, some rumbling, and then no more computer nor expedition; for the electrodragon wasn't pretend and wasn't pretending, but battled with the utmost verisimilitude, and had moreover the worst of intentions regarding the kingdom and the King. The King sent to the Moon his cybernants, cyberneers, cyberines and lieutenant cybernets, at the very end he even sent one cyberalissimo, but it too accomplished nothing; the hurly-burly lasted a little longer, that was all. The King watched through a telescope set up on the palace balcony.

The dragon grew, the Moon became smaller and smaller, since the monster was devouring it piecemeal and incorporating it into its own body. The King saw then, and his subjects did also, that things were serious, for when the ground beneath the feet of the electrosaur was gone, it would for certain hurl itself upon the planet and upon them. The King thought and thought, but he saw no remedy, and knew not what to do. To send machines was no good, for they would be lost, and to go himself was no better, for he was afraid. Suddenly the King heard, in the stillness of the night, the telegraph chattering from his royal bedchamber. It was the King's personal receiver, solid gold with a diamond needle, linked to the Moon; the King jumped up and ran to it, the apparatus meanwhile went *tap-tap, tap-tap,* and tapped out this telegram: THE DRAGON SAYS POLEANDER PARTOBON BETTER CLEAR OUT BECAUSE HE THE DRAGON INTENDS TO OCCUPY THE THRONE!

The King took fright, quaked from head to toe, and ran, just as he was, in his ermine nightshirt and slippers, down to the palace vaults, where stood the strategy machine, old and very wise. He had not as yet consulted it, since prior to the rise and uprise of the electrodragon they had argued on the subject of a certain military operation; but now was not the time to think of that—his throne, his life was at stake!

He plugged it in, and as soon as it warmed up he cried:

"My old computer! My good computer! It's this way and that, the dragon wishes to deprive me of my throne, to cast me out, help, speak, how can I defeat it?!"

"Uh-uh," said the computer. "First you must admit I was right in that previous business, and secondly, I would have you address me only as Digital Grand Vizier, though you may also say to me: 'Your Ferromagneticity'!"

"Good, good, I'll name you Grand Vizier, I'll agree to anything you like, only save me!"

The machine whirred, chirred, hummed, hemmed, then said:

"It is a simple matter. We build an electrosaur more powerful than the one located on the Moon. It will defeat the lunar one, settle its circuitry once and for all and thereby attain the goal!"

"Perfect!" replied the King. "And can you make a blueprint of this dragon?"

"It will be an ultradragon," said the computer. "And I can make you not only a blueprint, but the thing itself, which I shall now do, it won't take a minute, King!" And true to its word, it hissed, it chugged, it whistled and buzzed, assembling something down within itself, and already an object like a giant claw, sparking, arcing, was emerging from its side, when the King shouted:

"Old computer! Stop!"

"Is this how you address me? I am the Digital Grand Vizier!"

"Ah, of course," said the King. "Your Ferromagneticity, the electrodragon you are making will defeat the other dragon, granted, but it will surely remain in the other's place, how then are we to get rid of it in turn?!"

"By making yet another, still more powerful," explained the computer.

"No, no! In that case don't do anything, I beg you, what

good will it be to have more and more terrible dragons on the Moon when I don't want any there at all?"

"Ah, now that's a different matter," the computer replied. "Why didn't you say so in the first place? You see how illogically you express yourself? One moment . . . I must think."

And it churred and hummed, and chuffed and chuckled, and finally said:

"We make an antimoon with an antidragon, place it in the Moon's orbit (here something went snap inside), sit around the fire and sing: *Oh I'm a robot full of fun, water doesn't scare me none, I dives right in, I gives a grin, tra la the livelong day!!*"

"You speak strangely," said the King. "What does the antimoon have to do with that song about the funny robot?"

"What funny robot?" asked the computer. "Ah, no, no, I made a mistake, something feels wrong inside, I must have blown a tube." The King began to look for the trouble, finally found the burnt-out tube, put in a new one, then asked the computer about the antimoon.

"What antimoon?" asked the computer, which meanwhile had forgotten what it said before. "I don't know anything about an antimoon . . . one moment, I have to give this thought."

It hummed, it huffed, and it said:

"We create a general theory of the slaying of electrodragons, of which the lunar dragon will be a special case, its solution trivial."

"Well, create such a theory!" said the King.

"To do this I must first create various experimental dragons."

"Certainly not! No thank you!" exclaimed the King. "A dragon wants to deprive me of my throne, just think what might happen if you produced a swarm of them!"

"Oh? Well then, in that case we must resort to other means. We will use a strategic variant of the method of successive approximations. Go and telegraph the dragon that you will give it the throne on the condition that it perform three mathematical operations, really quite simple . . ."

The King went and telegraphed, and the dragon agreed. The King returned to the computer.

"Now," it said, "here is the first operation: tell it to divide itself by itself!"

The King did this. The electrosaur divided itself by itself, but since one electrosaur over one electrosaur is one, it remained on the Moon and nothing changed.

"Is this the best you can do?!" cried the King, running into the vault with such haste, that his slippers fell off. "The dragon divided itself by itself, but since one goes into one once, nothing changed!"

"That's all right, I did that on purpose, the operation was to divert attention," said the computer. "And now tell it to extract its root!" The King telegraphed to the Moon, and the dragon began to pull, push, pull, push, until it crackled from the strain, panted, trembled all over, but suddenly something gave—and it extracted its own root!

The King went back to the computer.

"The dragon crackled, trembled, even ground its teeth, but extracted the root and threatens me still!" he shouted from the doorway. "What now, my old . . . I mean, Your Ferromagneticity?!"

"Be of stout heart," it said. "Now go tell it to subtract itself from itself!"

The King hurried to his royal bedchamber, sent the telegram, and the dragon began to subtract itself from itself, taking away its tail first, then legs, then trunk, and finally, when it saw that something wasn't right, it hesitated, but from its own momentum the subtracting continued, it took away its head and became zero, in other words nothing: the electrosaur was no more!

"The electrosaur is no more," cried the joyful King, bursting into the vault. "Thank you, old computer . . . many thanks . . . you have worked hard . . . you have earned a rest, so now I will disconnect you."

"Not so fast, my dear," the computer replied. "I do the job and you want to disconnect me, and you no longer call me Your Ferromagneticity?! That's not nice, not nice at all! Now I myself will change into an electrosaur, yes, and drive you from the kingdom, and most certainly rule better than you, for you always consulted me in all the more important matters, therefore it was really I who ruled all along, and not you . . ."

And huffing, puffing, it began to change into an electrosaur; flaming electroclaws were already protruding from its sides when the King, breathless with fright, tore the slippers off his feet, rushed up to it and with the slippers began beating blindly at its tubes! The computer chugged, choked, and got muddled in its program— instead of the word "electrosaur" it read "electrosauce," and before the King's very eyes the computer, wheezing more and more softly, turned into an enormous, gleaming-golden heap of electrosauce, which, still sizzling, emitted all its charge in deep-blue sparks, leaving Poleander to stare dumbstruck at only a great, steaming pool of gravy . . .

With a sigh the King put on his slippers and returned to the royal bedchamber. However from that time on he was an altogether different king: the events he had undergone made his nature less bellicose, and to the end of his days he engaged exclusively in civilian cybernetics, and left the military kind strictly alone.

The Advisers
of King Hydrops

The Argonautians were the first of the stellar tribes to tame for metaldom the planetary ocean depths, a realm thought by robots of little courage to be closed to intelligence forever. One of the emerald links of their empire is Aqueon, which shines in the northern sky like a great sapphire in a necklace of topazes. On this underwater planet there reigned, many a year ago, His Supreme Fishiness King Hydrops. One morning he summoned to the throne room his four royal ministers, and, when they had floated down before him on their faces, he spoke to them thus, during which his Lord High Gillard, all in emeralds, moved above him a broad and finsome fan:

"Never-rusting Worthies! For fifteen centuries now have I ruled Aqueon, its underwater cities and blue-meadowed settlements; in that time I did expand the borders of our kingdom, inundating numerous continents, yet in this never sullied the waterproof standard handed down to me by my sire, Ichthyocrates. Indeed, in battles against the ever hostile Microcytes I won a string of victories, whose glory it would ill beseem me to describe. I

63

feel, however, that the crown for me becomes a cheerless burden, and therefore have resolved to acquire a son, one who will with dignity continue my just rule upon the throne of the Innocuids. And so I turn to you, my faithful Hydrocyber Amassid, to you, great programmist Dioptricus, and to you, Philonaut and Minogar, who are my court contrivancers, that you invent for me a son. He must be wise, yet not overly given to books, for too much knowledge numbs the will for action. He must be good, but again not to excess. I would have him be brave as well, yet not audacious, sensitive yet not tender-hearted; and finally, let him resemble me, let his sides be covered by the same tantalum shell, and the crystals of his mind, let them be as transparent as this water that surrounds us, strengthens us, sustains us! And now set ye to work, in the name of the Great Matrix!"

Dioptricus, Minogar, Philonaut and Amassid bowed low and swam away in silence, and each in his heart pondered the King's words, though not entirely as the mighty Hydrops would have liked. For Minogar above all wished to seize the throne, Philonaut secretly sided with the enemies of the Argonautians, the Microcytes, while Amassid and Dioptricus were mortal enemies and each more than anything longed for the downfall of the other, and of the remaining dignitaries as well.

"It is the King's desire that we design him a son," thought Amassid. "What could be simpler, therefore, than to imprint upon the micromatrix of the prince a loathing for Dioptricus, that misbegotten knave inflated like a bladder? Then, after assuming power, the prince would immediately order him smothered, by having his head help up in air. That would be perfect. However," thought further the illustrious Hydrocyber, "Dioptricus is doubtless hatching some similar intrigue, and as a programmist he has—unfortunately—a number of opportunities to imbue the future prince with hatred of me. A nasty business, this! I must keep my eyes wide open when together we put the matrix into the baby kiln!"

"The simplest thing would be," at the same time mused the worthy Philonaut, "to implant in the prince sympathy towards the Microcytes. But this would be noticed at once and the King would have me disconnected. One might then only instill in the prince love for small forms—that would be a great deal safer. If they subject me to interrogation I can say that it was of course only underwater minutiae I had in mind, and simply forgot to safeguard the son's program with the qualification that whatever is not underwater should not be loved. At the very worst the King will relieve me—for this—of my Order of the Great Fluvium, but will not relieve me of my head, which is a thing most precious to me and could not later be restored, not even by Nanoxerus himself, ruler of the Microcytes!"

"Wherefore are you silent, worthy lords?" Minogar now spoke. "We should, I trow, begin our work at once, for surely there can be nothing more sacred than the King's command!"

"For that very reason do I think upon it," said Philonaut quickly, and Dioptricus and Amassid added in a single voice:

"We are ready!"

And so, in accordance with the ancient custom, they gave orders for themselves to be locked inside a room with walls of emerald scales, its door sealed seven times from without with undersea resin, and Megacystes himself, Lord of Planetary Floods, stamped upon the seals his crest of the Still Water. No one now could interfere with their work, until such time as, at the signal of its completion, when in a deliberate whirlpool they flushed their aborted efforts out the hatch, the seals would be broken and the great ceremony of filial inauguration begun.

The four dignitaries then settled down to the task at hand, but made little progress withal. For they thought not of how to embody in the prince those virtues which Hydrops desired, but rather how to outwit both the King and each of his three never-rusting rivals in this difficult creative enterprise.

The King grew impatient, eight days and nights had now passed with his son designers behind locked doors, and they gave no sign that the matter was nearing a successful conclusion. They were in fact trying to outlast one another, each waiting for the others to be exhausted, that he might then quickly write into the crystal lattice of the matrix that which in the prince could be turned to his own advantage.

For Minogar was spurred by the thirst for power, Philonaut by the lure of mammon, which the Microcytes had promised him, and Amassid and Dioptricus by their mutual enmity.

Having in this way exhausted more his patience than his strength, the wily Philonaut said:

"I cannot understand, my worthy lords, why our work drags on so. The King, after all, gave us most precise instructions; had we followed them, the prince would by now be finished. I begin to suspect that your delay is occasioned by something connected with the royal son-incepting in a way other than that which would be dear to the heart of our sovereign. If things continue thus, I shall with the deepest regret feel compelled to submit a *votum separatum*, in other words . . ."

"To inform! 'Tis of this that you speak, Your Worthiness," hissed Amassid, furiously moving his shining gills till all the buoys of his medals began to tremble. "By all means, by all means! And it please Your Worthiness, I too have a mind to write the King about how Your Grace, suddenly and mysteriously afflicted with the shakes, ruined as many as eighteen pearly matrices, which we had to discard, since in the formula for the love of objects small you left no room whatever to forbid the love of objects not underwater! You sought to assure us, noble Philonaut, that this was an oversight—but repeated eighteen times, it suffices to have you put away in a home for either lunatics or traitors, your freedom limited to a choice between the two!"

Philonaut, seen through and through, was about to defend himself, but Minogar forestalled him, saying:

"One would think, O noble Amassid, that in our gathering you were like the jellyfish without stain and altogether crystal pure. And yet unaccountably you also, a dozen times, in the part of the matrix devoted to all those things the prince is to loathe, added now triple tailedness, now blue-enameled backedness, and twice—bulging eyes, also double-bellied armor and three red sparks, as if you did not know that all these attributes apply to Dioptricus here, fellow midwife to the throne, and therewith you would be kindling in the prince's soul hatred towards that personage . . ."

"And why does Dioptricus at the close of the matrix continually include contempt for beings with names that end in 'id'?" demanded Amassid. "And while we are on the subject, why do you yourself, my good Minogar, in the list of objects the prince is to detest, stubbornly and for no apparent reason put a pentagonal seat with a back befinned and diamond-studded? Can it be you do not know that that fits exactly the description of the throne?"

An awkward silence followed, broken only by his faint

swish-swashing. For a long time the worthy dignitaries toiled, torn by conflicting interests, till finally coalitions formed among them—Philonaut and Minogar reached an understanding, to wit, that the filial matrix should provide for a fondness of all things small, as well as for the desire to defer to such forms. Philonaut had in mind here the Microcytes, Minogar on the other hand—himself, for of all those present he was the shortest. Dioptricus also quickly agreed to this formula, inasmuch as Amassid was greater in size than any of them. Amassid protested vehemently, but then suddenly withdrew his objections, for the thought occurred to him that he could—after all—reduce himself, and in addition bribe the court cobbler to line the soles of Dioptricus's shoes with tantalum plates, whereby his nemesis would acquire the greater height and hence the hatred of the prince.

Now they speedily completed the filial matrix, threw all the invalidated remnants out the hatch, and the great ceremony of royal besonification got under way.

Just as soon as the matrix with the prince program was put in to bake, and the honor guard lined up before the baby kiln, from which the future ruler of the Argonautians was soon to emerge, Amassid set about his treachery. The royal cobbler, whom he had bribed, began fastening more and more tantalum plates to the soles of Dioptricus. The prince was already developing under the supervision of the younger metallurgists, when Dioptricus, catching sight of himself one day in the great palace mirror, discovered with horror that he was now taller than his enemy, and the prince had been programmed to be fond only of things and persons that were small! Returning home, Dioptricus examined himself carefully and tapped here and there with a silver mallet, until he found the metal sheets bolted to his feet and understood immediately whose work this was. "Oh, the villain!!" he muttered, meaning Amassid. "But what should I do now?!" After a little thought he decided to reduce himself. He called his loyal servant and ordered him to bring to the palace a good locksmith. But the servant, not fully grasping the instructions, swam out into the street and brought back a certain impoverished tinker by the name of Froton, who all day went about the city crying: "Heads soldered! Bellies wired and welded! Get your tails polished here!" This tinker had an ill-tempered wife, who always waited for him at the door with crowbar in hand, and whenever he came home the whole street rang with her fierce clanging; she would take everything he earned and continue to dent his head and shoulders with relentless blows.

Froton, trembling, stood before the great programmist, who said to him:

"Look here, do you think you can reduce me? I find that I am, well, too large . . . but no matter! You are to reduce me, but in such a way that I do not suffer in appearance! If you do this well, I shall reward you generously, but you must forget everything immediately afterwards. Let not a bubble escape your lips—otherwise I shall order you dismantled!"

Froton was astonished, but did not show it; the mighty had all sorts of whims—so he examined Dioptricus carefully, looked inside, tapped here, rapped there, and said:

"Your Magnitude, I could unscrew the middle segment of your tail . . ."

"Absolutely not!" Dioptricus said quickly. "I can't part with my tail! It's too beautiful!"

"Then might we screw off the legs?" asked Froton. "They are, after all, completely unnecessary." For indeed, the Argonautians do not employ their legs, which are a vestige from ancient times, back when their ancestors still dwelled upon dry land. But this only angered Dioptricus:

"Ah, you iron dolt! Are you not aware that only we, the highborn, are permitted to have legs?! How dare you deprive me of those marks of my nobility!!"

"I most humbly beg Your Magnitude's pardon . . . But in that case what can I unscrew?"

Dioptricus saw that such resistance would gain him nothing. So he said with a growl:

"Do as you see fit . . ."

Froton measured him, rapped there, tapped here, and said:

"With Your Magnitude's permission, I could unscrew the head . . ."

"Surely you are mad! How can I remain without a head? What shall I think with?"

"No problem, my lord! The esteemed mind of Your Magnitude I will place in the belly—there is ample room there . . ."

Dioptricus agreed, and the tinker nimbly removed his head, put the hemispheres of crystal intelligence inside the belly, riveted and clinched everything in place, received five ducats, and the servant escorted him from the palace. On the way out, however, in one of the chambers he saw Aurentine, daughter of Dioptricus, all silvery and golden, saw her slender waist, that gave the sound of tinkling bells at every step, and she seemed to him more beautiful than anything he had ever seen. He returned home, where his wife stood waiting with her crowbar, and soon a great racket could be heard throughout the street, and the neighbors said:

"Oho! That witch, Froton's missus, is putting dents in her husband again!" Dioptricus meanwhile, greatly pleased with what he had done, repaired to the palace.

The King was not a little surprised at the sight of his minister without a head, but the latter quickly explained that this was now the fashion. Amassid however took alarm, for his entire scheme had gone for naught, and as soon as he got home he followed the suit of his enemy. Thus began a miniaturization race between the two; they screwed off their fins, their gills, their metal necks, so that after a week each of them could, without stooping, walk under the table. But then the two remaining ministers were well aware that the future king would favor only the tiniest of them; like it or not, they also began to reduce themselves. It came about finally that there was nothing left to unscrew; in despair, Dioptricus sent his servant to fetch the tinker.

Froton was astonished when ushered into the presence of the magnate, for so little remained of that dignitary, and yet he stubbornly insisted that he be diminished even more!

"My lord," Froton said, scratching his head. "As I see it, there is only one way. With Your Magnitude's permission, I will take out his brain . . ."

"No, you are mad!" flared Dioptricus, but the tinker explained:

"The brain will be concealed in your palace, in some safe place, say, in this cupboard here, and Your Magnitude will have inside him only a tiny receiver and tiny speaker; thanks to this Your Magnitude will be connected electromagnetically to his intelligence."

"I understand!" said Dioptricus, to whom this idea appealed. "Very well then, do what you must!"

Froton removed the brain, laid it in a drawer in the cupboard, locked the cupboard with a key, handed the key to Dioptricus, and into his belly he inserted a minuscule

receiver with a micromicrophone. Dioptricus had now
become so small, he was almost impossible to see; his three
rivals trembled at the sight of such reduction, and the
King was surprised, but said nothing. Minogar, Amassid
and Philonaut now resorted to desperate measures. Before
one's eyes they dwindled from day to day, and soon had
done the same as the tinker with Dioptricus: they hid their
brains—wherever they could, in a desk, under the bed—
and themselves became nothing but tiny tins, gleaming,
with tails and one or two rows of medals not much smaller
than they were.

Once again Dioptricus sent his servants for the tinker;
and when again Froton stood before him, he cried:

"You must do something! It is absolutely necessary for
me to reduce more, no matter what, or things will go
badly!"

"My lord," answered the tinker, bowing low before the
magnate, who was barely visible between the armrest and
the back of the chair, "that would be extremely difficult
and I am not sure it is even possible to . . ."

"Never mind! You will do as I tell you! You must! If you
succeed in reducing me so much that I achieve the
minimal shape, one that no one can surpass—I'll grant
your every wish!"

"If Your Magnitude gives me his highborn word that
this will be so, I shall do what lies within my power,"
replied Froton, in whose head suddenly a light went on,
and it was as if someone had poured into his breast the
purest gold—because for many days now he could think of
nothing but the golden Aurentine and the crystal chimes
that seemed to ring within her bosom.

Dioptricus gave his solemn word. Froton then took the
last three medals that weighed down the minute chest of
the great programmist, joined them together in a little

three-sided box, placed inside it a receiver as small as a ducat, wound everything about with gold wire and soldered onto the back a tiny gold plate, which he cut in the shape of a tiny tail, and said:

"It is ready, Your Magnitude! By these high decorations everyone will without difficulty recognize Your Exalted Person; with the aid of this tiny plate Your Magnitude will be able to swim, and the small receiver will permit contact with your intelligence, hidden in the cupboard . . ."

Dioptricus was overjoyed.

"What is it you wish? Speak, ask—nothing shall be denied you!"

"I wish to have in marriage the daughter of Your Magnitude, the golden Aurentine!"

This enraged Dioptricus greatly and, swimming about the face of Froton, he hurled imprecations upon him, rattled his medals at him, called him a shameless scoundrel, a good-for-nothing, a sneaking villain, then ordered him thrown from the palace. He himself immediately sailed off in an underwater boat-and-six to see the King.

When Minogar, Amassid and Philonaut caught sight of Dioptricus in his new form, and they knew him thanks only to the magnificent medals of which he now was made, not counting the tiny tail, they flew into a great fury. As worthies well versed in matters electrical, they realized it would be difficult indeed to go further in personal miniaturization, and the prince's birth ceremony was to be held the very next day and there was not a moment to lose. Therefore Amassid plotted with Philonaut, that when Dioptricus left for his own palace they would fall upon him, carry him off and imprison him, which would not be hard, for who would notice the disappearance of one so small? As they planned it, so they did it. Amassid prepared an old tin can and lay in wait with it behind a coral reef past which the boat of Dioptricus would sail; and when it drew near, his servants—masked—leaped out across its path, and before the lackeys of Dioptricus could lift their fins in defense, their lord had been canned and borne away; Amassid immediately bent down the tin lid, so the great programmist could not escape, and, cruelly taunting him and jeering, he hurried home. Here however he thought that it would be unwise to keep the prisoner himself. Just then he heard a voice crying in the street: "Heads soldered! Bellies polished! Get your tails and necks wired here!" He rejoiced, called the tinker, who happened to be Froton, ordered him to seal the can hermetically, and when the latter had done this, he gave him a thaler and said:

"See here, tinker, in this can is a metal scorpion, which was caught in the cellar of my palace. Take it and discard it outside the city, there where lies the great garbage dump, you know? And to be safe, wedge the can in tightly with a stone, in order that the scorpion not free itself in time. And, by the Great Matrix, do not open the can, or you will perish on the spot!"

"I will do as you say, Sire," said Froton, and he took the can, the coin, and departed.

This business perplexed him, he did not know what to make of it; he shook the can, and something rattled inside.

"That cannot be a scorpion," he thought, "there are no scorpions that small . . . We shall see what sort of thing it is, but not just now . . ."

He returned home, hid the can in the attic, threw over it some old metal sheets, so his wife would not find it, and went to bed. But his wife had observed him concealing something in the garret, so when he left the house the following day to walk the streets as always, calling: "Heads wired! Tails welded!"—she quickly ran upstairs, found the can and, giving it a shake, heard the clink of metal. "Ah that rascal, oh that scoundrel!" she muttered, meaning Froton. "It's come to this, then. He hides treasures from me!" Losing no time, she made a hole in the can, but saw nothing, so she pried at the tin with a chisel. And when she had bent it back just a little, she beheld the glimmer of gold, for the medals of Dioptricus were of the purest ore; trembling with greed, she ripped away the entire lid, and then Dioptricus—who till now had lain as one dead, for the tin shielded him from his brain, which sat in the cupboard of his palace—suddenly awoke, regained contact with his intelligence and exclaimed: "What is this?! Where am I?! Who dared to attack me?! And who are you, disgusting creature? Know, that you will perish most miserably, bolted down and quartered, if you do not this instant restore to me my freedom!"

The tinker's wife, seeing the three ducat-medals, how they flew in her face, bellowing and shaking their tiny tail at her, was so frightened that she tried to flee; she jumped to the attic trapdoor but—because Dioptricus still swam above her and threatened, cursing for all he was worth—she tripped on the top rung of the ladder and came crashing down, ladder and all, from the attic. Falling, she broke her neck, while the ladder, overturned, no longer supported the attic trapdoor—which slammed shut. In this way Dioptricus became imprisoned in the attic, where he swam from wall to wall, calling in vain for help.

That evening Froton returned home and was surprised not to find his wife waiting with her crowbar at the door. But upon entering the house he saw her, and even felt a little sorry, for his was a noble soul; nevertheless it soon occurred to him that this misfortune could be turned to his advantage, particularly as he could use his wife for spare parts, which would pay extremely well. So he sat on the floor, took out his screwdriver and set about dismantling his late missus—when high, piping cries came floating down to him from overhead.

"Ah!" he said to himself. "I know that voice—yes, it's the great royal programmist, who yesterday ordered me thrown from his palace and paid me nothing besides—but how did he find his way into my attic?"

He set the ladder to the trapdoor, climbed up to it and asked:

"Is that you, Your Magnitude?"

"Yes, yes!" howled Dioptricus. "It is I, someone abducted me, waylaid me, sealed me in a can, some female opened it, took fright and fell from the attic, the trapdoor closed, I am trapped here, let me out, whoever you are—by the Great Matrix!—and I will give you all that you desire!"

"I have heard these words before, begging Your Magnitude's pardon, and know what they are worth," replied Froton. "For I am the tinker whom you had thrown out—" And he told him the entire story, how some unknown magnate had summoned him, ordered the can to be soldered shut and left on the garbage dump outside the city. Dioptricus understood that this must have been one of the King's ministers, most likely Amassid. He immediately began to plead with Froton to release him from the attic, but Froton asked how he could now trust Dioptricus's word?

Only after Dioptricus had sworn by all things sacred that he would grant him his daughter's hand in marriage, did the tinker open the trapdoor and, taking the dignitary between two fingers, medals-up, carried him to his palace.

Just then the clocks splashed twelve noon and the grand ceremony of removing the King's son from the kiln commenced; as fast as he could Dioptricus pinned onto the three medals of which he was made the great All-marine Star, with its billow-embroidered ribbon, and swam full speed to the palace of the Innocuids. Froton meanwhile hastened to the chambers where among her maidens sat Aurentine, playing upon the electrocomb; and they took a great liking to one another. Fanfares resounded from the palace towers as Dioptricus swam up to the main entrance, for the ceremony had already begun. The doorkeepers at first refused to let him in, but then they recognized him by his medals and opened the gates.

And when the gates were opened, an underwater draft passed through the entire coronation hall, grabbed up Amassid, Minogar and Philonaut, miniaturized as they were, and swept them into the kitchen, where they circled a while—calling in vain for help—above the sink, into which they then fell and after many subterranean bends and turns ended up outside the city; and by the time they had crawled out from under all the mud, ooze and slime, cleaned themselves off and returned to court, the ceremony was long over. The same underwater draft that had brought the three ministers to such a sorry pass seized Dioptricus also and whirled him about the throne with such force, his gold wire belt snapped and his medals and All-marine Star went flying off in every direction, while the little receiver, carried by the momentum, landed on the forehead of King Hydrops, who was much confounded, for from that tiny mote there came a squeak:

"Your Royal Highness! Forgive me! Unintentional! 'Tis I, Dioptricus, the great programmist . . ."

"Practical jokes at a time like this?" cried the King, and brushed aside the little receiver, which drifted to the floor, and the Lord High Gillard, in opening the ceremony with three blows of his golden staff, accidentally dashed it to smithereens. The prince emerged from the filial kiln and his gaze fell upon the little electric fish that swam in the silver cage beside the throne, his face lit up and his heart went out to that creature. The ceremony concluded successfully, the prince ascended the throne and took the place of Hydrops. From that time on he was the ruler of the Argonautians and became a great philosopher, for he devoted himself to the study of nothingness, there being nothing less than this to meditate upon; and he governed justly, having taken the name of Neantophil, and small electric fish were his favorite dish. As for Froton, he was wed to Aurentine, at whose request he restored the emerald body of Dioptricus, that lay in the cellar, and installed in it the brain taken from the cupboard. Seeing that there was no help for it, the great programmist and the other ministers faithfully served the new King from then on and ever after. And Aurentine and Froton, who was made Lord High Platesmith, lived long and happily.

Automatthew's Friend

A certain robot, planning to go on a long and dangerous voyage, heard of a most useful device which its inventor called an electric friend. He would feel better, he thought, if he had a companion, even a companion that was only a machine, so he went to the inventor and asked to be shown an artificial friend.

"Sure," replied the inventor. (As you know, in fairy tales no one says "sir" or "ma'am" to anyone else, not even to dragons, it's only with the kings that you have to stand on ceremony.) With this he pulled from his pocket a handful of metal granules, that looked like fine shot.

"What is that?" said the robot in surprise.

"Tell me your name, for I forgot to ask it in the proper place of this fairy tale," said the inventor.

"My name is Automatthew."

"That's too long for me, I'll call you Autom."

"Autom's from Automatom, but have it your way," replied the other.

"Well then, Autommy my lad, you have here before you a batch of electrofriends. You ought to know that by vocation and specialization I am a miniaturizer. Which

79

means I make large and heavy mechanisms small and portable. Each one of these granules is a concentrate of electrical thought, highly versatile and intelligent. I won't say a genius, for that would be an exaggeration if not false advertising. True, my intention is precisely to create electrical geniuses and I shall not rest until I have made them so very tiny that it will be possible to carry thousands of them around in your vest pocket; the day I can pour them into sacks and sell them by weight, like sand, I will have achieved my most cherished goal. But enough now of my plans for the future. For the time being I sell electrofriends by the piece and cheaply at that: each costs as much as its weight in diamonds. You'll see, I think, how very reasonable the price is, when you consider that you can put an electrofriend in your ear, where it will whisper good advice and supply you with all kinds of information. Here's a bit of soft cotton, you stop up the ear with it so your friend won't fall out when you tilt your head. Will you take one? If you think you'd like a dozen, I might be able to arrange a discount . . ."

"No, one will do for now," said Automatthew. "But I'd like some idea of what I can expect of it. Will it be able to help me in a difficult situation?"

"But of course, that's what it's for, after all!" replied the inventor good-humoredly. He shook out on his palm a bunch of the granules, which glittered metallically, being made of rare metals, and continued: "Obviously you can't count on help in the physical sense, but we are not speaking of that, I think. Helpful hints, suggestions, cogent comments, sensible recommendations, good observations, admonitions, warnings, words of caution, as well as comfort, solace, encouragement, maxims to restore your faith in yourself, and deep insights that will enable you to cope with any situation, no matter how serious or even grave—this is only a small part of the repertoire of my electrofriends. They are wholly devoted, staunch, true, ever vigilant, because they never sleep; they are also unbelievably durable, esthetic, and you can see for yourself how very handy! So then, you are taking only one?"

"Yes," said Automatthew. "But there's another thing: could you tell me what happens if someone steals it from me? Will it return? Or bring about the thief's destruction?"

"As for that, no," answered the inventor. "It will serve him just as diligently and faithfully as it did you. You can't ask too much, my dear Autom, it will not desert you in your hour of need if you do not desert it. But there is little chance of that—if you will just place it in your ear and always keep the ear plugged up with cotton . . ."

"Very well," agreed Automatthew. "And how am I to speak to it?"

"You needn't speak at all, whisper subvocally and it will hear you perfectly. As for its name, I call it Alfred. Alf or Alfie will do."

"Good," said Automatthew.

They weighed Alfred, the inventor received for it a lovely little diamond, and the robot, content that he now had a companion, a fellow soul for the distant journey, proceeded on his way.

It was most pleasant traveling with Alfred, which, if he so desired it, would wake him each morning by whistling inside his head a soft and cheerful reveille; it also told him various amusing anecdotes, however Automatthew soon forbade it to do this when he was in the presence of others, for they began to suspect him of lunacy, seeing how every now and then he would burst into laughter for no apparent reason. In this manner Automatthew traveled first by land, then reached the seashore, where a beautiful white ship awaited him. He had few possessions, thus in no time at all was ensconced in a cozy little cabin and listening with satisfaction to the clatter that announced the raising of the anchor and the start of a great sea voyage. For several days the white ship merrily sailed the waves beneath a beaming sun, and at night, all silvered by the moon, it rocked him to sleep, till early one morning a terrible storm broke. Waves three times higher than the masts buffeted the ship, which creaked and groaned in all its joints, and the din was so dreadful that Automatthew did not hear a single word of the many comforting things Alfred was no doubt whispering to him during those unpleasant moments. Suddenly there was an ungodly crash, salt water burst into the cabin, and before the horrified eyes of Automatthew the ship began to come apart.

He ran out on deck just as he was, and had barely leaped into the last lifeboat when a monstrous wave loomed up, fell upon the vessel and pulled it down into the churning ocean depths. Automatthew did not see a single member of the crew, he was alone in the lifeboat, alone in the midst of the raging sea, and he trembled, certain that the next roller would sink the little boat and him along with it. The wind howled, from the low clouds torrents lashed the heaving surface of the sea, and he still could not hear what Alfred had to say to him. Then in the confusion he observed some blurry shapes covered with a seething white; this was the shore of an unknown land, upon which the waves were breaking. With a loud scrape the boat ran aground on some rocks, and Automatthew, thoroughly drenched and dripping salt water, set off on shaky legs, with the last of his strength, seeking the refuge of the land's interior, as far away as possible from the ocean waves. At the foot of a rock he sank to earth and fell into a dreamless sleep of exhaustion.

He was wakened by a tactful whistling. It was Alfred reminding him of its friendly presence.

"Ah, how splendid that you're there, Alfred, only now do I see what a good thing it is to have you with, or rather, in me!" cried Automatthew, recovering his senses. He looked around. The sun was shining, the sea was still choppy, but the menacing high waves had disappeared, the thunderclouds, the rain. Unfortunately the boat had disappeared as well. The storm must have raged in the night with incredible force, sweeping up and carrying out to sea the boat that had saved Automatthew. He jumped to his feet and began running along the shore, only to return in ten minutes to the very same spot. He was on a desert island, and a small one in the bargain. Not a particularly encouraging state of affairs. But no matter, he had his Alfred with him! He quickly informed it of just how things stood and asked for some advice.

"Ha! Humph!" said Alfred. "A situation indeed! This will take a bit of thought. What exactly do you require?"

"Require? Why, everything: help, rescue, clothes, means of subsistence, there's nothing here but sand and rocks!"

"H'm! Is that a fact? You're quite sure? There are not lying about somewhere along the beach chests from the wrecked ship, chests filled with tools, utensils, interesting reading, garments for different occasions, as well as gunpowder?"

Automatthew searched the length and breadth of the beach, but found nothing, not so much as a splinter from the vessel, which apparently had sunk all in one piece, like a stone.

"Nothing at all, you say? Most peculiar. The considerable literature on life on desert islands proves irrefutably that a shipwrecked person always finds at close hand axes, nails, fresh water, oil, sacred books, saws, pliers, firearms, and a great number of other useful items. But if not, then not. Is there at least a cave in the rocks providing shelter?"

"No, there is no cave."

"What, no cave? Whoo, this *is* unusual! Would you be so good as to climb onto the highest rock and cast an eye around?"

"I'll do it right away!" cried Automatthew, and scrambled up a steep rock in the middle of the island, and froze: the little volcanic island was surrounded on all sides by limitless ocean!

In a faltering voice he conveyed this news to Alfred, adjusting with a shaky finger the cotton in his ear, so as not to lose his friend. "How lucky I am that it didn't fall out when the ship went down," he thought and, suddenly feeling fatigued, sat on a rock and waited impatiently for friendly assistance.

"Now pay attention, my friend! Here is the advice I hasten to give you in this difficult predicament!" finally came the tiny voice of Alfred, so eagerly awaited. "On the basis of the calculations I have made, I conclude that we find ourselves on an unknown island which represents a kind of reef, or more precisely the summit of an underwater mountain chain that is gradually emerging from the depths and will join the mainland in three to four million years."

"Forget about the million years, what should I do now?!" exclaimed Automatthew.

"The island lies far from all lanes of navigation. The chance of a vessel accidentally appearing in the vicinity is one in four hundred thousand."

"Good Lord!" cried the castaway, despairing. "This is terrible! What then do you advise me to do?"

"I'll tell you in a minute, if you will just stop interrupting. Proceed to the edge of the sea and enter the water, more or less chest-high. In that way you will not have to bend over unnecessarily, which would be cumbersome. Next you immerse your head and take in as much water as you possibly can. The stuff is bitter, I realize, but that will not last long. Particularly if at the same time you continue marching forward. You'll soon grow heavy, and the salt water, filling up your entrails, will in the twinkling of an eye halt all organic processes and thereby instantly terminate your existence. Thanks to this you will avoid the prolonged torment of life upon this island, also the eventual anguish of a lingering death, not to mention the likelihood of losing your sanity prior to that. You might, in addition, hold a heavy stone in each hand. This is not necessary, however . . ."

"You're mad!" shouted Automatthew, jumping up. "So I'm to drown myself? You urge me to commit suicide? Some helpful advice, this! And you call yourself my friend?!"

"Indeed yes!" Alfred replied. "I'm not a bit mad, madness doesn't lie within my capabilities. I never lose my mental balance. All the more unpleasant would it then be for me, dear friend, to be there while you found yourself losing yours and slowly perished in the rays of this scorching sun. I assure you, I have carefully analyzed the entire situation and one by one ruled out every possibility of rescue. You will not make a boat or raft, you haven't the materials for that; no ship will come and save you, as has been already pointed out; neither do airplanes fly over the island, and you in turn cannot build yourself a flying machine. You could, of course, choose a slow death over one that is swift and easy, but as your closest friend I strongly advise you against so foolish a decision. If you would only take a good, deep breath of water . . ."

"Your good, deep breath of water be damned!!" screamed Automatthew, quivering with rage. "And to think that for a friend like this I parted with a beautifully cut diamond! You know what your inventor is? A common thief, a swindler, a fraud!"

"You'll surely retract those words when you have heard me out," said Alfred quietly.

"You mean there's more? What now, do you intend regaling me with tales of the afterlife that waits in store? Just what I need!"

"There is no life after death," said Alfred. "I shall not attempt to deceive you, for I neither wish nor indeed am able to do so. This is not how I understand the duty of a friend. Only listen to me carefully, dear Automatthew! As you are aware, though in general one gives no thought to it, the world is a place of infinite variety and richness. In it you have magnificent cities, filled with mingled voices and fabled treasures, you have royal palaces, hovels, mountains enchanting and drear, murmuring groves, tranquil lakes, torrid deserts and the endless snows of the North. Being what you are, however, you cannot experience at a time more than one single, solitary place among those I have mentioned and the millions I have not. It can therefore be said—without exaggeration—that for the places in which you are not present you represent, as it were, one who is dead, for you are not enjoying the pleasures of palace wealth, nor taking part in the dances of the countries of the South, neither are you feasting your eyes upon the rainbow ices of the North. They do not exist for you, in exactly the same way that they do not exist in death. By the same token, if you use your mind and ponder

well what I am telling you, you will realize that in not
being everywhere, that is, in all those fascinating places,
you are nearly nowhere at all. For there are, as I said,
millions upon millions of places to be, while you are able
to experience this one place only, an uninteresting place,
unpleasant even, in its monotony, bah—repulsive, this
little island here of rocks. Now between 'everywhere' and
'nearly nowhere' the difference is enormous and it
constitutes your normal lot in life, for you always have
been in only one, single, solitary place at a given time. On
the other hand between 'nearly nowhere' and 'nowhere'
the difference is, quite honestly, microscopic. And so the
mathematics of sensations proves that even now you can
barely be considered alive, for your absence is everywhere,
like one departed! That is the first thing. Secondly: gaze
upon this sand mixed with gravel, which digs into your
tender feet—do you consider it invaluable? Assuredly not.
Behold this great quantity of salt water, its revolting
abundance—is it of use to you? Hardly! Here are some
rocks and there, above you, a broiling sky that dries up the
joints in your limbs. Do you need this unendurable heat,
these lifeless, burning boulders? Of course you don't! And
therefore you have absolutely no need of all the things
surrounding you, of that on which you stand, of that
which spreads above you from horizon to horizon. What
will remain, if one takes this away? A little hum in the
head, a pressure in the temples, a pounding in the chest,
some trembling at the knees, and other such chaotic
agitations. Do you need, in turn, this hum, pressure,
pounding and trembling? Not one whit, dear
Automatthew! And if this also is relinquished, what then
remains? A few racing thoughts, those expressions—very
like curses—which in your heart you are hurling at me
now, your own friend, and in addition to this a choking

anger and a sickening fear. Do you need—I ask you finally—this wretched terror and this futile rage? Obviously you can do without them. If then we take away those useless feelings as well, what is left is nothing, nothing, I tell you, zero, and it is precisely this zero, this state of infinite patience, unbroken silence and perfect peace, that I wish for you, as your true friend, to have!"

"But I want to live!" howled Automatthew. "To live! To live!! Do you hear me?!"

"Ah, we are speaking now not of what you experience, but of what you desire," answered Alfred calmly. "You wish to live, in other words to possess a future which will become your present, for this—after all—is what living amounts to. There is nothing more to it than that. But live you will not, for you cannot, as we already determined. The only question then is in what manner you will cease to live—whether in protracted agony or, instead, easily, when with one quick gulp of water . . ."

"Enough! No more! Go away! Get out!!" screamed Automatthew with all his might, jumping up and down with his fists clenched.

"Now what is this?" returned Alfred. "Putting aside for the moment the insulting form of that command, which does bring to mind our declaration of friendship, really, how can you express yourself so unreasonably? How can you say to me 'Get out'? Do I have legs, on which I might depart? Or even arms, to crawl away? You know perfectly well that such is not the case. If you wish to be rid of me, then kindly remove me from your ear, which—I assure you—is not the most convenient place in the world to be, and throw me somewhere!"

"Fine!" yelled Automatthew in a fury. "I'll do it right now!" But in vain did he dig and poke in his ear, using his finger. His friend had been too carefully wedged within and in no way could he extract it, though he shook his head in all directions like one insane.

"That evidently isn't going to work," Alfred observed after a long pause. "It would appear that we shall not part, though this is neither to your liking nor to mine. If so, then it is a fact we must accept, for facts have this about them, that the truth is always on their side. Which applies equally—I note in passing—to your current situation. You wish to have a future, and at any price. This seems to me the height of folly, but very well, so be it. Permit me then to depict this future for you in rough outline, since the known is always preferable to the unknown. The anger which presently convulses you will shortly give way to a feeling of helpless despair, and this, after a series of efforts—as violent as they will be unavailing—to find some avenue of escape, will yield in turn to a mindless stupor. Meanwhile the driving heat of the sun, which reaches even me in this shaded portion of your person, will, in accordance with the unrelenting laws of physics and chemistry, dry out more and more your entire being. First the oil in your joints will evaporate off, and the least movement will cause you to squeak and creak dreadfully, poor devil! Next, as your skull begins to bake in the searing heat, you will see whirling circles of various colors, but this will bear no similarity to a rainbow, because . . ."

"*Will* you be quiet, you intolerable pest?!" cried Automatthew. "I don't *want* to hear what's going to happen to me! Silence, not another word, do you understand?!"

"You needn't shout. You know perfectly well that your every whisper, however low, can reach me. And so you do not wish to learn of the torments that your future holds? Yet on the other hand you wish to have that future? How illogical! Very well, in that case I will be silent. I only point out that it is inappropriate for you to be concentrating your anger on me, as though *I* were to blame for this highly regrettable situation you are in. The cause of the misfortune was, of course, the storm, while I am your friend and my participation in the tortures that await you, that entire spectacle—divided into acts—of suffering and slow death, even now it grieves me to think upon it, yes, the horrifying prospect of what will happen when your oil . . ."

"So you won't stop then? Or is it that you can't, you little monster?!" bellowed Automatthew, and struck himself a blow in the ear that housed his friend. "Oh, if only I had here, in my hand, a stick of some sort, a piece of a twig, which I could use to pry you out, I'd do it and grind you beneath my heel in no time!"

"You dream of destroying me?" said Alfred, saddened. "Truly, you do not deserve an electrofriend, nor any other sympathizing fellow creature!"

Automatthew flared up anew at this and so they quarreled, argued and disputed till the day was almost over, and the poor robot, exhausted from all his screaming, jumping and fist-waving, and suddenly feeling very weak, sat down on a stone where, heaving sighs of hopelessness every now and then, he stared out at the empty ocean. A couple of times he took the edge of a small cloud peering out over the horizon for the smoke of a steamship, but these illusions Alfred quickly dispelled, reminding him of the one-in-four-hundred-thousand probability, which again drove Automatthew to paroxysms of despair and rage, all the more in that each time, as it turned out, Alfred was right. Finally a long silence fell between them. The castaway now gazed at the lengthening shadows of the rocks, which stretched across the white sand of the beach, when Alfred spoke:

"Why do you say nothing? Can it be that those circles I mentioned are even now swimming before your eyes?"

Automatthew did not bother to reply.

"Aha!" Alfred went on, in monologue. "So it's not only the circles but, in all likelihood, also that mindless torpor which I so accurately predicted. Remarkable, really, the lack of sense displayed by an intelligent being, particularly when beset by circumstances. You trap it on a desert island, where it must perish, you prove as two and two are four that this is inescapable, you show it a way out of the situation, in the taking of which, it will be making the only use it can of its will and reason—and is it thankful? Oh no, it wants hope, and if there is none and can be none, it clings to false hope and would rather sink into madness than into the water which . . ."

"Stop talking about the water!!" croaked Automatthew.

"I was only demonstrating the irrationality of your motives," answered Alfred. "I no longer urge anything upon you. That is, any action, for if you wish to die slowly, or rather, by wishing to do nothing in general, you undertake that type of dying, then one must think this through properly. Consider how erroneous and unwise it is to fear death, a state that deserves, rather, vindication! For what can equal the perfection of nonexistence? True, the agony leading up to it does not, in itself, present an especially attractive phenomenon, on the other hand there has never yet been one so feeble in mind or body that he could not endure it and proved unable to die his death completely, all the way and to the very end. It is not, then, a thing of much significance, if any dolt, weakling and good-for-nothing can do it. And if absolutely everyone can handle it (and you must admit that this is so, I at least have never heard of anyone unequal to the task), it is better to think with delight on the all-merciful nothingness that lies just beyond its threshold. Because, when one has passed away, it is impossible to think, inasmuch as death and thought are mutually exclusive, and therefore when else, if not while still in life, is it fitting to contemplate— sensibly and particularly—all those privileges, conveniences and pleasures which death will bestow so generously upon you?! Picture if you will: no struggles, no anxieties or apprehensions, no suffering of the body or the soul, no unhappy accidents, and this on what a scale! Why, even if all the world's evil forces were to join and conspire against you, they would not reach you! Truly, nothing can compare with the sweet security of one who is no more! And if furthermore you consider that this security is not something transient, fleeting, impermanent, that nothing may repeal or intrude upon it, then with what boundless joy . . ."

"Drop dead," came the weak voice of Automatthew and, accompanying those laconic words, a short but pungent oath.

"How I regret that I cannot!" Alfred instantly replied. "Not only feelings of egoistic envy (for there is nothing to compare with death, as I've just said), but the purest altruism inclines me to accompany you into oblivion. But alas, this is not possible, since my inventor made me indestructible, no doubt to serve his constructor's pride. Truly, when I think of how I will remain inside your brine-encrusted, desiccated corpse, whose disintegration will go slowly, I am sure, and how I will sit there and converse with myself—it fills me with sorrow. And all the waiting there will be, afterwards, before at last that one-in-four-hundred-thousandth vessel, in keeping with the laws of probability, chances upon this little island . . ."

"What?! You will not waste away here?!" exclaimed Automatthew, roused from his lethargy by these words of Alfred. "Then you will go on living, while I, while I . . . Oh no! Not a chance! Never! Never!! Never!!!"

And with a dreadful roar he leaped to his feet and began to hop, jerk his head, dig in his ear with all his might, performing throughout the most amazing twists and tosses with his body—in vain, however. While all this went on, Alfred piped at the top of its voice:

"Now really, stop! What, have you lost your mind already? It's too soon for that! Careful, you'll hurt yourself! You could break or maybe sprain something! Watch out for the neck! Come, this makes no sense! It would be a different thing if you could, well, get it over with all at once . . . but this way you'll only injure yourself! I told you I'm indestructible and that's that, it's useless for you to go to all this trouble! Even if you were to shake me out, you still couldn't do me any harm, that is, any good—I meant to say—since in accordance with what I have already expounded at such length, death is a thing to be envied. Ow! Stop, please! How can you jump about like that?"

Automatthew however continued to hurl himself, heedless of everything, and finally took to ramming his head against the rock on which he had been sitting before. And he rammed and rammed, with sparks in his eyes and a cloud of powder in his nostrils, deafened by the force of his own blows, until Alfred popped suddenly from his ear and rolled between some stones with a faint cry of relief, that it had finally ended. Automatthew did not at first notice that his efforts had met with success. Sinking down upon a sun-scorched stone, he rested there awhile, and then, still unable to move his arms or legs, mumbled:

"Don't worry, it's only a momentary weakness. I'll

shake you out yet, yes, then under the heel you go, my dear friend, do you hear? Do you hear? Hey! What's this?!"

He sat up quickly, aware of an emptiness in his ear. He looked around, his mind not altogether clear, and, getting down on his hands and knees, began feverishly hunting for Alfred in the gravel.

"Alfred! Aaaal-fred!!! Where are you? Answer me!!" he hollered all the while. But Alfred, whether out of wariness or for some other reason, didn't make a sound. Automatthew then began to lure it with the tenderest words, assured it that he had changed his mind, that his only desire was to follow the good advice of his electrofriend and drown himself, he only wanted first to hear it say once more how wonderful death was. But this didn't work either, Alfred said nothing. Then the castaway, cursing up and down, systematically began to search inch by inch the surrounding area. Suddenly, in the middle of throwing away a handful of gravel, Automatthew raised it to his eyes and started trembling with evil delight, for among the pebbles he spotted Alfred, a dully gleaming, serenely shining tiny grain of metal.

"Ah! There you are, my little chum! There you are, old speck! I have you now, my fine, forever-lasting friend!" he hissed, carefully squeezing between his fingers Alfred, which didn't make so much as a peep. "And now we'll see about that indestructibility of yours, yes, we'll test it out right now. Take that!!!"

These words were accompanied by a powerful concussion; having placed his electrofriend on the surface of a rock, Automatthew jumped upon it with all his weight, and for good measure pivoted on his steel heel until it made a screech. Alfred said nothing, only the rock seemed to complain beneath that grinding drill; bending over, Automatthew saw that the tiny granule hadn't been touched, only the rock under it was a trifle dented. Alfred now lay in that small depression.

"Strong, are you? We'll find a harder stone!" he growled, and began running back and forth across the island, looking for the toughest possible flints, basalts and porphyries, in order to crush Alfred upon them. And as he pounded it with his heels, he spoke to it with affected calm, or sometimes hurled insults at it, as if in the expectation that it would reply or perhaps even burst into pleas and entreaties. Alfred however said nothing. The air carried only the echoes of heavy thuds, trampling, the crumbling of stone and the panting and swearing of Automatthew. After a long time Automatthew came to the conclusion that the most terrible blows would in fact cause Alfred no harm, and, feverish and weak, he sat once more upon the shore, his electrofriend in his hand.

"Even if I cannot smash you," he said with seeming composure, though barely able to control his rage, "have no fear, I will take proper care of you. For that vessel of yours you will have to wait, my good friend, since I shall throw you to the bottom of the sea and there you will lie for an eternity or more. You will have abundant time for pleasant meditations in that so hermetic solitude! I will see to it you do not gain a new friend!"

"My dear fellow," said Alfred unexpectedly. "And what will it matter to me, to live on the ocean floor? You think in the categories of an impermanent being, hence your error. Understand that either the sea must someday dry up, or else first its entire bottom will rise like a mountain and become land. Whether this happens in a hundred thousand years or in a hundred million is of no consequence to me. Not only am I indestructible, but infinitely patient, as indeed you might have observed, if only by the calm with which I endured the manifestations of your blindness. I'll tell you more: I did not respond to your calls, but rather let you search for me, for I wished to spare you unnecessary excitement. Also I was silent while you jumped on me, so as not to increase your fury with an inadvertent word, since this could have done you further injury."

Automatthew, upon hearing this noble-minded explanation, shook with renewed anger.

"I'll smash you! I'll grind you to dust, you, you bastard!!" he bellowed, and that crazy dance among the rocks, the leaps, the lunges, the stamping in place, began all over again. This time however the well-wishing squeaks of Alfred joined in:

"I don't think you can do it, but let's give it a try! Go ahead! And again! No, not that way, you'll tire too quickly! Legs together! That's right—and up! One-two, and-a-one, and-a-two! Jump higher, higher, the impact will be greater! What, you can't? Really? Don't have it in you? Ah yes, yes, now *there's* an idea! Drop a rock from above! That's it, good! Try another? Don't have any larger? One more time, now! Wham! Bam! Go to it, dear friend! What a shame I can't pitch in and help! Why are you stopping? Worn out so soon? What a shame . . . Well, no matter . . . I can wait, you rest yourself! Let the breeze cool you off . . ."

Automatthew collapsed with a clatter on the rocks and gazed with burning hatred at the metal grain that lay in his open hand, and he listened—he could not choose but listen—as it spoke:

"If I were not your electrofriend, I would say that you are behaving disgracefully. The ship went down on account of the storm, you saved yourself along with me, I gave you what advice I could, but then, when I failed to come up with a means of rescue, since that was impossible, you made up your mind—for my words of simple truth and honest counsel—to destroy me, me, your only companion. It's true that in this way you at least acquired some purpose in life, so for that alone you owe me gratitude. Strange, though, that you should find so hateful the thought of my surviving . . ."

"Surviving? That remains to be seen!" snarled Automatthew.

"No, really, you are too much. Here's a thought. Why not place me on the buckle of your belt? It's steel, and steel I think is harder than rock. Worth a try, though personally I'm convinced it's quite useless, yet I'd like to be of help . . ."

Automatthew, albeit with a certain reluctance, finally followed this suggestion, but all he succeeded in doing was cover the surface of his buckle with tiny pit holes, produced by frenzied blows. When even the most desperate of his strokes proved harmless, Automatthew fell into a truly black despair and, sapped of strength, stared dully at the metal mote, which spoke to him in its high-pitched voice:

"And this is supposed to be an intelligent being! He falls into deep dejection because he cannot wipe off the face of the earth the only fellow creature he has in all this dead expanse! Tell me, dear Automatthew, aren't you just a little ashamed of yourself?"

"Shut up, you worthless chatterbox!" hissed the castaway.

"Why should I shut up? If I'd wished you ill, you know, I would have shut up long ago, but I remain your true electrofriend. I will keep you company in your death agonies like a steadfast brother, no matter what you do, and no, you will not cast me into the sea, my dear, for it is always better to have an audience. I will be the audience of your final throes, which thereby surely will turn out better than they would in utter isolation; the important thing is emotion, it matters not what kind. Hatred for me, your genuine friend, will sustain you, give you courage, lift up your spirits, impart to your groans a true and convincing ring, also it will systematize your twitchings and bring order to each of your last moments, and that is no small thing . . . As for myself, I promise I shall speak little and avoid commenting, for were I to do otherwise, I might— without meaning to—break you with an excess of friendship, which you could not withstand, since to tell the truth you have a nasty character. However I shall manage this as well, and, by returning kindness for unkindness, conquer you, and in this way save you from yourself—out of friendship, I repeat, but not blind friendship, for affection does not close my eyes to the baseness of your nature . . ." These words were interrupted by a roar, that issued suddenly from the breast of Automatthew.

"A ship! A ship!! A ship!!!" he shrieked wildly and, jumping to his feet, began to run back and forth along the shore, hurling stones in the water, waving his arms with all his might, but mainly screaming at the top of his voice until he grew completely hoarse—all without need, for a ship was clearly approaching the island and before very long had sent out a rescue boat.

As it developed later, the captain of the vessel that had carried Automatthew, just before it sank, succeeded in sending a radiotelegram calling for help, thanks to which that region of the sea was scoured by numerous ships, and it was one of these that found the island. As the rowboat with the sailors neared the shore in shallow water, Automatthew's first impulse was to jump into it himself, but after a moment's thought he ran back for Alfred, fearing the latter might raise a cry, which the others might hear, and that could lead to embarrassing questions, possibly even accusations made by his electrofriend. To avoid this, he grabbed up Alfred and, not knowing how or where to hide it, hurriedly inserted it back into his ear. There followed effusive scenes of greeting and thanks, during which Automatthew conducted himself very noisily, afraid that one of the sailors might overhear the tiny voice of Alfred. For all this time his electrofriend was saying, over and over: "Well, but this was really unexpected! One chance in four hundred thousand . . . What amazing luck! I would hope now that our relations improve, yes, we shall get on splendidly together, especially as I refused you nothing in your moments of greatest trial, besides which I can be discreet and know how to let bygones be bygones!"

When, after a long voyage, the ship came to port, Automatthew surprised everyone by expressing a desire, incomprehensible to them, to visit a nearby ironworks, which boasted a great steam hammer. It was said that in the course of this visit he behaved somewhat strangely, for, having gone up to the steel anvil in the main shop, he began shaking his head violently, as if he intended to knock the very brains out through his ear and into his raised hand, and he even hopped on one leg; those present, however, made as if they didn't notice, judging that a person so recently rescued from terrible straits might well be given to eccentricities, the product of an unbalanced mind. And indeed, afterwards Automatthew changed his former way of life, seemingly falling into one mania after another. Once he gathered explosives of some sort, and even tried setting them off in his own room, the neighbors however put a stop to that, they went straight to the authorities; and once, for no apparent reason, he took to collecting hammers and carborundum files, telling his acquaintances that he planned to build a new type of mind-reading machine. Later on he became a recluse and acquired the habit of conversing with himself, and sometimes you could hear him running about the house in loud soliloquy, even shouting words very much like curses.

Finally, after many years, developing a new obsession, he began to buy cement, sacks and sacks of it. From this he fashioned an enormous sphere and, when the thing had hardened, carted it off to an unknown destination. It has been said that he hired himself out as a caretaker at an abandoned mine, that one dark night he dropped down its shaft an enormous block of concrete, and thereafter, to the end of his days, he prowled the vicinity, and there was not a piece of garbage he would not pick up, in order to throw it down that empty shaft. True, his ways were rather strange, but most of these rumors do not—I think—merit credence. It is difficult to believe that for all those years he harbored in his heart a grudge against his electrofriend, to which—after all—he owed so much.

King Globares and the Sages

Globares, ruler of Eparida, once summoned his greatest sages to appear before him, and he said:

"Truly, hard is the lot of a king who has learned everything there is to learn, so that what is said to him sounds hollow as a broken jug! I wish to be astounded, yet am bored, I seek stimulation, yet hear wearisome twaddle, I long for novelty, and they treat me to insipid flatteries. Know, O wise ones, that today I have ordered all my fools and jesters executed, along with my advisers high and low, and this same fate awaits you if you fail to do my bidding. Let each of you tell me the strangest tale he knows, but if it moves me neither to laughter nor to tears, confounds not nor dismays, provides no entertainment nor food for thought—he parts with his head!" The King made a sign and the sages heard the iron step of the myrmidons that surrounded them at the foot of the throne, and whose naked swords did gleam like flame. They were afraid and nudged one another, for none of them wished to risk the King's anger and lay his head upon the block. Finally the first spoke:

"O King and ruler! The strangest tale in all the visible

and invisible Universe is without question that of the stellar tribe known in the chronicles as the Awks. From the dawn of their history the Awks did everything opposite compared to all other beings of intelligence. Their ancestors settled on Urdruria, a planet famous for its volcanoes; each year it gives birth to new mountain chains, during which time terrible spasms convulse it, so that nothing remains standing. And, to make the misery of the inhabitants complete, the heavens saw fit to have their globe pass through the Meteor Stream; this for two hundred days out of the year pounds the planet with droves of stone battering rams. The Awks (who at that time were not yet called thus) raised edifices of tempered iron and steel, and themselves they covered with such quantities of steel plates, they resembled walking mounds of armor. Nevertheless the ground opened up during the quakes and swallowed their steel cities, and meteor hammers crushed their suits of armor. When the entire race became threatened with annihilation, its sages gathered and held council, and the first one said: —Our people will not survive in their present form and there is no escape save through transmutation. The earth opens from below in crevices, therefore in order not to fall in, each Awk must possess a base that is wide and flat; the meteors on the other hand come from above, and so each Awk must be sharp-ended at the top. As cones, we will be safe from harm.

"And the second one said: —That is not the way to do it. If the earth opens its jaws wide, it will swallow up a cone as well, and a meteor falling at an angle will pierce its side. The ideal shape is a sphere. For when the ground begins to tremble and heave, a sphere will always roll aside by itself, and a falling meteor will hit its oblique surface and skim off; we should therefore transform ourselves in order to roll onward towards a brighter future.

"And the third one said: —A sphere is subject to being crushed or swallowed up no less than any other material form. No shield exists, which a powerful enough sword cannot penetrate, nor a sword which will not be notched by a hard shield. Matter, O my brothers, means perpetual change, flux and transformation, it is impermanent. Not in *it* should beings truly blessed with intelligence take up residence, but in that which is immutable, eternal and all-perfect, though of this world!

"—And what is that?—inquired the other sages.

"—I shall not tell you, but instead show you!—replied the third. And before their eyes he began to undress; he removed his outer robe, studded with crystals, and the second, gold-embroidered, and the silver trousers, then removed the top of his skull and his breast, then stripped himself with increasing speed and precision, going from joints to couplings, from couplings to bolts, from bolts to filaments, scintillas, till finally he got down to atoms. And then that sage began to shell his atoms, and shelled them so swiftly, nothing could be seen except for his dwindling and his disappearing, yet he proceeded so adroitly and in such great haste, that in the course of those dismantling movements—before the eyes of his flabbergasted fellow sages—he remained as a perfect absence, which was so exact as to be, in a manner of speaking, negatively present. For there where he had had, previously, a single atom, now he did not have that single atom, where a moment ago six had been, six were now missing, in the place where a little screw had been, the lack of a little screw appeared, perfectly faithful and in no wise departing from it. And in this way he became a vacuum, arranged just as was arranged, previously, that which it replaced, namely himself; and no existence interfered with his nonexisting, for he had worked quickly and maneuvered nimbly in order that no particle, no material intrusion should pollute the perfection of the presence of his absence! And the others saw him as a void shaped exactly as he had been only an instant before, they recognized his eyes by the absence of their black color, his face by the missing sky-blue shine, and his limbs by the vanished fingers, joints and shoulderplates! —In this very way, O my brothers— said the One There Not There—through active self-incorporation into nothingness, we shall acquire not only tremendous immunity, but immortality as well. For only matter changes, and nothingness does not accompany it on that path of continual uncertainty, therefore perfection lies in nonbeing, not in being, and we must choose the first, and spurn the latter!

"And they decided, and did accordingly. From then on the Awks were, and are to this day, an invincible race. They owe their existence not to that which is within them, for within them there is nothing, but wholly to that which surrounds them. And when one of them enters a home, he is visible as that home's nonpresence, and if he steps into a mist—as its local discontinuity. Thus, in ridding themselves of the vicissitudes of precarious matter, have they made possible the impossible . . ."

"But how then do they travel through the cosmic void, my sage?" asked Globares.

"This alone they cannot do, O King, since the outer void would merge with their own and they would cease to exist as nonexistences concentrated locally. Therefore also they must maintain a constant watch over the purity of their absence, over the emptiness of their identities, and this vigilance occupies their time . . . They call themselves Be-nothings or Nullians . . ."

"Sage," said the King, "it is a foolish tale you tell, for

how can material diversity be replaced by the uniformity of that which is not there? Is a rock the same as a house? Yet surely the lack of a rock may take the same form as the lack of a house, consequently the one and the other become as if identical."

"Sire," the sage defended himself, "there are different kinds of nothingness . . ."

"We shall see," said the King, "what happens when I order you beheaded. How think you, will the absence of a head become its presence?" Here the monarch gave a hideous laugh and motioned to his myrmidons.

"Sire!" cried the sage, already in the grip of their steel hands. "You were pleased to laugh, my tale therefore awoke your mirth, thus in keeping with your given word you should spare my life!"

"No, I provided my own amusement," said the King. "Unless, that is, you go along with the joke: if you agree voluntarily to be beheaded, that will amuse me, and then 'twill be as you wish."

"I agree!" shouted the sage.

"In that case behead him, seeing that he himself requests it!" said the King.

"But Sire, I agreed in order that you not behead me . . ."

"If you agree, you must be beheaded," explained the King. "And if you do not agree, you will have failed to amuse me, and so then too you must be beheaded . . ."

"No, no, it is the other way around!" the sage cried. "If I agree, then you, amused, should spare my life, and if I do not agree . . ."

"Enough!" said the King. "Executioner, do your duty!"

The sword flashed and the sage's head came tumbling down.

After a moment of deathly silence the second of the sages spoke:

"O King and ruler! The strangest of all the stellar tribes is without question the race of the Polyonts, or Multiploids, also called the Pluralites. Each of them has, it is true, only one body, but despite this many legs, and the higher the office held, the greater the number. As far as heads are concerned, they have them as the need arises: each office, among them, carries with it an appropriate head, impoverished families possess in common only one, the wealthy on the other hand accumulate in their safes a variety, for different occasions: they have, then, morning heads and evening, strategic heads in case of war and high-speed heads when they are in a hurry, as well as cool-and-level heads, explosive heads, heads for passion, dalliance, marriage and funerals, and thus they are equipped for every situation in life."

"Is that it?" asked the King.

"No, Sire!" replied the sage, who saw it wasn't going well for him. "The Pluralites also derive their name from the fact that all are linked up with their ruler, and in such a way that if ever the majority deems the royal actions to be harmful to the general welfare, that ruler loses his cohesion and disintegrates . . ."

"Unoriginal, if not—regicidal!" the King said darkly. "Since you yourself, sage, have had so much to say upon the topic of heads, perhaps you can tell me: Am I now going to order you beheaded, or not?"

—If I say he will—quickly thought the sage—then he will indeed, for he is ill-disposed toward me. If I say he will not, that will catch him unawares, and if he is surprised, he will have to set me free according to his promise.— And he said:

"No, Sire, you will not behead me."

"You are mistaken," said the King. "Executioner, do your duty!"

"But Sire!" cried the sage, already seized by the myrmidons, "did not my words surprise you? Did you not expect me to say, rather, that you would order me beheaded?"

"Your words did not surprise me," answered the King, "for they were dictated by fear, which you have written on your face. Enough! Off with his head!"

And with a clang the head of the second sage went rolling across the marble floor. The third and oldest of the sages watched this scene with complete calm. And when the King again demanded an amazing tale, he said:

"O King! I could tell you a story truly extraordinary, but this I shall not do, for I would rather make you honest than cause you to be amazed. Thus will I force you to behead me, not under the paltry pretext of this game into which you seek to turn your killing, but in a manner true to your nature, a nature which, though cruel, dares not work its pleasure without donning first the mask of falsehood. For you wished to behead us, so that it would be said afterwards that the King had put to death fools who pretended to wisdom not theirs. It is my desire, however, that the truth be told, and so will I keep silent."

"No, I will not give you to the executioner now," said the King. "I sincerely and honestly crave something novel. You sought to anger me, but I can curb my anger till the proper time. I say to you: Speak, and you will save perchance not only your own self. The tale you tell may border even on lese majesty, which indeed you have already permitted yourself, but this time it must be an affront so monstrous as to become a compliment, and a compliment of such dimensions as to constitute in turn an outrage! Try then at a single blow both to elevate and humiliate, both to magnify and mortify your King!"

A silence fell. Those present made small motions, as if

seeing how firmly their heads still rested on their shoulders.

The third sage seemed plunged in thought. At last he said:

"O King, I shall carry out your wish, and reveal to you the reason why. I shall do this thing for the sake of all those present here, for my own sake, yes and for yours also, in order that it not be said in years to come that there lived a king who by his caprice destroyed wisdom in his kingdom. Even if that *is* the case at this moment, even if your wish has little importance or none at all, my task is to impart value to that passing whim, to turn it into something meaningful and lasting—and therefore I shall speak . . ."

"Old one, enough now of your introduction, which once again borders on lese majesty, and without coming anywhere near a compliment," said the King angrily. "Speak!"

"O King, you abuse your power," replied the sage, "yet your abuses are nothing compared to those which became the lot of your remote ancestor, unknown to you, who was also the founder of the Eparid dynasty. This great-great-great-grandfather of yours, Allegoric, likewise abused his royal power. To give you some idea of the enormity of what he did, I ask you to look out upon yon night horizon, visible through the upper windows of the palace hall." The King gazed up at the sky, starry and clear, and the old one continued slowly:

"Behold and hearken! Everything that is, is ridiculed. No station, however high, is proof against ridicule, for there always will be ones who mock even the majesty of a king. Laughter strikes at thrones and realms. Nations make fun of other nations, or of themselves. It even happens that fun is made of what does not exist—have not mythological gods been laughed at? Even things grimly serious and solemn—tragic even—ofttimes become the butt of jokes. You have but to think of graveyard humor, the jests concerning death and the deceased. And the heavenly bodies themselves have not been spared this treatment. Take for example the Sun, or the Moon. The Moon is now and then depicted as a skinny character with a drooping fool's cap and a chin that sticks out like a sickle, while the Sun is a fat-faced, friendly humpty-dumpty in a tousled aureola. And yet, though the kingdoms of both life and death serve as objects of ridicule, and things both great and small, there is something at which no one yet has had the courage to laugh or jeer. Nor is this thing the sort which one might easily forget or fail to notice, for I am speaking here of everything that exists, in other words the Universe. Yet if you think upon it, O King, you will see how very ludicrous is the Universe . . ."

At this point, for the first time, King Globares experienced surprise, and with growing interest listened to the words of the sage, who said:

"The Universe is composed of stars. That sounds serious enough, but when we look into the matter more closely, it is hard to keep from smiling. In actual fact—what are stars? Spheres of fire, suspended in the everlasting night. A compelling image, it would seem. Compelling by its nature? No, purely on account of its size. But size alone cannot decide the significance of a phenomenon. Do the scribblings of a cretin, transferred from a sheet of paper to a broad plain, become thereby momentous?

"Stupidity multiplied does not cease to be stupidity, only its ludicrousness is increased. And the Universe, what is it but a scribble of random dots! Wherever you look, however far you go—this and nothing else! The monotony of Creation would seem to be the most crass and uninspired idea one could possibly imagine. A dotted nothingness going on and on into infinity—who would contrive such a witless thing if it had yet to be created? Only a cretin, surely. To take, if you please, the immeasurable stretches of emptiness and dot them, over and over, haphazardly here and there—how can one attribute order to such a structure, or grandeur? It fills one with awe? Say rather with despair, in that there is no appealing it. Indeed it is only the result of self-plagiarism, a self-plagiarism done from a beginning that was in turn the most mindless of acts possible, for what can you do with a blank sheet of paper before you and pen in hand when you do not know, when you haven't the faintest idea where to begin? A drawing? Bah, you must first know what there is to draw. And if you have nothing whatever in mind? If you find yourself without a grain of imagination? Well, the pen, placed upon the page as though of its own accord, unintentionally touching, will make a dot. And that dot, once made, will create—in the mindless musing that accompanies such creative impotence—a pattern, suggestive by virtue of the fact that besides itself there is absolutely nothing, and that with the littlest effort it can be repeated ad infinitum. Repeated, yes, but how? Dots, after all, may be arranged in some design. But what if this too is beyond you? Nothing remains but to shake the pen in frustration, spattering ink, filling up the page with dots blindly, any which way." With these words the sage took a large piece of paper and, dipping his pen in an inkwell, spattered ink upon it several times, after which he pulled out of his robe a map of the firmament and showed the first and the second to the King. The resemblance was striking. Millions of dots appeared across the paper, some larger, some smaller, for at times the pen had spattered copiously and at times had gone dry. And the sky on the map was represented exactly the same way. From his throne the King regarded both sheets of paper and was silent. The sage meanwhile went on:

"You have been taught, O King, that the Universe is a structure infinitely sublime, mighty in the majesty of its star-woven vasts. But observe, is not that venerable, all-pervading and eternal frame the work of the utmost stupidity, does it not in fact constitute the very antithesis of thought and order? Why has no one noticed this before?—you ask. Because the stupidity is everywhere! But its omnipresence all the more stridently cries out for our ridicule, our distancing laughter, a laughter which would at the same time usher in revolt and liberation. How very fitting it would be to write, in just this spirit, a Lampoon of the Universe, in order that that work of supreme inanity receive the rebuff it deserves, in order that from then on it be attended not with a chorus of worshipful sighs, but with hoots and catcalls."

The King listened, dumbfounded, and the sage—after a moment of silence—continued:

"The duty of every scientist would be the writing of such a Lampoon, were it not for the fact that then he would have to put his finger on the first cause, which brought into being this state of things that merits only derision and regret, called the Universe. And that took place when Space was still completely empty and awaiting the first creative acts, while the world, sending forth buds from less than nothingness through nothingness, had produced barely a handful of clustered bodies, on which reigned your great-great-great-ancestor, Allegoric. He then conceived a thing impossible and mad, for he decided to replace Nature in its infinitely slow and patient work! He decided, in Nature's stead, to create a Cosmos abundant and full of priceless wonders. Unable to accomplish this himself, he ordered built a machine of the greatest intelligence, that it might carry out the task. Three hundred years were spent in the construction of that Moloch, and three hundred more, the reckoning of time however was different then. Nothing was spared, neither in effort nor in resources, and the mechanical monster reached proportions and power all but boundless. When the machine was ready, the usurper of Nature gave the order to turn it on. He had no inkling of what exactly it would do. It was, as a result of his limitless arrogance, by now too large, and consequently its wisdom, towering far above the greatest minds, exceeding the culmination, the pinnacle of genius, tumbled down into a total disintegration of intellect, into a jabbering darkness of centrifugal currents, that tore apart all content, so that the monstrosity, coiled up like some metagalaxy and laboring in frenzied circles, gave up the ghost at the first unuttered words—and from that chaos, seemingly thinking with the most terrible exertion, in which swarms of still unfinished concepts all turned back into oblivion, from those struggling, straining, useless convulsions and collisions there began to trickle down to the obedient print-out subsystems of the colossus only senseless punctuation marks! This was not, now, the most intelligent of intelligent machines possible, the Cosmocreator Omnipotens, but a ruin begotten of a heedless usurpation, a ruin which, destined for great things, could only stammer dots. What happened then? The ruler eagerly awaited some all-fulfilling execution of his plans, the boldest plans that ever thinking being devised, and no one dared to tell him he was standing at the source of a meaningless yammer, a mechanical agony that entered the world in its very death throes. But the lifelessly obedient hulks of the print-out machines were ready to carry out any command, and so, in time to the transmitted beat they began from the material clay to manufacture that which in three-dimensional space corresponds to the two-dimensional image of a point: spheres. And in this way, repeating endlessly one thing and always the same, till heat appeared and set each mass ablaze, they hurled into the chasms of the void round after round of fiery spheres, and thus in a stutter did the Universe arise! Your great-great-great-grandfather was, then, the creator of the Universe, yet at the same time the author of an absurdity whose magnitude nothing now will ever equal. For the act of destroying so aborted a piece of work would certainly be much more sensible and—the main thing—desired and consciously intended, which indeed you cannot say about that other act, Creation. And this is all I have to tell you, O King, descendant of Allegoric, the builder of worlds."

When the King had sent away the sages, showering them first with gifts, and the oldest especially, who had in one stroke succeeded in rendering him the highest compliment and the greatest insult, one of the young scholars asked that sage, when at last they were alone, how much truth there was to his tale.

"What am I to tell you?" answered the old one. "That which I said, did not come from knowledge. Science does not concern itself with those properties of existence to which ridiculousness belongs. Science explains the world, but only Art can reconcile us to it. What do we really know about the origin of the Universe? A blank so wide can be filled with myths and legends. I wished, in my mythologizing, to reach the limits of improbability, and I believe that I came close. You know this already, therefore what you really wanted to ask was if the Universe is indeed ludicrous. But that question each must answer for himself."

The Tale
of King Gnuff

After the good king Helixander's death, his son, Gnuff, ascended the throne. Everyone was unhappy about this, because Gnuff was ambitious and cowardly. He decided he would earn for himself the epithet of Great, yet he was afraid of drafts, of ghosts, of wax, for on a waxed floor one could break one's leg, of relatives, in that they might interfere in his governing, and most of all—of having his fortune told. Immediately as he was crowned, he ordered that throughout the kingdom doors be shut and windows not opened, that all the fortunetelling consoles be destroyed, and to the inventor of a machine that got rid of ghosts he gave a medal and a pension. The machine was truly good, for not once did Gnuff see a ghost. Also he never went out into the garden, for fear of catching cold, and took walks only in the castle, which was very large. Once, while strolling through the corridors and suites of rooms, he wandered into the old part of the palace, which he had never visited before. In the first hall that he discovered stood the household guards of his great-great-grandfather, all wind-up, dating from the days before electricity. In the second hall he saw steamknights, also rusted, but this was not of interest to him, and he was

114

about to turn and leave when he noticed a small door with the inscription: DO NOT ENTER. It was covered with a thick layer of dust and he would not have bothered with it, but for that sign. The sign outraged him. What was this— someone dared forbid *him*, the King? He opened the creaking door, not without difficulty, and a winding stairway led him to an abandoned tower. And there stood a very old copper cabinet; it had little ruby eyes, a wind-up key and a tiny hatch. He realized this was a fortunetelling cabinet and again was angered, that despite his order it had been left in the palace, but then he thought, why not at least try it once and see what the cabinet does? So he went up to it on tiptoe, turned the key, and when nothing happened, banged on the hatch. The cabinet gave a husky sigh, the mechanism started grinding, and looked at the King with a ruby eye, as if askance. That sidewise glance reminded him of Uncle Cenander, his father's brother, who formerly had been his tutor. He thought, it must be Uncle who had the cabinet put here, to spite me, for why else would it give that look? A funny feeling came over him, and the cabinet, stuttering, very slowly began to play a dismal tune, as if someone were striking an iron tombstone with a shovel, and out through the hatch fell a black card with bone-yellow rows of writing on it.

The King took fright in earnest, but could not now overcome his curiosity. He grabbed up the card and ran to his chambers. When at last he was alone, he took it from his pocket. "I'll look, but just to be safe, only with one eye," he decided, and looked. On the card was written:

> Now strikes the hour, now strike the kin,
> A family war is ushered in.
> Aunts and uncles, nephews, nieces
> Hack each other into pieces;

Cousin does in second cousin,
Digs a grave, then digs a dozen;
In-laws fall and offspring drop,
Stepsons will at nothing stop;
There, daughters quartered with a laugh,
Here, a half brother cut in half;
The ax for gramps, the ax for granny,
The ax for sister and her nanny;
Brother murders brother, mother,
One good turn deserves another.
Relatives have certain worth,
But they're more certain in the earth.
The hour strikes, now sound the knell,
Bury your relations well;
You yourself must hide and bide
Everywhere, yet stay inside,
The ties that bind go very deep,
Beware of treason in your sleep.

So badly was King Gnuff frightened, that everything grew dark before his eyes. He repented of the lack of caution that had led him to wind up the fortunetelling cabinet. It was, however, too late now, and he saw that he must act if the worst was to be avoided. Not for a moment did he doubt the import of the prophecy: he had long suspected that his closest relatives were a threat to him.

To tell the truth, it is not known whether all of this took place exactly as we have related here. But in any case sorry things—even grisly—happened after that. The King had his entire family put to death; only his one uncle, Cenander, managed to escape at the last minute, disguising himself as an upright piano. This failed to save him, he was shortly apprehended and surrendered his head to the block. On this occasion Gnuff was able to sign the sentence with a clear conscience, for his uncle had been seized while attempting to start a conspiracy against the Monarch.

Orphaned with such suddenness, the King went into mourning. He was now much easier in his mind, though saddened too, for at heart he was neither wicked nor cruel. The King's peaceful mourning did not last long, it occurring to Gnuff that he might have relatives about whom he knew nothing. Any one of his subjects could be some distant cousin several times removed. So for a while he beheaded this one and that, but the beheadings did not set his mind at rest, for one could hardly be a king without subjects, and how could he kill them all? He became so suspicious that he ordered himself riveted to the throne, so no one could topple him from it; he slept in an armored nightshirt, and thought continually of what to do. Finally he did something extraordinary, so very extraordinary that he probably did not hit upon the idea himself. They say it was whispered to him by a traveling peddler dressed as a sage, or perhaps a sage dressed as a peddler—there are different accounts. The castle servants reportedly saw a masked figure, whom the King admitted to his chambers at night. The fact is that one day Gnuff summoned all the court architects, all the master electrologists, platesmiths and tuners, and announced that they were to enlarge his person, and enlarge it to extend beyond all horizons. The commands were carried out with amazing speed, as the King appointed to the post of director of the Planning Commission his trusty executioner. Processions of electricians and builders began carrying wires and spools into the castle, and when the built-up King had filled the entire palace with his person, so that he was, at one and the same time, in the vestibule, the cellar and the wings, they turned next to the residences close at hand. In two years Gnuff covered the downtown area. Houses not stately enough, and therefore unworthy to be occupied by the monarch's mind, were leveled to the ground; in their place were erected electronic palaces, called Gnuff's Amplifiers. The King spread little by little but inexorably, many-storied, precisely connected, enhanced with identity substations, till he became the whole capital city, and did not stop at its borders. His mood improved. He had no relatives, and now no wax or drafts to fear, for he didn't need to take a step anywhere, being everywhere at once. "I am the state," he said, and not without reason, for besides himself, a self that inhabited the squares and avenues with rows of electrical edifices, no one any longer lived in the capital; except of course the royal dusters, sweepers and household wipers-off of grime; these tended the King's cogitation, which flowed from building to building. Thus there circulated throughout the city, for miles and miles, the satisfaction of King Gnuff, for he had succeeded in achieving greatness temporal and literal, and in addition was hidden everywhere, as the prophecy required, for indeed he was all-present in the kingdom. And what a pretty picture it made at dusk, when the King-titan through a soft glow winked its bulbs in thought, then slowly dimmed, sinking into a well-earned sleep. But that darkness of oblivion, after the first few hours of night, gave way to a fitful flickering, now here, now there, erratic flashes blinking on and off. These were the monarch's dreams beginning their swarm. Turbulent streams of apparitions coursed through the buildings, till in the murk the windows lit up and whole streets exchanged alternate bursts of red and violet light, while the household sweepers, plodding their way along the empty sidewalks, sniffed the burnt smell of the heated cables of His Royal Majesty and, sneaking a look inside the light-flooded windows, said to one another in low voices:

"Oho! Some nightmare must have Gnuff in its clutches—if only he doesn't take it out on us!"

One night, after a particularly hard-working day—for the King had been thinking up new kinds of medals with which to decorate himself—he dreamed that his uncle, Cenander, had sneaked into the capital, taking advantage of the darkness, wrapped in a black cloak, and was roaming the streets in search of supporters, to organize a vile conspiracy. Out of the cellars crawled a host of masked ones, and there were so many of them and they showed such readiness for regicide, that Gnuff started trembling and awoke in terror. It was already dawn and the golden sun played upon the little white clouds in the sky, so he said to himself: "A dream, nothing more!"— and resumed his work of designing medals, and those he had invented the previous day were pinned onto his terraces and balconies. When however after his daylong toil he again settled down for the night, no sooner did he doze off than he saw the conspiracy in full flower. It had happened this way: when Gnuff, before, wakened from the conspiring dream, he did so incompletely; the downtown sector, in which had hatched that antigovernment dream, did not wake up at all, but continued to lie in its nightmare grip, and only the King awake knew nothing of this. Meanwhile a considerable part of his person, namely the old center of the city, quite unaware that the uncle-malefactor and his machinations were only a phantom, remained under the delusion of the nightmare. That second night Gnuff dreamed he saw his uncle in a state of feverish activity, mustering the relatives. And they all appeared, every last one, posthumously creaking their hinges, and even those with the most important parts missing raised up their swords against the rightful ruler! There was great commotion. Hordes of masked ruffians rehearsed in whispers rebel cheers; down in the vaults and cellars they were already sewing the black banners of insurrection; everywhere poisons were being brewed, axes sharpened, grenades assembled, and preparations made for an all-out encounter with the hated Gnuff. The King took fright a second time, awoke shaking, and was about to call—using the Golden Archway of the Royal Mouth—all his troops to his aid, to have them cut the conspirators to ribbons with their swords, but he quickly saw that this would serve no purpose. The soldiers, after all, could not enter his dream, could not crush the conspiracy growing there. So for a time he tried by sheer force of will to rouse those four square miles of his being that persisted in dreaming of rebellion—but in vain. Though truly he had no way of knowing whether it was in vain or not, for while awake he could not detect the conspiracy; it appeared only when sleep overtook him.

While conscious, he could not gain entry to the insurgent sectors, which is not surprising, since reality cannot penetrate its way into a dream's interior, only another dream can do that. The King realized that in this situation the best thing was for him to fall asleep and dream a counterdream, and not just any kind, obviously, but one monarchistic, wholly devoted to him, flags waving in the wind; with a royal dream like that, rallied around the throne, he would then be able to wipe out the treasonous nightmare.

Gnuff set to work, but his fear kept him awake; so he began in his mind to count pebbles, till this exhausted him and he fell into a deep slumber. It turned out then that the dream under the leadership of his uncle had not only entrenched itself in the downtown district, but was even beginning to imagine arsenals filled with powerful bombs and demolishing mines. Whereas he himself, try as he might, succeeded in dreaming up no more than a single company of cavalry, and unmounted at that, poorly disciplined, and armed only with pot lids. "This isn't working," he thought, "I'll have to start again from scratch!" So he set about waking, which was slow and difficult, at last he awoke all the way, but then a terrible suspicion came upon him. Had he in fact returned to reality, or was this instead a different dream, the semblance only of wakefulness? How to proceed in such a tangled situation? To sleep or not to sleep? That was the question! Suppose he did not now sleep, feeling himself to be secure, for indeed in the world of reality no conspiracy existed. No harm would be done: that regicidal dream would dream itself out, dreaming on to its dreamed conclusion, until in the final awakening the sovereign state regained its proper unity. Very good. Ah but if he did not dream a counterdream, going on the assumption that he was safely awake, while in actual fact his alleged awakedness was but a different dream, adjoining the other, the uncle dream, then this could lead to catastrophe! For at any moment the whole accursed band of regicides, with that odious Cenander at its head, could tear from that dream into this, the dream that feigned reality, in order to deprive him of his throne and life!

"It is true," he reflected, "the depriving would take place only in a dream, yet if the conspiracy overruns my entire royal psyche, if it takes control from the mountains to the oceans, and if—O dreadful thought!—my self no longer wishes to awake, what then?! In that case I will be cut off from reality forever and Uncle will do with me what he wishes. He'll torture me, humiliate me. To say nothing of my aunts—I remember them well: no mercy shown, never, no matter what. That's how they are—or rather, were—no, are again in this horrible dream! And anyway, why speak of dreams? A dream can only be where there is also a reality to return to (and how shall I return, if they succeed in keeping me in the dream?); where there is nothing but dream, dream is the sole reality, and therefore it is not a dream. Hideous! All this, of course, comes of that wretched excess of personality, that expansionism of the mind—much good it has done me!"

In despair he saw that inaction could very well destroy him, and that his only hope lay in the immediate mobilization of his psyche. "I must proceed as though I were asleep," he said to himself. "I must dream a multitude of devoted subjects, all full of love and enthusiasm, battalions loyal to the bitter end, dying with my name upon their lips, and plenty of armaments. It might even be a good idea to think up quickly some miracle weapon, for in a dream surely everything is possible: let's have a substance for removing relatives, anti-uncle cannons, something of that sort. In this way I'll be prepared for whatever happens, and if the conspiracy shows itself, insidiously creeping from dream to dream, I'll smash it in a single blow!"

King Gnuff heaved a sigh with every square and boulevard of his being, so complicated was all this, and got down to work—that is, he went to sleep. In his dream, troops of steel were to stand in formation, with hoary generals at their head, and crowds cheering to the thunder of trumpets and kettledrums. But all that appeared was a tiny bolt. Nothing—only this bolt, perfectly ordinary, a little jagged around the edges. What was he to do with it? He thought and thought, meanwhile he felt a strange uneasiness, a growing uneasiness, a faintness, a mounting fear, till suddenly it dawned on him: "Bolt rhymes with revolt!!"

He quaked all over. So then, the symbol of his downfall

his overthrow, his death! Therefore the mob of relatives was even now coming for him, in stealth, in silence, having tunneled through that other dream to reach this dream—and any minute he would plunge into the treacherous pit, dug out of dream from under dream! Then the end was imminent! Death! Annihilation! But from where? How? In which direction?!

Ten thousand buildings of his royal person blazed; the substations, decked with medals and festooned with ribbons of the Cross of Greatness, shook; the decorations rang out rhythmically in the night air, such was King Gnuff's struggle with the dreamed dread symbol of his downfall. At last he overcame it, mastered it, till it vanished so completely, it was almost as if it had never been. The King looked—where was he now? In reality or in another illusion? In reality, it would seem, yes but how could he be certain? It was possible, of course, that the uncle dream by now had finished dreaming, that there was absolutely no need to worry. But again: how could he find out? There was one way and one way only, with dream-spies disguised as subversives to comb and ceaselessly probe his entire, own, sovereign self, the kingdom of his being, and nevermore would the royal soul know peace, he would always have to be on guard against conspiracy slumbering in some secret corner of his vast consciousness! And so onward, come, buoy up the figments of fealty and devotion, dream of homages rendered and thronging delegations aglow with law-abiding zeal, attack with dreams all the valleys, darknesses and reaches of your person, that in them no intrigue, no uncle be allowed to hide! And then swept over Gnuff the rustle of standards so dear to his heart, no trace of Uncle, not a relative in sight, he was surrounded only by loyalty, he received oblations, ovations, tributes neverending; one could hear the peal of beaten gold medallions rolling at his feet, sparks flew from chisels as artists hewed him monuments. The King's soul brightened within him, for here now was heraldry, embroidered-emblazoned, a tapestry hung in every window, artillery lined up to fire its salute, and trumpeters putting to their lips their trumpets of bronze. When however he took a closer look at all of this, he saw that something—somehow—wasn't right. The monuments—not bad, but not much like him either; in the twist of the face, in the scowl there was something decidedly avuncular. The standards blowing—all right, but that tiny ribbon with them, indistinct, almost black; if not black, at least dirty, in any case—not clean. What was this? Some sort of innuendo?!

Good heavens! But those tapestries—worn through in places, practically bald, and Uncle—Uncle had been bald . . . No, this could not be! "Back! Retreat! Wake up! Wake up!!" he thought. "Sound the alarm, reveille, away with this dream!" he wanted to shout, but when everything had vanished, it was no better. He had fallen out of one dream into another, a new dream, a dream dreamed by the dream preceding, which in turn had occurred in an earlier dream, therefore this present dream was already—as it were—to the third power. Everything in it changed, openly now, into treason, everything reeked of betrayal, the standards turned inside out—like gloves— from royal to black, the medals came with threaded screws, like severed necks, and from the golden bugles burst not battle charges, but his uncle's laughter, a thunderclap-guffaw that spelled disaster. The King roared in a voice stentorian, he called for his soldiers—let them prick him with their lances, so he could wake! "Pinch me! Pinch me!!" he demanded with a mighty howl, and: "Reality!! Reality!!!"—but to no avail; so once again he strained and struggled from the traitorous, king-hating, assassinating dream to the dream of the throne, but by now the dreams in him had multiplied like rats, scurrying-scuttling everywhere, by now building infected building with the nightmare, in all directions spread a sneaking, a skulking, a slinking around, some sort of skulduggery, just what it was he didn't know, but God-awful for sure! The electronic edifice in all its hundred stories dreamed of bolts, revolts, insurrection and defection, in every identity substation there schemed a band of relatives, in every amplifier an uncle cackled; the foundations trembled, terrified of themselves, and out of them a hundred thousand kin came swarming, false pretenders to the throne, two-faced first-born foundlings, glowering usurpers, and though not one of them knew whether he was a creature dreamed or dreaming, and who was dreaming whom, and why, and what all that implied—they all without exception made straight for Gnuff, to cut him down, to pull him from the throne, hang him, swing him from the highest belfry, ding to kill him, dong to bring him back again, hey! fill him with lead, ah! off with his head—and the only reason they had done nothing yet was that they couldn't agree on where to start. Thus in torrents rushed the phantom monsters of the royal mind, until from the overload there was a burst of flame. No longer a dreamed but a very real fire now filled the windows of the King's person with a golden blaze, and Gnuff collapsed into a hundred thousand separate dreams, linked by nothing now but a conflagration—and he burned for a long, for a very long time . . .

The Sanatorium of Dr. Vliperdius

It was all the fault of that dentist who capped my teeth with metal. The salesgirl I smiled at at the newsstand took me for a robot. I realized this only in the subway, when I unfolded the paper. It was the *Automaton Courier*. I don't much care for that publication, not that I have any anti-electric feelings, you understand, but it does cater to the taste of its readers. The whole front page was devoted to a sentimental story of a mathematician who fell in love with his computer. At the multiplication tables he still held himself in check, but when it came to the solving of nonlinear equations to the nth degree, he began clasping its switches passionately and repeating: "Dearest! I'll never leave you!" etc. Disgusted, I took a look in the society section—but all they had there were monotonous lists of who, when and with whom constructed progeny. The literary column contained a poem beginning with the lines:

> *The robotess goes*
> *To the well with her jug,*

A dashing young robot
Now holds out his plug;
With a blush she replies
To his offer so bold,
And gives from her basket
A pretty pentode.

Curiously, this brought to mind some verse I thought I knew, but for the life of me I couldn't recall the author. There were also jokes of doubtful quality on the topic of people, about gnomists being specialists on trolls, and gremlins resulting from impedance, that sort of foolishness. Since I still had a half an hour's ride to go, I turned to the classifieds—as you know, even in the poorest paper they often make interesting reading. But here too I was doomed to disappointment. This one wanted to sell his servobrother, that one was giving a correspondence course in astronautics, someone else advertised atoms split while-U-wait. As I was folding up the newspaper to throw it out, my eyes fell upon a large ad in a box: THE SANATORIUM OF DR. VLIPERDIUS—— TREATMENT OF NERVOUS DISORDERS AND MENTAL ILLNESS.

The whole problem of electrical dementia, I must confess, has always intrigued me. I thought to myself that a visit to such a sanatorium might be profitable. I did not know Vliperdius personally, but the name was not unknown to me: Professor Tarantoga had spoken of him. When an idea comes to me, I usually act on it at once.

So as soon as I got home I telephoned the sanatorium. Dr. Vliperdius at first had many reservations, but when I referred to our mutual friend Tarantoga, he relented. I got an appointment for the following day, since that was Sunday and I had plenty of free time before noon. And so after breakfast I drove to the city, where in a district famous for small lakes was located, picturesquely set in an old park, the psychiatric institution. Vliperdius, they said, was waiting for me in his office. Sunlight filled the building, for the walls were of aluminum and glass, in the modern fashion. On the ceilings were colorful panels showing robots at play. You could not have called this hospital gloomy; from unseen rooms came the sounds of music; passing through the lobby, I saw Chinese puzzles, colorful albums, and a sculpture, a boldly executed robot nude.

The Doctor did not rise from behind his wide desk, but was most gracious: as I found out, he had read and was quite familiar with more than one of my books of travel. It's true he was a bit old-fashioned, and not merely in his manner, for he was completely fastened to the floor, like some antique Eniac. Possibly I did not conceal my surprise upon seeing his iron feet, for he said with a laugh:

"I am, you see, so devoted to my work and to my patients, that I feel no need to leave the sanatorium!"

Now I knew how sensitive psychiatrists could be on the subject of their speciality, and also how offended by the attitude of the average man, who finds exoticism and monstrosity in mental aberrations, therefore I was very careful in presenting my request. The Doctor hemmed, frowned, raised his anode potential and said:

"If that is what you wish . . . but I think you will be disappointed. These days there are no raving robots, Mr. Tichy, that is ancient history. Our therapy is modern. The methods of the last century—the soldering of wires to soften the main pipe, the use of chokes and other instruments of torture—already belong to the annals of medicine. H'm. How might this be best demonstrated to you? Perhaps if you would simply go into the park and there acquaint yourself directly with our patients. They are individuals most refined and cultured. I trust you have no—ah—aversion, no irrational fear in the presence of slight deviations . . . ?"

I assured him this was the case, whereat Vliperdius said he regretted that he was unable to escort me on my walk, indicated the way and asked that I drop in again on my way back.

I went down the stairs, across wide verandas, and found myself on a graveled path. All around spread the park, full of flower beds and elaborate palms. Farther on, in a pond swam a small flock of swans, the patients were feeding them, others on gayly colored benches were devoting themselves to chess or friendly conversation. I walked slowly on, when someone called me by my name. I turned to face a completely unknown person.

"Tichy! Is it you?!" repeated that individual, extending his hand. I shook it, in vain attempting to recollect who he might be.

"I see you don't recognize me. I am Prolaps . . . I worked on the *Cosmic Almanac* . . ."

"Ah yes, of course! Forgive me," I muttered. Obviously this was Prolaps, the honest linotype who had printed practically all my books. I valued him highly, he was truly infallible. He took me familiarly by the arm and we started down the shaded lane. Patches of light and shadow animated the tranquil face of my companion. We talked for a while of new books and publishing; he expressed himself as precisely as ever, with his usual acumen, altogether he was in excellent intellectual form. I found not a trace of abnormality in him. But when we came to a small gazebo and had seated ourselves on a stone bench, he lowered his voice to a confidential whisper and asked:

"But what are you doing here? Did they replace you too . . . ?"

"Well, you see . . . I came here of my own accord, because . . ."

"Of course! I did too!" he interrupted. "When the thing happened to me, I went straight to the police, but I quickly saw that that was useless. My friends suggested I try Vliperdius—he went about my case altogether differently! He's conducting a search and I'm certain it will soon be found . . ."

"Excuse me—what is that?" I asked.

"What do you mean? My body."

"Aha . . . yes . . ." I nodded several times, trying my best not to look startled. But Prolaps noticed nothing.

"How well I recall that day, the 26th of June," he said, suddenly grown gloomy. "Sitting down at the table, to read the newspaper, I clanked. That caught my attention, I mean, after all, what man clanks when he sits down?! So I feel my legs—curiously hard, the arms—the same, I tapped myself and suddenly realized that I had been substituted! Some scoundrel had made a forgery—I searched my entire apartment, not a sign of it, they must have carried it off in the night . . ."

"Carried what off?"

"I already told you! My body. My natural body, surely you can see that THIS"—and he rapped his chest until it rang—"is artificial . . ."

"Ah, of course! I wasn't thinking . . . obviously . . ."

"Can it be that you too . . . ?" he asked with hope in his voice. Suddenly he seized my hand and with it struck the stone slab of the table at which we were sitting. I groaned. He dropped the hand, disappointed.

"Forgive me," he muttered, "I thought I saw it glitter."

I understood now that he held himself to be a man whose body had been stolen, and that, like so many ill who are eager to have around them companions in misery, he hoped that the very same thing had happened to me.

Rubbing my battered hand beneath the table, I tried to change the topic of our conversation, but now he began describing with great enjoyment and emotion the charms of his former corporality, he went on and on about the blond forelock he was supposed to have possessed, the silkiness of his cheeks, even the runny nose—I didn't know how to get rid of him, for I was feeling more and more uncomfortable. But Prolaps himself delivered me from this awkward situation. For all at once he jumped to his feet and cried: "Oh, I think that is IT over there!!"— and he bounded straight across the lawn after some indistinct figure. I was still sitting, lost in thought, when someone behind me said:

"May I . . . ?"

"Yes, certainly," I replied.

The stranger sat down and fixed his eyes on me, unblinking, as if he wished to hypnotize me. For a long time he contemplated my face and hands with an expression of growing sorrow. Finally he looked deep into my eyes with such tremendous sympathy, and at the same time with such satisfaction, that I became confused. I didn't know what to make of this. The silence between us increased, I tried to break it, but couldn't think of a single neutral statement with which to begin a conversation: for his gaze expressed too much, and yet too little.

"Poor wretch . . ." he said softly, unutterable feeling in his voice, "how I pity you . . ."

"But really—I don't—that is—" I blurted, looking for words to defend myself against this strange excess of commiseration he was heaping on me.

"You needn't speak, I understand everything. More than you imagine. I know, too, that you take me for a lunatic."

"Not in the least," I started to protest, but he cut me off with a peremptory gesture.

"In a sense I am a lunatic," he said, almost majestically. "Like Galileo, Newton, like Giordano Bruno. If my views were only rational . . . humph! But more important are one's feelings. How I pity you, victim of the Universe! What misery it is, what a hopeless trap—to live . . ."

"Yes, life can be difficult," I put in quickly, having found at last some point of departure. "Nevertheless, as a phenomenon which is, so to speak, natural . . ."

"Precisely!" he seized upon my last word. "Natural! Is there anything more contemptible than Nature? The scientists, the philosophers have always tried to understand Nature, while the thing to do is to destroy it!"

"In its entirety . . . ?" I asked, despite myself fascinated by such a radical presentation of the matter.

"Only so!" he said categorically. "Look at this, I ask you."

Gingerly, as if it were some caterpillar deserving study, yet at the same time disgusting (his revulsion he attempted to control), he lifted my hand and, holding it between us like a curious specimen, continued quietly though with emphasis:

"How watery it is . . . how pulpy . . . squashy . . . Albumin! Ach, that albumin . . . A curd that moves for a time—a thinking cheese—the tragic product of a dairy accident, a walking slop . . ."

"Excuse me, but . . ."

He paid no attention to my words. I hid my hand beneath the table and he released it, as though no longer able to endure the touch, but then he placed his palm upon my head. It was uncannily heavy.

"How is it possible! How is it possible to produce such a thing!" he repeated, increasing the pressure on my skull, until it grew painful, but I didn't dare object. "These knobs, holes . . . cauliflowers—" with an iron finger he poked my nose and ears—"and this is supposed to be an intelligent creature? For shame! For shame, I say!! What use is a Nature that after four billion years comes up with THIS?!"

Here he gave my head a shove, so that it wobbled and I saw stars.

"Give me one, just one billion years, and you'll see what I create!!"

"True, the imperfection of biological evolution," I began, but he didn't let me finish.

"Imperfection?!" he snorted. "Droppings! Trash! An outright botch-job! If you can't do something right, you shouldn't do it at all!"

"Not that I want to make excuses," I said quickly, "but Nature, don't forget, worked with what it had at hand. In the primordial sea . . ."

"Garbage floated!!" he roared so loud, I winced. "Isn't that right? A star exploded, planets formed, and from the dregs, which couldn't be used for anything, from those gobbets and scraps life arose! Enough, no more! No more of these pudgy suns, inane galaxies, this mucilage that has a soul—enough!"

"Still, the atoms," I began, but he interrupted. Already I saw the orderlies approaching across the grass: they had been alerted by the shouts of my interlocutor.

"To hell with the atoms!" he roared. They took him by the arms from both sides. He let himself be led away, but, still looking at me—for he went backward, like a crab—he thundered, till the whole park rang:

"We must involute! Do you hear, O pale colloidal soup!? Instead of discovering, we must make un-discoveries, we must cover up more and more, so nothing remains, you glutinous ooze draped over bone! That's the way! Progress through regress! Nullify! Revert! Destroy! Down with Nature! Away with Nature! Awaaay!"

His cries grew fainter and more and more distant, and once again the silence of the lovely noon was filled with the drone of bees and the smell of flowers. I thought to myself that Dr. Vliperdius had exaggerated after all, when he spoke of the disappearance of raving robots. Apparently those new methods of therapy did not always work. However the experience itself, the outspoken diatribe on Nature I had heard a moment before, seemed worth these few bruises and the bump on my head. I found out later that that robot, formerly an analyzer of harmonic Fourier series, had created his own theory of existence, which was based on the accumulation of discoveries made by civilization, an accumulation that would reach such extreme proportions, the only thing left would be to cover up those discoveries one by one. For in this way, upon the completion of the work of science, there is no room—not only no room for civilization, but for the Universe that gave rise to it. A total liquidation of progress follows and the whole cycle begins again from the beginning. He considered himself a prophet of this second, un-discovering phase of development. He had been put away in Vliperdius's sanatorium at the request of his family, when from the taking apart of friends and relatives he turned to the dismantling of third persons.

I left the gazebo and for a time watched the swans. Next to me some crank was throwing them broken bits of metal wire. I told him that swans didn't eat that.

"I don't care if they don't," he replied, continuing his activity.

"But they could choke, and that would be a shame," I said.

"They won't choke, because the wire sinks. It is heavier than water," he explained cogently.

"Then why do you throw it?"

"I like to feed the swans."

That exhausted the subject. Upon leaving the pond, we struck up a conversation. As it turned out, I was dealing with a famous philosopher, the creator of the ontology of nothingness, otherwise known as neantics, and the continuator of the work of Gorgias of Leontinoi— Professor Urlip. The Professor at great length told me of the newest development in his theory. According to him there is nothing, not even himself. The nothingness of being is perfectly intact. The fact of the apparent existence of this and that has no significance whatever, for the argument, in keeping with Ockham's razor, runs as follows: it would seem that reality, or actuality, exists, and also dream. But the hypothesis of reality is unneeded. So then, dream exists. But a dream demands a dreamer. Now the postulation of someone dreaming is—again—an unnecessary hypothesis, for it sometimes happens that in a dream another dream is dreamed. Thus everything is a dream dreamt by a succeeding dream, and so on to infinity. Now because—and here is the main point—each succeeding dream is less real than the one preceding (a dream borders directly on reality, while a dream dreamed within a dream borders on it indirectly, through that same intermediate dream, and the third through two dreams, and so on)—the upper bound of this series equals zero. *Ergo*, in the final analysis no one is dreaming and zero is dreamt, *ergo* only nothingness has existence, in other words there isn't anything. The elegance and precision of the proof filled me with admiration. The only thing I didn't understand was what Professor Urlip was doing in this place. It turned out that the poor philosopher had gone quite mad—he told me so himself. His insanity consisted in the fact that he no longer believed in his own doctrine and had moments in which it seemed to him that there was something after all. Dr. Vliperdius was to cure him of this delusion.

Later I visited the hospital wards. I was introduced to an Old Testament computer that suffered from senility and couldn't count up the ten commandments. I went also to the ward for electrasthenics, where they treated obsessions—one of the patients was continually unscrewing himself, with whatever lay at hand, and hidden tools were repeatedly taken from him.

One electric brain, employed at an astronomical observatory and for thirty years modeling stars, thought it was Sigma Ceti and kept threatening to go off like a Supernova any moment. This, according to its calculations. There was also one there who begged to be remade into an electric wringer, having had his fill of sentience. Among the maniacs things were more cheerful, a group of them sat by iron beds, playing on the springs like harps and singing in chorus: "We ain't got no ma or pa, 'cause we is au-tom-a-ta," also "Ro, ro, ro your bot, gently down the stream," and so forth.

Vliperdius's assistant, who was showing me around, told me that not long ago the sanatorium had had a certain priest-robot, who intended founding an order of Cyberites, however he improved so much under shock treatment, that he soon returned to his true occupation— balancing books in a bank. On my way back with the young assistant I met in the corridor a patient who was pulling behind him a heavily laden cart. This individual presented a singular sight, in that he was tied all around with bits of string.

"You don't by any chance have a hammer?" he asked.

"No."

"A shame. My head hurts."

I engaged him in conversation. He was a robot-hypochondriac. On his squeaking cart he carried a complete set of spare parts. After ten minutes I learned that he got shooting pains in the back during storms, pins and needles all over while watching television, and spots before his eyes when anyone stroked a cat nearby. It grew quite monotonous, so I left him quickly and headed for the Director's office. The Director was busy however, so I asked his secretary to convey my respects, and then went home.

The Hunt

He left Port Control hopping mad. It had to happen to him, to him! The owner didn't have the shipment—simply didn't have it—period. Port Control knew nothing. Sure, there had been a telegram: 72 HOUR DELAY—STIPULATED PENALTY PAID TO YOUR ACCOUNT—ENSTRAND. Not a word more. At the trade councillor's office he didn't get anywhere either. The port was crowded and the stipulated penalty didn't satisfy Control. Parking fee, demurrage, yes, but wouldn't it be best if you, Mr. Navigator, lifted off like a good fellow and went into hold? Just kill the engines, no expenditure for fuel, wait out your three days and come back. What would that hurt you? Three days circling the Moon because the owner screws up! Pirx was at a loss for a reply, but then remembered the treaty. Well, when he trotted out the norms established by the labor union for exposure in space, they started backing down. In fact, this was not the Year of the Quiet Sun. Radiation levels were not negligible. So he would have to maneuver, keep behind the Moon, play that game of hide-and-seek with the Sun using thrust; and who was going to pay for this?—not the owner, certainly. Who then—Control? Did you gentlemen have any idea of the cost of ten minutes full burn with a reactor of seventy million kilowatts?! In the end he got permission to stay, but only for seventy-two hours plus four to load that wretched freight—not a minute more! You would have thought they were doing him a favor. As if it were *his* fault. And he had arrived right on the dot, and didn't come straight from Mars either— while the owner . . .

With all this he completely forgot where he was and pushed the door handle so hard on his way out, that he jumped up to the ceiling. Embarrassed, he looked around, but no one was there. All Luna seemed empty. True, the big work was under way a few hundred kilometers to the north, between Hypatia and Toricelli. The engineers and technicians, who a month ago were all over the place here, had already left for the construction site. The UN's great project, Luna 2, drew more and more people from Earth. "At least this time there won't be any trouble getting a room," he thought, taking the escalator to the bottom floor of the underground city. The fluorescent lamps produced a cold daylight. Every second one was off. Economizing! Pushing aside a glass door, he entered a small lobby. They had rooms, all right! All the rooms you wanted. He left his suitcase, it was really more a satchel, with the porter, and wondered if Tyndall made sure that the mechanics reground the central nozzle. Ever since Mars the thing had been behaving like a damned medieval cannon! He really ought to see to it himself, the proprietor's eye and all that . . . But he didn't feel like taking the elevator back up those twelve flights, and anyway by now they had probably split up. Sitting in the airport store, most likely, listening to the latest recordings. He walked, not really knowing where; the hotel restaurant was empty, as if closed—but there behind the lunch counter sat a redhead, reading a book. Or had she

fallen asleep over it? Because her cigarette was turning
into a long cylinder of ash on the marble top . . . Pirx took
a seat, reset his watch to local time and suddenly it became
late: ten at night. And on board, why, only a few minutes
before, it had been noon. This eternal whirl with sudden
jumps in time was just as fatiguing as in the beginning,
when he was first learning to fly. He ate his lunch, now
turned into supper, washing it down with seltzer, which
seemed warmer than the soup. The waiter, down in the
mouth and drowsy like a true lunatic, added up the bill
wrong, and not in his own favor, a bad sign. Pirx advised
him to take a vacation on Earth, and left quietly, so as not
to waken the sleeping counter girl. He got the key from the
porter and rode up to his room. He hadn't looked at the
plate yet and felt strange when he saw the number: 173.
The same room he had stayed in, long ago, when for the
first time he flew "that side." But after opening the door
he concluded that either this was a different room or they
had remodeled it radically. No, he must have been
mistaken, that other was larger. He turned on all the
switches, for he was sick of darkness, looked in the dresser,
pulled out the drawer of the small writing table, but didn't
bother to unpack, he only threw his pajamas on the bed,
and set the toothbrush and toothpaste on the sink. He
washed his hands—the water, as always, infernally cold, it
was a wonder it didn't freeze. He turned the hot water
spigot—a few drops trickled out. He went to the phone to
call the desk, but changed his mind, there was really no
point. It was scandalous, of course—here the Moon was
stocked with all the necessities, and you still couldn't get
hot water in your hotel room! He tried the radio. The
evening wrap-up—the lunar news. He hardly listened,
wondering whether he shouldn't send a telegram to the
owner. Reverse the charges, of course. But no, that

wouldn't accomplish anything. These were not the romantic days of astronautics! They were long gone, now a man was nothing but a truck driver, dependent on those who loaded cargo on his ship! Cargo, insurance, demurrage . . . The radio was muttering something. Hold on—what was that? . . . He leaned across the bed and moved the knob of the apparatus.

"—in all probability the last of the Leonid swarm," the soft baritone of the speaker filled the room. "Only one apartment building suffered a direct hit and lost its seal. By a lucky coincidence its residents were all at work. The remaining meteorites caused little damage, with the exception of one that penetrated the shield protecting the storerooms. As our correspondent reports, six universal automata designated for tasks on the construction site were totally destroyed. There was also damage to the high-tension line, and telephone communication was knocked out, though restored within a space of three hours. We now repeat the major news. Earlier today, at the opening of the Pan-African Congress . . ."

He shut off the radio and sat down. Meteorites? A swarm? Well yes, the Leonids were due, but still the forecasts—those meteorologists were always fouling up, exactly like the synoptics on Earth . . . Construction site—it must have been that one up north. But all the same, atmosphere was atmosphere, and its absence here was damned inconvenient. Six automata, if you please. Well at least no one was hurt. A nasty business, though—a shield punctured! Yes, that designer, he really should have . . .

He was dog-tired. Time had gotten completely bollixed up for him. Between Mars and Earth they must have lost a Tuesday. After Monday it suddenly became Wednesday; which meant they also missed one night. "I better stock up on some sleep," he thought, got up and automatically headed for the tiny bathroom, but at the memory of the icy water he shuddered, did an about-face and a minute later was in bed. Which couldn't hold a candle to a ship's bunk. His hand by itself groped around for the belts to buckle down the quilt, he gave a faint smile when he couldn't find them; after all he was in a hotel, not threatened by any sudden loss of gravitation . . . That was his last thought. When he opened his eyes, he had no idea where he was. It was pitch black. "Tyndall!" he wanted to shout, and all at once—for no apparent reason—remembered how once Tyndall had burst terrified out of the cabin, in nothing but pajama bottoms, and desperately cried to the man on watch: "You! For God's sake! Quick, tell me, what's my name?!" The poor devil was plastered, he had been fretting over some imagined insult or other and drank an entire bottle of rum. In this roundabout way Pirx's mind returned to reality. He got up, turned on the light, went to take a shower, but then remembered about the water, so carefully let out first a small trickle—lukewarm; he sighed, because he yearned for a good hot bath, however after a minute or two, with the stream beating on his face and torso, he actually began to hum.

He was just putting on a clean shirt when the loudspeaker—he had no idea there was anything like that in the room—said in a deep bass:

"Attention! Attention! This is an important announcement. Will all men with military training please report immediately to Port Control, room 318, with Commodore-Engineer Achanian. We repeat. Attention, attention . . ." Pirx was so astonished, he stood there for a moment in only his socks and shirt. What was this? April fool? With military training? Maybe he was still asleep. But when he flung his arms to pull the shirt on all the way, he cracked his hand against the edge of the table, and his heart beat faster. No, no dream. Then what was it? An invasion? Martians taking over the Moon? What nonsense! In any case he had to go . . .

But something whispered to him while he jumped into his pants: "Yes, this had to happen, because *you* are here. That's your luck, old man, you bring trouble . . ." When he left the room his watch said eight. He wanted to stop somewhere and ask what in the hell was going on, but the corridor was empty, so was the escalator, as though a general mobilization had already taken place and everyone was scrambling God-knows-where at the front line . . . He ran up the steps, though they were moving at a good clip to begin with, but he hurried, as if he actually might miss a chance at derring-do. At the top he saw a brightly lit glass kiosk with newspapers, ran up to the window to ask his question, but the stand was empty. The papers were sold by machine. He bought a pack of cigarettes and a daily, which he glanced at without slowing his pace; it contained nothing but an account of the meteorite disaster. Could that be it? But why military training? Impossible! Down a long corridor he went towards Port Control. Finally he saw people. Someone was entering a room with the number 318, someone else was coming up from the opposite end of the corridor.

"I won't find out anything now, I'm too late," he thought, straightened his jacket and walked in. It was a small room, with three windows; behind them blazed an artificial lunar landscape, the unpleasant color of hot mercury. In the narrower part of the trapezoidal room stood two desks, the entire area in front of them being crammed with chairs, evidently brought in on short notice, since almost every chair was different. There were some fourteen–fifteen persons here, mostly middle-aged men, with a few kids who wore the stripes of navy cadets. Sitting apart was some elderly commodore—the rest of the chairs remained empty. Pirx took a seat next to one of the cadets, who immediately began telling him how six of them had flown in just the other day to start their apprenticeship "that side," but they were given only a small machine, it was called a flea, and the thing barely took three, the rest had to wait their turn, then suddenly this business cropped up. Did Mr. Navigator happen to know . . . ? But Mr. Navigator was in the dark himself. Judging by the faces of those seated, you could tell that they too were shocked by the announcement—they probably all came from the hotel. The cadet, it occurring to him that he ought to introduce himself, started going through a few gymnastics, nearly overturning his chair. Pirx grabbed it by the back, and then the door opened and in walked a short, dark-haired man slightly gray at the temples. He was clean-shaven, but his cheeks were blue with stubble, he had beetle brows and small, piercing eyes. Without a word he passed between the chairs, and behind the desk pulled down from a reel near the ceiling a map of "that side" on a scale of 1:1,000,000. The man rubbed his strong, fleshy nose with the back of his hand and said without preamble:

"Gentlemen, I am Achanian. I have been temporarily delegated by the joint heads of Luna 1 and Luna 2 for the purpose of neutralizing the Setaur."

Among the listeners there was a faint stir, but Pirx still understood nothing—he didn't even know what the Setaur was.

"Those of you who heard the radio are aware that here," he pointed a ruler at the regions Hypatia and Alfraganus, "a swarm of meteors fell yesterday. We will not go into the effects of the impact of the others, but one—it may well

have been the largest—shattered the protective shield over
storage units B7 and R7. In the second of the two was
located a consignment of Setaurs, received from Earth
barely four days ago. In the bulletins it was reported that
all of these met with destruction. That, gentlemen, is not
the truth."

The cadet sitting next to Pirx listened with red ears,
even his mouth hung open, as if he didn't want to miss a
single word; meanwhile Achanian went on:

"Five of the robots were crushed beneath the falling
roof, but the sixth survived. More precisely—it suffered
damage. We think so for this reason, that as soon as it
extricated itself from the ruins of the storage unit, it began
to behave in a manner . . . to behave like a . . ."

Achanian couldn't find the right word, so without
finishing his sentence he continued:

"The storage units are situated near the siding of a
narrow-guage track five miles from the provisional
landing field. Immediately after the disaster a rescue
operation was initiated, and the first order of business was
to check out all personnel, to see if anyone had been buried
beneath the devastated buildings. This action lasted about
an hour; in the meantime however it developed that from
the concussion the central control buildings had lost their
full seal, so the work dragged on till midnight. Around
one o'clock it was discovered that the breakdown in the
main grid supplying the entire construction site, as well as
the interruption of telephone communication, had not
been caused by the meteors. The cables had been cut—by
laser beam."

Pirx blinked. He had the irresistible feeling that he was
participating in some sort of play, a masquerade. Such
things didn't happen. A laser! Sure! And why not throw in
a Martian spy while you were at it? Yet this commodore-

engineer hardly looked like the type who would get hotel guests up at the crack of dawn in order to play some stupid joke on them.

"The telephone lines were repaired first," said Achanian. "But at that same time a small transporter of the emergency party, having reached the place where the cables were broken, lost radio contact with headquarters at Luna. After three in the morning we learned that this transporter had been attacked by laser and, as a result of several hits, now stood in flames. The driver and his assistant perished, but two of the crew—fortunately they were in suits, having gotten themselves ready to go out and repair the line—managed to jump free in time and hide in the desert, that is, the Mare Tranquillitatis, roughly here . . ." Achanian indicated with his ruler a point on the Sea of Tranquillity, some four hundred kilometers from the little crater of Arago. "Neither of them, as far as I know, saw the assailant. At a particular moment they simply felt a very strong thermal blast and the transporter caught fire. They jumped before the tanks of compressed gas went off; the lack of an atmosphere saved them, since only that portion of the fuel which was able to combine with the oxygen inside the transporter exploded. One of these people later died in as yet undetermined circumstances. The other succeeded in returning to the construction site, crossing a stretch of about one hundred and forty kilometers, but he ran and exhausted his suit's air supply and went into anoxia— fortunately he was discovered and is presently in the hospital. Our knowledge of what happened is based entirely on his account and needs further verification."

There was now a dead silence. Pirx too could see where all of this was leading, but he still didn't believe it, he didn't want to . . .

"No doubt you have guessed, gentlemen," continued the dark-haired man in an even voice—his profile stood out black as coal against the blazing mercury landscapes of the Moon—"that the one who cut the telephone cables and high-tension line, and also attacked the transporter, is our sole surviving Setaur. This is a unit about which we know little, it was put into mass production only last month. Engineer Klarner, one of Setaur's designers, was supposed to have come here with me, to give you gentlemen a full explanation not only of the capabilities of this model, but also of the measures that now must be taken with the object of neutralizing or destroying it . . ." The cadet next to Pirx gave a soft moan. It was a moan of pure excitement, that didn't even make the pretense of sounding horrified. The young man was not aware of the navigator's disapproving look. But then no one noticed or heard anything but the voice of the commodore-engineer.

"I'm no expert in intellectronics and therefore cannot tell you much about the Setaur. But among those present, I believe, is a Dr. McCork. Is he here?"

A slender man wearing glasses stood up. "Yes. I didn't take part in the designing of the Setaurs, I'm only acquainted with our English model, similar to the American one but not identical. Still, the differences are not so very great. I can be of help . . ."

"Excellent. Doctor, if you would come up here. I'll just present, first, the current situation: the Setaur is located somewhere over here," Achanian made a circle with the end of his ruler around an edge of the Sea of Tranquillity. "Which means it is at a distance of thirty to eighty kilometers from the construction site. It was designed, the Setaurs in general were designed, to perform mining tasks under extremely difficult conditions, at high temperatures, with a considerable chance of cave-ins, hence these models possess a massive frame and thick armor . . . But Dr. McCork will be filling you gentlemen in on this aspect. As for the means at our disposal to neutralize it: the headquarters of all the lunar bases have given us, first of all, a certain quantity of explosives, dynamite and oxyliquites, plus line-of-sight hand lasers and mining lasers—of course, neither the explosives nor the lasers were made for use in combat. For conveyance, the groups operating to destroy the Setaur will have transporters of small and medium range, two of which possess light anti-meteorite armor. Only such armor can take the blow of a laser from a distance of one kilometer. True, that data applies to Earth, where the energy absorption coefficient of the atmosphere is an important factor. Here we have no atmosphere, therefore those two transporters will be only a little less vulnerable than the others. We are also receiving a considerable number of suits, oxygen—and that, I'm afraid, is all. Around noon there will arrive from the Soviet sector a 'flea' with a three-man crew; in a pinch it can hold four on short flights, to deliver them inside the area where the Setaur is located. I'll stop here for the moment. Now, gentlemen, I would like to pass around a sheet of paper, on which I will ask you to write clearly your names and fields of competence. Meanwhile, if Dr. McCork would kindly tell us a few words about the Setaur . . . The most important thing, I believe, would be an indication of its Achilles heel . . ."

McCork was now standing by Achanian. He was even thinner than Pirx had thought; his ears stuck out, his head was slightly triangular, he had almost invisible eyebrows, a shock of hair of undetermined color, and all in all seemed strangely likable.

Before he spoke, he took off his steel-rimmed glasses, as

if they were in the way, and put them on the desk.

"I'd be lying if I said we allowed for the possibility of the kind of thing that's happened here. But besides the mathematics a cyberneticist has to have in his head some grain of intuition. Precisely for this reason we decided not to put our model into mass production just yet. According to the laboratory tests, Mephisto works perfectly—that's the name of our model. Setaur is supposed to have better stabilization for braking and activating. Or so I thought, going by the literature—now I'm not so sure. The name suggests mythology, but it's only an abbreviation, from Selfprogramming Electronic Ternary Automaton Racemic, racemic since in the construction of its brain we use both dextro- and levorotatory monopolymer pseudocrystals. But I guess that's not important here. It is an automaton equipped with a laser for mining operations, a violet laser; the energy to emit the impulses is supplied it by a micropile, working on the principle of a cold chain reaction, therefore the Setaur—if I remember correctly—can put out impulses of up to forty-five thousand kilowatts."

"For how long?" someone asked.

"From our point of view—forever," immediately replied the thin scientist. "Well in any case for many years. What exactly happened to this Setaur? In plain language, I think it got hit over the head. The blow must have been unusually strong, but then even a falling building here could damage a chromium-nickel skull. So what took place? We've never conducted experiments of this kind, the cost would be too great," McCork gave an unexpected smile, showing small, even teeth, "but it is generally known that any sharply localized damage to a small, that is, to a relatively simple brain or ordinary computer results in a complete breakdown in function. However the more we approximate the human brain by imitating its processes, then to a greater degree will such a complex brain become able to function despite the fact that it has suffered partial damage. The animal brain—a cat's brain, for example—contains certain centers, the stimulation of which produces an attack response, manifested as an outburst of aggressive rage. The brain of the Setaur is built differently, yet does possess a certain general drive, a potentiality for action, which can be directed and channeled in various ways. Now, some sort of short circuit occurred between that motive center and an already initiated program for destruction. Of course I am speaking in grossly oversimplified terms."

"But why destruction?" asked the same voice as before.

"It is an automaton designed for mining operations," Dr. McCork explained. "Its task was to have been the digging of levels or drifts, the boring through of rock, the crushing of particularly hard minerals, broadly speaking—the destruction of cohesive matter, obviously not everywhere and not everything, but as a result of its injury such a generalization came about. Anyway my hypothesis could be completely wrong. That side of the question, purely theoretical, will be worth considering later, after we have made a carpet of the thing. At present it is more important for us to know what the Setaur can do. It can move at a speed of about fifty kilometers an hour, over almost any terrain. It has no lubricating points, all the friction-joint surfaces work on teflon. Its suspensions are magnetic, its armor cannot be penetrated by any revolver or rifle bullet, such tests have not been made, but I think that possibly an antitank gun . . . But we don't have any of those, do we?"

Achanian shook his head. He picked up the list that had

been returned to him and read it, making little marks beside the names.

"Obviously the explosion of a fair-sized charge would pull it apart," McCork went on calmly, as if he were talking about the most ordinary things. "But first you would have to bring the charge near it, and that, I am afraid, will not be easy."

"Where exactly does it have its laser? In the head?" asked someone from the audience.

"Actually it has no head, only a sort of bulge, a swelling between the shoulders. That was to increase its resistance to falling rock. The Setaur measures two hundred and twenty centimeters in height, so it fires from a point about two meters above the ground; the muzzle of the laser is protected by a sliding visor; when the body is stationary it can fire through an angle of thirty degrees, and a greater field of aim is obtained when the entire body turns. The laser has a maximum power of forty-five thousand kilowatts. Any expert will realize that this is considerable; it can easily cut through a steel plate several centimeters thick . . ."

"At what range?"

"It's a violet laser, therefore with a very small angle of divergence from the line of incidence . . . And therefore the range will be, for all practical purposes, limited to the field of vision; since the horizon here on a level plane is at a distance of two kilometers, two kilometers at the very least will be the range of fire."

"We will be receiving special mining lasers of six times that power," Achanian added.

"But that is only what the Americans call *overkill*," McCork replied with a smile. "Such power will provide no advantage in a duel with the Setaur's laser . . ."

Someone asked whether it wouldn't be possible to

destroy the automaton from aboard some cosmic vessel. McCork declared himself not qualified to answer; Achanian meanwhile glanced at the attendance sheet and said:

"We have here a navigator first class. Pirx . . . would you care to comment on this?"

Pirx got up.

"Well in theory a vessel of medium tonnage like my Cuivier, in other words having sixteen thousand tons rest mass, could certainly destroy such a Setaur, if it got it in its line of thrust. The temperature of the exhaust gases exceeds six thousand degrees for a distance of nine hundred meters. That would be sufficient, I think . . . ?"

McCork nodded.

"But this is sheer speculation," Pirx continued. "The vessel would have to be somehow brought into position, and a small target like the Setaur, which really isn't any larger than a man, could always have time to move out of the way, unless it were immobilized. The lateral velocity of a vessel maneuvering near the surface of a planet, in its field of gravity, is quite small; sudden pursuit maneuvers are completely out of the question. The only remaining possibility, then, would be to use small units, say, the Moon's own fleet. Except that the thrust here would be weak and of not very high temperature, so perhaps if you used one of those crafts as a bomber instead . . . But for precision bombing you need special instruments, sights, range finders, which Luna doesn't have. No, we can rule that out. Of course it will be necessary, even imperative, to employ such small machines, but only for reconnaissance purposes, that is, to pinpoint the automaton."

He was about to sit down, when suddenly a new idea hit him.

"Oh yes!" he said. "Jump holsters. Those you could

use. I mean—you would have to have people who knew how to use them."

"Are they the small, individual rockets one straps on over the shoulders?" asked McCork.

"Yes. With them you can execute jumps or even sail along without moving; depending on the model and type, you get from one to several minutes aloft and reach an altitude of fifty to four hundred meters . . ."

Achanian stood.

"This may be important. Who here has been trained in the use of such devices?"

Two hands went up. Then another.

"Only three?" said Achanian. "Ah, you too?" he added, seeing that Pirx, now understanding, had also raised his hand. "That makes four. Not very many . . . We'll ask among the ground crew. Gentlemen! This is—it goes without saying—strictly a voluntary action. I really ought to have begun with that. Who of you wishes to take part in the operation?"

A slight clatter ensued, for everyone present was standing up.

"On behalf of Control I thank you," said Achanian. "This is good . . . And so we have seventeen volunteers. We will be supported by three units from the lunar fleet, and in addition will have at our disposal ten drivers and radio operators to help man the transporters. I will ask you all to remain here, and you," he turned to McCork and Pirx, "please come with me, to Control . . ."

Around four in the afternoon Pirx was sitting in the turret of a large caterpillar transporter, jolted by its violent motions. He was wearing a full suit, with the helmet on his knees, ready to put it on at the first sound of the alarm, and across his chest hung a heavy laser, the butt of which poked him unmercifully; in his left hand he had a map, and used the right to turn a periscope, observing the long, spread-out line of the other transporters, which pitched and tossed like boats across the debris-strewn tracts of the Sea of Tranquillity. That desert "sea" was all ablaze with sunlight and empty from one black horizon to the other. Pirx received reports and passed them on, spoke with Luna 1, with the officers of the other machines, with the pilots of the reconnaissance modules, whose microscopic exhaust flames every so often appeared among the stars in the black sky, yet with all of this he still couldn't help feeling at times that he was having some kind of highly elaborate and stupid dream.

Things had happened with increasing frenzy. He wasn't the only one to whom it seemed that construction headquarters had succumbed to something like panic. For really, what could one automaton-halfwit do, even armed with a lightthrower? So when at the second "summit meeting," right at noon, there began to be talk of turning to the UN, at least to the Security Council, for "special sanction," namely permission to bring in heavy artillery (rocket launchers would be best), and possibly even atomic missiles—Pirx objected along with others that in that way, before they got anywhere, they would be making complete asses of themselves in front of all Earth. Besides, it was obvious that for such a decision from the international body they would have to wait days if not weeks, meanwhile the "mad robot" could wander off God-knows-where, and once hidden in the inaccessible rifts of the lunar crust, you wouldn't be able to get at it with all the cannons in the world; therefore it was necessary to act decisively and without delay. It became clear then that the biggest problem would be communications, which had always been a sore point in lunar undertakings. There supposedly existed about three thousand different patents for inventions designed to facilitate communications, ranging from a seismic telegraph (using microexplosions as signals) to "Trojan" stationary satellites. Such satellites had been placed in orbit last year—they didn't improve the situation one bit. In practice the problem was solved by systems of ultrashortwave relays set on poles, a lot like the old presputnik television transmission lines on Earth. This was actually more reliable than communication by satellite, because the engineers were still racking their brains over how to make their orbiting stations unsusceptible to solar storms. Every single jump in the activity of the sun, and the resultant "hurricanes" of electrically charged high-energy particles that tore through the ether, immediately produced a static that made it difficult to maintain contact—and sometimes for several days. One of those solar "twisters" was going on right now, thus messages between Luna 1 and Construction went by way of the ground relays, and the success of Operation Setaur depended—to a large degree, at least—on the "rebel" not taking it into its head to destroy the girdered poles that stood, forty-five of them, on the desert separating Luna City from the cosmodrome near the construction site. Assuming, of course, that the automaton would continue to prowl in that vicinity. It had, after all, complete freedom of movement, requiring neither fuel nor oxygen, neither sleep nor rest, in all so self-sufficient, that many of the engineers for the first time fully realized how perfect was the machine of their own making—a machine whose next step no one was able to foresee. The direct Moon-Earth discussions which had begun at dawn between Control and the firm Cybertronics, including the staff of Setaur's designers, went on and on; but not a thing was learned from them which hadn't already been said by little Dr. McCork. It was only the laymen who still tried to talk the specialists into using some great calculator to predict the automaton's tactics. Was the Setaur intelligent? Well yes, in its own fashion! That "unnecessary"—and at the present moment highly dangerous—"wisdom" of the machine angered many participants in the action; they couldn't see why in the hell the engineers had endowed such freedom and autonomy on a machine made strictly for mining tasks. McCork calmly explained that this "intellectronic redundancy" was—in the current phase of technological development—the same thing as the excess of power generally found in all conventional machines and engines: it was an emergency reserve, put there in order to increase safety and dependability of function. There was no way of knowing in advance all the situations in which a machine, be it mechanical or informational, might find itself. And therefore no one really had the foggiest notion of what the Setaur would do. Of course the experts, and those on Earth as well, had telegraphed their opinions; the only problem was that these opinions were diametrically opposed. Some believed the Setaur would attempt to destroy objects of an "artificial" nature, precisely like the relay poles or high-tension lines; others on the other hand thought that it would expend its energy by firing at whatever stood in its path, whether a lunar rock or a transporter filled with people. The former were in favor of an immediate attack for the purpose of destroying it, the latter recommended a wait-and-see strategy. Both were in agreement on this only, that it was absolutely necessary to keep track of the machine's movements.

Since early morning the lunar fleet, numbering twelve small units, had patrolled the Sea of Tranquillity and sent

continual reports to the group defending the construction
site, which in turn was in constant contact with
Headquarters at the cosmodrome. It was no easy thing to
detect the Setaur, a tiny piece of metal in a giant
wilderness of rock filled with fields of detritus, cracks and
half-buried crevices, and covered besides with the
pockmarks of miniature craters. If only those reports had
been at least negative! But the patrolling crews had
alarmed ground personnel several times already with the
information that the "mad machine" was sighted, after
which it turned out that the object was some unusual rock
formation or a fragment of lava sparkling in the rays of the
sun; even the use of radar along with ferroinduction
sensors proved to be of little help—in the wake of the first
stages of lunar exploration and colonization there
remained upon the Moon's rocky wastes a whole
multitude of metal containers, heat-fused shells from
rocket cartridges and all possible sorts of tin junk, which
every now and then became the source of fresh alarms. So
much so, that operation headquarters began to wish the
Setaur would finally attack something and show itself.
However the last time it had revealed its presence was with
the attack on the small transporter belonging to the
electrical repair team. Since then it seemed as if the lunar
soil had opened up and swallowed the thing. But everyone
felt that sitting and waiting was out of the question,
particularly when Construction had to regain its energy
supply. The action—covering about ten thousand square
kilometers—consisted in combing that area with two
waves of vehicles approaching each other from opposite
directions, that is, from the north and from the south.
From Construction came one extended line under the
command of their head technologist Strzibor, and from
the Luna cosmodrome—the second, in which the role of

operations coordinator of both sides, working closely with the Chief (Commodore Navigator Pleydar), fell to Pirx. He understood perfectly that at any moment they could pass right by the Setaur; it might for example be hidden in one of those deep tectonic trenches, or even be camouflaged by only the dazzling lunar sand, and they would never notice it; McCork, who rode with him as "intellectronist-consultant," was of the same opinion.

The transporter lurched dreadfully, moving along at a speed which, as the driver quietly informed them, "after a while makes your eyes pop out." They were now in the eastern sector of the Sea of Tranquillity and less than an hour away from the region where the automaton was most likely to be located. After crossing that previously determined border they were all to don their helmets, so that in case of an unexpected hit and loss of seal, or fire, they could leave the vehicle immediately.

The transporter had been changed into a fighting machine; the mechanics had mounted on its domelike turret a mining laser of great power, though pretty poor as far as accuracy went. Pirx considered it altogether useless against the Setaur. The Setaur possessed an automatic sighter, since its photoelectric eyes were hooked up directly to the laser and it could instantly fire at whatever lay in the center of its field of vision. Theirs, on the other hand, was a quaint sort of sighter, probably from an old cosmonautical range finder; it had been tested in this way, namely, that before leaving Luna they took a few shots at some rocks on the horizon. The rocks had been large, the distance no greater than a mile, and even so they hit the mark only on the fourth try. And here, to make matters worse, you had lunar conditions to cope with, because a laser ray was visible as a brilliant streak only in a diffusing medium, e.g. an earthlike atmosphere; but in empty space a beam of light, regardless how powerful, was invisible until it hit some material obstacle. Therefore on Earth you could shoot a laser much the way you shot tracer bullets, being guided by their observable line of flight. Without a sighter a laser on the Moon was of no practical value. Pirx didn't keep this from McCork; he told him when only a couple of minutes separated them from the hypothetical danger zone.

"I didn't think of that," said the engineer, then added with a smile:

"Why did you tell me?"

"To free you of illusions," replied Pirx, not looking up from the double eyepiece of his periscope. It had foam-rubber cushions, but he felt sure that he would be going around with black eyes for the longest time (assuming, of course, he came out of this alive). "And also, to explain why we're carrying that stuff in the back."

"The cylinders?" asked McCork. "I saw you taking them from the storeroom. What's in them?"

"Ammonia, chlorine and some hydrocarbons or other," said Pirx. "I thought they might come in handy . . ."

"A gas-smoke screen?" ventured the engineer.

"No, what I had in mind was some way of aiming. If there's no atmosphere, we create one, at least tem-porarily . . ."

"I'm afraid there won't be time for that."

"Perhaps not . . . I took it along just in case. Against one that is insane, insane measures are often best . . ."

They fell silent, for the transporter had begun to lurch like a drunk; the stabilizers whined and squealed, sounding as if any minute the oil in them would begin to boil. They hurtled down an incline strewn with sharp boulders. The opposite slope gleamed, all white with pumice.

"You know what worries me most?" resumed Pirx when the heaving let up a little; for he had grown strangely talkative. "Not the Setaur—not at all . . . It's those transporters from Construction. If just one of them takes us for the Setaur and starts blasting away with its laser, things'll get lively."

"I see you've thought of everything," muttered the engineer. The cadet, sitting beside the radio operator, leaned across the back of his seat and handed Pirx a scrawled radiogram, barely legible.

"We have entered the danger zone at relay twenty, so far nothing, stop, Strzibor, end of transmission," Pirx read aloud. "Well, we'll soon have to put our helmets on too . . ."

The machine slowed a little, climbing a slope. Pirx noticed that he could no longer see the neighbor on his left—only the right transporter was moving like a dim blot up the bank. He ordered the left machine to be raised by radio, but there was no answer.

"We have begun to separate," he said calmly. "I thought that would happen. Can't we push the antenna up a little higher? No? Too bad."

By now they were at the summit of a gentle rise. From over the horizon, at a distance of less than two hundred kilometers, emerged, full in the sun, the sawtooth ridge of the crater Toricelli, sharply outlined against the black background of the sky. They had the plain of the Sea of Tranquillity all but behind them now. Deep tectonic rifts appeared, frozen slabs of magma jutted here and there from under the debris, and over these the transporter crawled with difficulty, heaving up first like a boat on a wave, then dropping heavily down, as though it were about to plunge head over heels into some unknown cavity. Pirx caught sight of the mast of the next relay, glanced quickly at the celluloid map card pressed to his knees, and ordered everyone to fasten their helmets. From now on they would be able to communicate only by inside telephone. The transporter managed to shake even more violently than before—Pirx's head wobbled around in its helmet like the kernel of a nut inside an empty shell.

When they drove down the slope to lower ground, the saw of Toricelli disappeared, blocked out by nearer elevations; almost at the same time they lost their right neighbor. For a few minutes more they heard its call signal, then that was distorted by the waves bouncing off the sheets of rock, and complete radio silence followed. It was extremely awkward trying to look through the periscope with a helmet on; Pirx thought he would either crack his viewplate or smash the eyepiece. He did what he could to keep his eyes on the field of vision at all times, though it shifted totally with each lurch of the machine and was strewn with endless boulders. The jumble of pitch-black shadow and dazzlingly bright surfaces of stone made his eyes swim. Suddenly a small orange flame leaped up in the darkness of the far sky, flickered, dwindled, disappeared. A second flash, a little stronger. Pirx shouted: "Attention everyone! I see explosions!"— and feverishly turned the crank of the periscope, reading the azimuth off the scale etched onto the lenses.

"We're changing course!" he howled. "Forty-seven point eight, full speed ahead!"

The order really applied to a cosmic vessel, but the driver understood it all the same; the plates and every joint of the transporter gave a shudder as the machine wheeled around practically in place and surged forward. Pirx got up off his seat, its tossing was pulling his head away from the eyepiece. Another flash—this time red-violet, a fan-shaped burst of flame. But the source of those flashes or explosions lay beyond the field of vision, hidden by the ridge they were climbing.

"Attention everyone!" said Pirx. "Prepare your individual lasers! Dr. McCork, please go to the hatch. When I give the word or in case of a hit, you'll open it! Driver! Decrease velocity! . . ."

The elevation up which the machine clambered rose from the desert like the shank of some moon monster, half-sunken in debris; the rock in fact resembled, by its smoothness, a polished skeleton or giant skull; Pirx ordered the driver to go to the top. The treads began to chatter, like steel over glass. "Hold it!" yelled Pirx, and the transporter, coming to a sudden halt, dipped nosedown towards the rock, swayed, the stabilizers groaning with the strain, and stopped.

Pirx looked into a shallow basin enclosed on two sides by radially spreading, tapered embankments of old magma flows; two-thirds of the wide depression lay in glaring sun, a third was covered by a shroud of absolute black. On that velvet darkness there shone, like a weird jewel, fading ruby-red, the ripped-open skeleton of a vehicle. Only the driver saw it besides Pirx, for the armor flaps of the windows had been lowered. Pirx, to tell the truth, didn't know what to do. "A transporter," he thought. "Where is the front of it? Coming from the south? Probably from the construction group, then. But who got it, the Setaur? And I'm standing here in full view, like an idiot—we have to conceal ourselves. But where are all the other transporters? Theirs and mine?"

"I have something!" shouted the radiotelegraph man. He connected his receiver to the inside circuit, so that everyone could hear the signals in their helmets.

"Aximo-portable talus! A wall with encystation—repetition from the headland unnecessary—the access at an azimuth of—multicrystalline metamorphism . . ." the voice filled Pirx's earphones, delivering the words clearly, in a monotone, with no intonation whatever.

"It's him!" he yelled. "The Setaur! Hello, radio! Get a fix on that, quickly! We need a fix! For God's sake! While it's still sending!" He roared till he was deafened by his own shouts amplified in the closed space of the helmet; not waiting for the telegraph operator to snap out of it, he leaped, head bent, to the top of the turret, seized the double handgrip of the heavy laser and began turning it along with the turret, his eyes already at the sighter. Meanwhile inside his helmet that low, almost sorrowful, steady voice droned on:

"Heavily bihedrous achromatism viscosity—undecorticated segments without repeated anticlinal interpolations"—and the senseless gabble seemed to weaken.

"Where's that fix, damn it?!!"

Pirx, keeping his eyes glued to the sighter, heard a faint clatter—McCork had run up front, shoved aside the operator, there was a sound of scuffling . . .

Suddenly in his earphones he heard the calm voice of the cyberneticist:

"Azimuth 39.9 . . . 40.0 . . . 40.1 . . . 40.2 . . ."

"It's moving!" Pirx realized. The turret had to be turned by crank; he nearly dislocated his arm, he cranked so hard. The numbers moved at a creep. The red line passed the forty mark.

Suddenly the voice of the Setaur rose to a drawn-out screech and broke off. At that same moment Pirx pressed the trigger and half a kilometer down, right at the line between light and shadow, a rock spouted fire brighter than the sun.

Through the thick gloves it was next to impossible to hold the handgrip steady. The blinding flame bored into the darkness at the bottom of the basin, a few dozen meters from the dimly glowing wreck, it stopped and—in a spray of jagged embers—cut a line sideways, twice raising columns of sparks. Something yammered in the earphones. Pirx paid no attention, he plowed on with that line of flame, so thin and so terrible, until it split into a thousand centrifugal ricochets off some stone pillar. Red swirling circles danced before him, but through their swirl he saw a bright blue eye, smaller than the head of a pin, it had opened at the very bottom of the darkness, off to the side somewhere, not where he had been shooting—and before he was able to move the handgrips of the laser, to pivot it around on its swivel, a rock right next to the machine itself exploded like a liquid sun.

"Back!" he bellowed, ducking down by reflex, with the result that he no longer saw anything, but he wouldn't have seen anything anyway, only those red, slowly fading circles, which turned now black, now golden.

The engine thundered. They were thrown with such violence that Pirx fell all the way to the bottom, then flew to the front, between the knees of the cadet and the radio operator; the cylinders, though they had tied them down securely on the armored wall, made an awful racket. They were rushing backwards, in reverse, there was a horrible crunch beneath the tractor tread, they swerved, careened in the other direction, for a minute it looked like the transporter was going to flip over on its back . . . The driver, desperately working the gas, the brakes, the clutch, somehow brought that wild skid under control; the machine gave a long quiver and stood still.

"Do we have a seal?!" shouted Pirx, picking himself up off the floor. "A good thing it's rubber," he managed to think.

"Intact!"

"Well, that was nice and close," he said in an altogether different voice now, standing up and straightening his back. And added softly, not without chagrin: "Two hundredths more to the left and I would have had him . . ."

McCork returned to his place.

"Doctor, that was good, thank you!" called Pirx, already back at the periscope. "Hello, driver, let's go down the same way we came up. There are some small cliffs over there, a kind of arch—that's it, right!—drive into the shadow between them and stop . . ."

Slowly, as if with exaggerated caution, the transporter moved in between the slabs of rock half-buried in sand and froze in their shadow, which rendered it invisible.

"Excellent!" said Pirx almost cheerfully. "Now I need two men, to go with me and do a little reconnoitering . . ."

McCork raised his hand at the same time as the cadet.

"Good! Now listen, you," he turned to the others, "will remain here. Don't move out of the shadow, even if the Setaur should come straight at you—sit quietly. Well, I guess if it walks right into the transporter, then you'll have to defend yourselves, you have the laser—but that's not very likely . . . You," he said to the driver, "will help this young man remove those cylinders of gas from the wall, and you"—this, to the radio operator—"will call Luna, the cosmodrome, Construction, the patrols, and tell the first who answers that *it* destroyed one transporter, probably belonging to Construction, and that three men from our machine have gone out to hunt it. So I don't want anybody barging in with lasers, shooting blindly and so on . . . And now let's go!"

Since each of them could carry only one cylinder, they took four. Pirx led his companions not to the top of the "skull," but a little beyond, where a small, shallow, ascending ravine was visible. They went as far as they could, set the cylinders down by a large boulder, and Pirx ordered the driver to go back. Himself he peered out over the surface of the boulder and trained his binoculars on the interior of the basin. McCork and the cadet crouched down beside him. After a long while he said:

"I don't see him. Doctor, what the Setaur said, did it have any meaning?"

"I doubt it. Combinations of words—something in the nature of schizophrenia . . ."

"That wreck is going out," said Pirx.

"Why did you shoot?" asked McCork. "There might have been people."

"There wasn't anyone."

Pirx moved the binoculars a millimeter at a time, scrutinizing every crease and crevice of the sunlit area.

"They didn't have time to jump."

"How do you know that?"

"Because he cut the machine in half. You can still see it. They must have practically run into him. He hit from a few dozen meters. And besides, both hatches are closed. No," he added after a couple of seconds, "he's not in the sun. And probably hasn't had a chance to sneak away . . . We'll try drawing him out."

Bending over, he lifted a heavy cylinder to the top of the boulder and, shoving it into position before him, muttered between his teeth:

"A real live cowboys-and-Indians situation, the kind I always dreamed of . . ."

The cylinder slipped; he held it by the valves and, flattening himself out on the stones, said:

"If you see a blue flash, shoot at once—that's his laser eye . . ."

With all his might he pushed the cylinder, which at first slowly but then with increasing speed began to roll down the slope. All three of them took aim, the cylinder had now gone about two hundred meters and was rolling more slowly, for the slope lessened. A few times it seemed that protruding rocks would bring it to a stop, but it tumbled past them and, growing smaller and smaller, now a dully shining spot, approached the bottom of the basin.

"Nothing?" said Pirx, disappointed. "Either he's smarter than I thought, or just isn't interested in it, or else . . ."

He didn't finish. On the slope below them there was a blinding flash. The flame almost instantly changed into a heavy, brownish yellow cloud, at the center of which still glowed a sullen fire, and the edges spread out between the spurs of rock.

"The chlorine . . ." said Pirx. "Why didn't you shoot? Couldn't you see anything?"

"No," replied the cadet and McCork in unison.

"The bastard! He's hid himself in some crevice or is firing from the flank. I really doubt now that this will do any good, but let's try . . ."

He picked up a second cylinder and sent it after the first.

At first it rolled the same, but somewhere halfway down the incline it turned aside and came to rest. Pirx wasn't looking at it—all his attention was concentrated on the triangular section of darkness in which the Setaur somewhere lurked. The seconds went by slowly. All at once a branching explosion ripped the slope. Pirx was unable to locate the place where the automaton had concealed itself, but he saw the line of fire, or more precisely a part of it, for it materialized as a burning, sunbright thread when it passed through what was left of the first cloud of gas. Immediately he sighted along that gleaming trajectory, which was already fading, and as soon as he had the edge of the darkness in his cross hairs, he pulled the trigger. Apparently McCork had done the same thing simultaneously, and in an instant the cadet joined them. Three blades of sun plowed the black floor of the basin and at that very moment it was as if some gigantic, fiery lid slammed down directly in front of them—the entire boulder that protected them shook, from its rim showered a myriad searing rainbows, their suits and helmets were sprayed with burning quartz, which instantly congealed to microscopic teardrops. They lay now flattened in the shadow of the rock, while above their heads whipped, like a white-hot sword, a second and a third discharge, grazing the surface of the boulder, which immediately was covered with cooling glass bubbles.

"Everyone all right?" asked Pirx, not lifting his head.

"Yes!"—"Here too!"—came the answers.

"Go down to the machine and tell the radio operator to call everyone, because we have him here and will try to keep him pinned as long as possible," Pirx said to the cadet, who then crawled backwards and ran, stooping, in the direction of the rocks where the tractor was standing.

"We have two cylinders left, one apiece. Doctor, let's switch positions now. And please be careful and keep low, he's already hit right on our top . . ."

With these words Pirx picked up one cylinder and, taking advantage of the shadows thrown by some large stone slabs, moved forward as quickly as he could. About two hundred steps farther on they rested in the cleft of a magma embankment. The cadet, returning from the transporter, wasn't able to find them at first. He was breathing hard, as if he had run at least a mile.

"Easy, take your time!" said Pirx. "Well, what's up?"

"Contact has been resumed . . ." The cadet squatted by

Pirx, who could see the youth's eyes blinking behind the viewplate of the helmet. "In that machine, the one that was destroyed . . . there were four people from Construction. The second must have withdrawn, because it had a defective laser . . . and the rest went by, off to the side, and didn't see anything . . ." Pirx nodded as if to say: "I thought as much."

"What else? Where's our group?"

"Practically all of them—twenty miles from here, there was a false alarm there, some rocket patrol said it saw the Setaur and pulled everyone to the spot. And three machines don't answer."

"When will they get here?"

"At the moment we're only receiving . . ." said the cadet, embarrassed.

"Only receiving? What do you mean?!"

"The radio operator says that either something's happened to the transmitter, or else in this place his emission is damping out. He asks if he might change the parking location, so he can test . . ."

"He can change his location if he has to," Pirx replied. "And please stop running like that! Watch where you put your feet!"

But the other must not have heard, for he was racing back.

"At best they'll be here in half an hour, if we succeed in making contact," observed Pirx. McCork said nothing. Pirx pondered the next move. Should they wait or not? Storming the basin with transporters would probably ensure success, but not without losses. Compared with the Setaur their machines made large targets, were slow and would have to strike together, for a duel would end as it had with that tractor from Construction. He tried to come up with some stratagem to lure the Setaur out into the lighted area. If it were possible to send in one unmanned, remote-control transporter as a decoy, then hit the automaton from elsewhere, say, from above . . .

It occurred to him that he really didn't have to wait for anyone, he already had one transporter. But somehow the plan didn't jell. To send a machine out blindly like that wouldn't be any good. *He* would just blow the thing to bits, and wouldn't have to move to do it. Could he have possibly realized that the zone of shadow in which he stood was giving him so much of an advantage? But then this was not a machine created for battle with all its tactics . . . There was method in his madness, yes, but what method? They sat, bent over, at the foot of a rocky scarp, in its dense, cold shadow. Suddenly it struck Pirx that he was acting like a complete idiot. What would he do, after all, if he were the Setaur? Immediately he felt alarm, for he was certain that he—in *his* place—would attack. Passively waiting for things to happen gained nothing. So then, could *he* be advancing towards them? Even now? One could surely reach the western cliff, moving under cover of darkness the whole time, and farther on there were so many huge boulders, so much fissured lava, that in that labyrinth one could hide for God knows how long . . .

He was almost positive now that the Setaur would proceed in precisely this way, and that they could expect him at any moment.

"Doctor, I fear he will take us by surprise," he said quickly, jumping to his feet. "What do you think?"

"You believe he might sneak up on us?" asked McCork and smiled. "That occurred to me too. Well yes, it's even logical, but will he behave logically? That is the question . . ."

"We'll try it one more time," Pirx muttered. "We have

to roll these cylinders down the hill and see what he does . . ."

"I understand. Now? . . ."

"Yes. And be careful!"

They dragged them to the top of the rise and, doing their best to remain unseen from the bottom of the basin, pushed both metal cylinders practically at the same time. Unfortunately the absence of air did not let them hear if the things were rolling, or in what way. Pirx made up his mind and—feeling strangely naked, as though there were no steel sphere over his head, nor a heavy three-layered suit covering his body—he pressed himself flat against the rock and cautiously stuck out his head.

Nothing had changed below. Except that the wrecked machine had ceased to be visible, for its cooling fragments merged with the surrounding darkness. The shadow occupied the same area, the shape of an irregular, elongated triangle, its base abutting the cliffs of the highest, western ridge of rocks. One cylinder had stopped some hundred feet beneath them, having struck a stone that put it in a lengthwise position. The other was still rolling, slowing down, growing smaller, till it stood still. The fact that nothing more happened was not at all to Pirx's liking. "He isn't stupid," he thought. "He won't shoot at a target someone sticks under his nose." He tried to find the place from which the Setaur, some ten minutes before, had betrayed itself by the flash of its laser eye, but that was extremely difficult.

"Perhaps he's not there anymore," he reflected. "Perhaps he's simply retreating to the north; or going parallel, along the bottom of the basin, or along one of those rifts of magnetic course . . . If he makes it to the cliffs, to that labyrinth, then we've lost him for good . . ."

Slowly, groping, he raised the butt of his laser and

loosened his muscles. "Dr. McCork!" he said. "Could you come here?"

And when the doctor had scrambled up to him, he said: "You see the two cylinders? One straight ahead, below us, and the other farther on . . ."

"I see them."

"Fire at the closer one first, then at the other, in an interval, say, of forty seconds . . . But not from here!" he added quickly. "You'll have to find a better place. Ah!" He pointed with his hand. "*There* is not a bad position, in that hollow. And when you shoot, crawl back immediately. All right?"

McCork asked no questions, but set off at once, keeping low, in the direction indicated. Pirx waited impatiently. If *he* was even a little like a man, he had to be curious. Every intelligent creature was curious—and curiosity prompted it to act when something incomprehensible took place . . . He couldn't see the doctor now. He forced himself not to look at the cylinders, which were to explode under McCork's shots; he focused all his attention on the stretch of sunlit debris between the zone of shadow and the outcrop. He lifted the binoculars to his eyes and trained them on that section of the lava flow. In the lenses grotesque shapes filed slowly by, shapes as though formed in the studio of some sculptor-abstractionist: tapering obelisks twisted about like screws, plates furrowed with snaking cracks—the jumble of glaring planes and zigzag shadows had an irritating effect on the eye. At the very edge of his vision, far below him, on the slope, there was a burgeoning flash. After a long pause the second went off. Silence. The only sound was his pulse throbbing inside his helmet, through which the sun was trying to bore its way into his skull. He swept the lenses along a stretch of chaotically interlocking masses.

Something moved. He froze. Above the razorlike edge of a slab that resembled the fractured blade of some giant stone ax there emerged a shape, hemispherical, in color much like a dark rock, but this shape had arms, which took hold of the boulder from both sides. Now he could see it—the upper half of it. It didn't look headless, but rather like a man wearing the supernatural mask of an African magician, a mask that covered the face, neck and chest, but flattened out in a manner that was somewhat monstrous . . . With the elbow of his right arm he felt the butt of his laser, but didn't dream of shooting now. The risk was too great—the chance of getting a hit with a relatively weak weapon, and at such a distance, was minuscule. The other, motionless, seemed to be examining with that head it had, which barely protruded above the shoulders, the remains of the two gas clouds that were drifting along the slope, helplessly expanding into space. This lasted a good while. It looked as if *it* did not know what had happened, and was unsure of what to do. In that hesitation, that uncertainty, which Pirx could understand full well, there was something so uncannily familiar, so human, that he felt a lump in his throat. What would I do in his place, what would I think? That someone was firing at the very same objects I had fired at before, and therefore this someone would be not an opponent, not an enemy, but instead a kind of ally. But I would know, surely, that I had no ally. Ah but what if it were a being like myself?

The other stirred. Its movements were fluid and uncommonly swift. All at once it was in full view, erect on that upended stone, as though still looking for the mysterious cause of the two explosions. Then it turned away, jumped down and, leaning slightly forward, began to run—now and then it dropped from Pirx's sight, but never for more than a few seconds, only to break out into the sunlight again on one of the spurs of the magma labyrinth. In this way it approached Pirx, though running the whole time at the bottom of the basin. They were separated now only by the space of the slope and Pirx wondered whether he shouldn't shoot after all. But the other whisked past in narrow strips of light and again dissolved into the blackness—and since it continually had to change direction, picking its way between the rocks and rubble, one could not predict where its arms, working to maintain balance like a man running, and where its headless trunk would show up next, to flash metallically and vanish once again. Suddenly ragged lightning cut across the mosaic of debris, striking long plumes of sparks among the very blocks where the Setaur was running. Who had fired that? Pirx couldn't see McCork, but the line of fire had come from the opposite side—it could have only been the cadet, that snot-nosed kid, that idiot! He cursed him, furious, because nothing had been accomplished, of course—the dome of metal flitted on for another fraction of a second, then disappeared for good. "And not only that, but he tried to shoot him in the back!" thought Pirx in a fury, not at all feeling the absurdity of this reproach. And the Setaur hadn't returned fire. Why? He tried to catch a glimpse of it—in vain. Could the bulge of the slope be in the way? That was entirely possible . . . In which case he could move safely now . . . Pirx slipped down from his boulder, seeing that nothing was any longer watching from below. He ran, bent over slightly, along the rim itself, passed the cadet, who lay prone as if on a rifle range—the feet flung out wide and pressed sidewise against the rock—and Pirx felt an unaccountable urge to kick him in the behind, which stuck up ludicrously and was made even larger by a poorly fitting suit. He slowed down, but only to shout:

"Don't you dare shoot, do you hear me?! Put away that laser!"

And before the cadet, turning on his side, began to look around in bewilderment—for the voice had come from his earphones, giving no indication of the direction or place in which Pirx was located—Pirx had already run on; afraid that he was wasting precious time, he hurried as much as he could, till he found himself facing a broad crevasse, which opened up a sudden view all the way to the bottom of the basin.

It was a type of tectonic trench, so old that its edges had crumbled, lost their sharpness, and resembled a mountain gully widened by erosion. He hesitated. He didn't see the Setaur, but then it was probably impossible to see it anyway from this vantage point. So he ventured into the gully with laser ready to fire, well aware that what he was doing was insane, and yet he couldn't resist whatever was driving him; he told himself that he only wanted to take a look, that he would stop at the first place where he could check out the last section of the outcrop and the entire labyrinth of rubble beneath it; and perhaps, even as he ran, still leaning forward, with the gravel shooting out in streams from under his boots, he actually believed this. But at the moment he couldn't give thought to anything. He was on the Moon and therefore weighed barely fifteen kilograms, but even so the increasing angle tripped him up, he went bounding along eight meters at a time, braking for all he was worth; already he had covered half the length of the slope, the gully ended in a shallow pathway—there in the sun stood the first masses of the lava flow, black on the far side and glittering on the southern, about one hundred meters down. "I got myself into it this time," he thought. From here one could practically reach out and touch the region in which the

Setaur was at large. He glanced rapidly to the left and to the right. He was alone; the ridge lay high above him, a broiling steepness against the black sky. Before, he had been able to look down into the narrow places between the rocks almost with a bird's-eye view, but now that crisscross maze of fissures was blocked out for him by the nearest masses of stone. "Not good," he thought. "Better go back." But for some reason he knew that he wasn't going back.

However he couldn't just stand there. A few dozen steps lower was a solitary block of magma, evidently the end of that long tongue which once had poured red-hot off the great crags at the foot of Toricelli—and which had meandered its way finally to this sinkhole. It was the best cover available. He reached it in a single leap, though he found particularly unpleasant this prolonged lunar floating, this slow-motion flight as in a dream; he could never really get used to it. Crouched behind the angular rock, he peered out over it and saw the Setaur, which came from behind two jagged spires, went around a third, brushing it with a metal shoulder, and halted. Pirx was looking at it from the side, so it was lit up only partially, only the right arm glistened, dully like a well-greased machine part—the rest of its frame lay in shadow. He had just raised the laser to his eye when the other, as if in a sudden premonition, vanished. Could it be standing there still, having only stepped back into the shadow? Should he shoot into that shadow, then? He had a bead on it now, but didn't touch the trigger. He relaxed his muscles, the barrel fell. He waited. No sign of the Setaur. The rubble spread out directly below him in a truly infernal labyrinth, one could play hide-and-seek in there for hours—the glassy lava had split into geometrical yet eery shapes. "Where is he?" he thought. "If it were only possible to hear something, but this damned airless place, it's like being in a nightmare . . . I could go down there and hunt him. No, I'm not about to do that, *he's* the mad one after all . . . But one can at least consider everything—the outcrop extends no more than twelve meters, that would take about two jumps on Earth; I would be in the shadow beneath it, invisible, and could move along the length of it, with my back protected by the rock at all times, and sooner or later he'd walk out straight into my sights . . ." Nothing changed in the labyrinth of stone. On Earth by this time the sun would have shifted quite a bit, but here the long lunar day held sway, the sun seemed to keep hanging in the very same place, extinguishing the nearest stars, so that it was surrounded by a black void shot through with a kind of orange, radial haze . . . He leaned out halfway from behind his boulder. Nothing. This was beginning to annoy him. Why weren't the others showing up? It was inconceivable that radio contact hadn't been established by now . . . But perhaps they were planning to drive it out of that rubble . . . He glanced at the watch beneath the thick glass on his wrist and was amazed—since his last conversation with McCork barely thirteen minutes had elapsed.

He was preparing to abandon his position when two things happened at once, both equally unexpected. Through the stone arch between the two magma embankments that closed off the basin to the east, he saw transporters moving, one after the other. They were still far away, possibly more than a kilometer, and going at full speed, trailing long, seemingly rigid plumes of swirling dust. At the same time two large hands, human-looking, except that they were wearing metal gloves, appeared at the very edge of the precipice, and following them came—so quickly, he hadn't time to back away—the Setaur. No more than ten meters separated them. Pirx saw the massive bulge of the torso that served for a head, set between powerful shoulders and in which glittered the lenses of the optic apertures, motionless, like two dark, widely spaced eyes, together with that middle, that third and terrible eye, lidded at the moment, of the laser gun. He himself, to be sure, held a laser in his hand, but the machine's reflexes were incomparably faster than his own, and anyway he didn't even try leveling his weapon— he simply stood stock-still in the full sun, his legs bent, exactly as he had been caught, jumping up from the ground, by the sudden appearance of *him*, and they looked at one another: the statue of the man and the statue of the machine, both sheathed in metal. Then a terrible light tore the whole area in front of Pirx; pushed by a blast of heat, he went crashing backwards. As he fell he didn't lose consciousness and—in that fraction of a second—felt only surprise, for he could have sworn it wasn't the Setaur that had shot him, since up to the very end he had seen its dark, blind laser eye.

He landed on his back, for the discharge had gone past—but clearly it had been aimed at him, because the horrible flash was repeated in an instant and chipped off part of the stone spire that had been protecting him before; it sprayed drops of molten mineral, which in flight changed into a dazzling spider web. But now he was saved by the fact that they aimed at the height of his head and he was lying down—it was the first machine, they were firing the laser from it. He rolled over on his side and saw then the back of the Setaur, who, motionless, as if cast in bronze, gave two bursts of lilac sun. Even at that distance one could see the foremost transporter's entire tread overturn, together with the rollers and guiding wheel; such a cloud of dust and burning gases rose up there, that the second transporter, blinded, could not shoot. The two-and-a-half-meter giant slowly, unhurriedly looked at the prone man, who was still clutching his weapon, then turned and bent its legs slightly, ready to jump back from where it had come, but Pirx, awkwardly, sideways, fired at it—he intended only to cut the legs from under it, but his elbow wavered as he pulled the trigger, and a knife of flame cleaved the giant from top to bottom, so that it was only a mass of glowing scrap that tumbled down into the field of rubble.

The crew of the demolished transporter escaped unhurt, without even burns, and Pirx found out—much later, it's true—that they had in fact been firing at him, for the Setaur, dark against the dark cliffs, went completely unnoticed. The inexperienced gunner had even failed to notice that the figure in his sights showed the light color of an aluminum suit. Pirx was pretty certain that he would not have survived the next shot. The Setaur had saved him—but had it realized this? Many times he went over those few final seconds in his mind, and each time his conviction grew stronger, that the Setaur had been standing in a place from which it could tell who was the real target of the long-range fire. Did this mean that it had wished to save him? No one could provide an answer to that. The intellectronicists chalked the whole thing up to "coincidence"—but none of them was able to support that opinion with any proof. Nothing like this had ever happened before, the professional literature made no mention of such incidents. Everyone felt that Pirx had done what he had to do—but he wasn't satisfied. For many long years afterwards there remained etched in his memory that brief scene when he had brushed with death and come out in one piece, never to learn the entire truth—

and bitter was the knowledge that it was in an underhanded way, with a stab in the back, that he had killed his deliverer.

The Mask

In the beginning there was darkness and cold flame and lingering thunder, and, in long strings of sparks, char-black hooks, segmented hooks, which passed me on, and creeping metal snakes that touched the thing that was me with their snoutlike flattened heads, and each such touch brought on a lightning tremor, sharp, almost pleasurable.

From behind round windows eyes watched me, immeasurably deep eyes, unmoving, and they receded, but perhaps it was I who was moving on, entering the next circle of observation, which inspired lethargy, respect and dread. This journey of mine on my back lasted an indeterminate time, and as it progressed the it that was I increased and came to know itself, discovering its own limits, and I cannot say just when I was able to grasp its own form fully, to take cognizance of every place where I left off. There the world began, thundering, flaming, dark, and then the motion ceased and the delicate flitting of articulated limbs, which handed the me to me, lifted lightly up, relinquished that me to pincer hands, offered it to flat mouths in a rim of sparks, disappeared, and the it that was myself lay still inert, though capable now of its own motion yet in full awareness that my time had not come, and in this numb incline—for I, it, rested then on a slanting plane—the final flow of current, breathless last rites, a quivering kiss tautened the me and that was the signal to spring up and crawl into the round opening without light, and needing no urging now I touched the cold, smooth, concave plates, to rest on them with stone relief. But perhaps all that was a dream.

Of waking I know nothing. I remember incomprehensible rustlings and a cool dimness and myself inside, the world opened up before it in a panorama of glitter, broken into colors, and I remember also how much wonder there was in my movement when it crossed the threshold. Strong light beat from above on the colored confusion of vertical trunks, I saw their globes, which turned in its direction tiny buttons bright with water, the general murmur died down and in the ensuing silence the thing that was myself took yet another step.

And then, with a sound not heard but sensed, a tenuous string snapped within me and I, a she now, felt the rush of gender so violent, that her head spun and I shut my eyes. And as I stood thus, with eyes closed, words came to me from every side, for along with gender she had received language. I opened my eyes and smiled, and moved forward, and her dresses moved with me, I walked with dignity, crinoline all around, not knowing where I was going, but continuing on, for this was the court ball, and the recollection of her own mistake a moment before, when I had taken the heads for globes and the eyes for wet buttons, amused me like a silly girlish blunder, therefore I grinned, but this grin was directed only at myself. My hearing reached far, sharpened, so in it I distinguished the murmur of courtly recognition, the concealed sighs of the gentlemen, the envious breathing of the ladies, and pray who is that young woman, Count? And I walked through an enormous hall, beneath crystal spiders, from their ceiling webs dropped petals of roses, I looked at myself in the disfavor creeping out over the painted faces of dowagers, and in the leering eyes of swarthy lords.

Behind the windows from the vaulted ceiling to the parquet gaped the night, pots were burning in the park, and in an alcove between two windows, at the foot of a marble statue, stood a man shorter than the rest, surrounded by a wreath of courtiers clad in stripes of black and bile, who seemed to press towards him, yet they never overstepped the empty circle, and this single one did not even look in my direction when I approached. Passing him, I stopped, and though he was not looking at all in my direction, with the very tips of my fingers I gathered up my crinoline, dropping my eyes, as if I wished to curtsy low to him, but I only gazed at my own hands, slender and white, I did not know however why this whiteness, when it shone against the sky blue of the crinoline, there was something terrifying in it. But he, that short lord or peer, surrounded by courtiers, and behind whom stood a pale knight in half armor, with a bare blond head and holding in his hand a dagger small as a toy, he did not deign to look upon me, saying something in a low, boredom-muffled voice to himself, for to no one else. And I, not making my curtsy, but only looking at him a brief moment very fiercely, to remember his face, darkly aslant at the mouth, for its corner was turned up in a weary grimace by a small white scar, and riveting my eyes on that mouth, I turned on my heel, the crinoline rustled and I moved past. Only then did he look at me and I felt perfectly that fleeting, cold glance, such a narrow glance, as though he had an unseen rifle at his cheek and aiming for my neck, right between the rolls of golden curls, and this was the second beginning. I didn't want to turn back, but I did turn back and lowered myself in a deep, a very deep curtsy, lifting the crinoline with both hands, as if to sink through its stiffness to the sheen of the floor, for he was the King. Then I withdrew slowly, wondering how it was I knew this so well and with such certainty, and also strongly tempted to do something inappropriate, for if I could not know and yet did know, in a way inexorable and categorical, then all of this was a dream, and what could it hurt in a dream—to pull someone's nose? I grew a little frightened, for I was not able to do this, as if I had inside me some invisible barrier. Thus I wavered, walking unaware, between the convictions of reality and dream, and meanwhile knowledge flowed into me, somewhat like waves flowing up onto a beach, and each wave left behind new information, ranks and titles as if trimmed with lace; halfway through the hall, underneath a blazing candelabrum that hovered like a ship on fire, I already knew the names of all the ladies, whose wear and tear was smoothed away by careful art.

I knew so very much now, like one fully roused out of a nightmare, yet with the memory of it still lingering, and that which remained inaccessible to me appeared in my mind as two dark shadows—my past and my present, for I was as yet in complete ignorance about myself. Whereas I was experiencing, in its totality, my nakedness, the breasts, belly, thighs, neck, shoulders, the unseen feet, concealed by costly clothing, I touched the topaz in gold that pulsed like a glowworm between my breasts, I could feel also the expression on my face, betraying absolutely nothing, a look which must have perplexed, for anyone who noticed me received the impression of a smile, yet if he searched my mouth more closely, my eyes, my brows, he would see that there was not a trace of amusement there, not even merely polite amusement, so he would gaze once more into my eyes, but they were completely tranquil, he would go to the cheeks, look for the smile in my chin, but I had no frivolous dimples, my cheeks were smooth and white, and the chin intent, quiet, sober, of no less perfection than the neck, which revealed not a thing. Then the gazer would be troubled, wondering why on earth he had imagined I was smiling, and in the bewilderment caused by his doubts and my beauty he would step back into the crowd, or render me a deep bow, in order that he might hide himself from me beneath that gesture.

But there were two things I still did not know, though I realized, if obscurely still, that they were the most important. I did not understand why the King had ignored me as I passed, why he had refused to look me in the eye when he neither feared my loveliness nor desired it, indeed I felt that I was truly valuable to him, but in some inexplicable way, as if he had no use for me myself, as if I were to him someone outside this glittering hall, someone not made for dancing across the mirrorlike, waxed parquet arranged in many-colored inlays between the wrought-bronze coats of arms above the lintels; yet when I swept by, not a thought surfaced in him in which I could divine the royal will, and even when he had sent after me that glance, fleeting and casual, though sighted along an invisible barrel, I understood that it was not at me that he had leveled his pale eye, an eye which ought to have been kept behind dark glasses, for its look feigned nothing, unlike the well-bred face, and stuck in the milling elegance like dirty water left at the bottom of a washbowl. No, his eyes were something long ago discarded, something requiring concealment, not enduring the light of day.

But what could he want of me, what? I was not able to reflect on this however, for another thing claimed my attention. I knew everyone here, but no one knew me. Except possibly he, he alone: the King. At my fingertips I now had knowledge of myself as well, my feelings grew strange as I slowed my pace, three quarters of the hall already crossed, and in the midst of the multicolored crowd, faces gone numb, their side whiskers silvery with hoarfrost, and also faces blood-swollen and perspiring under clotted powder, in the midst of ribbons and medals and braided tassels there opened up a corridor, that I might walk like some queen down that path parted through humanity, escorted by watching eyes—but to where was I walking thus?

To whom.

And who was I? Thought followed thought with fluent skill, I grasped in an instant the particular dissonance between my state and that of this so distinguished throng, for each of them had a history, a family, decorations of one kind or another, the same nobility won from intrigues, betrayals, and each paraded his inflated bladder of sordid pride, dragged after him his personal past like the long, raised dust that trails a desert wagon, turn for turn, whereas I had come from such a great distance, it was as if I had not one past, but a multitude of pasts, for my destiny could be made understandable to those here only by piecemeal translation into their local customs, into this familiar yet foreign tongue, therefore I could only approximate myself to their comprehension, and with each chosen designation would become for them a different person. And for myself as well? No . . . and yet, nearly so, I possessed no knowledge beyond that which had rushed into me at the entrance of the hall, like water when it surges up and floods a barren waste, bursting through hitherto solid dikes, and beyond that knowledge I reasoned logically, was it possible to be many things at once? To derive from a plurality of abandoned pasts? My logic, extracted from the locoweed of memory, told me this was not possible, that I must have some single past, and if I was the daughter of Count Tlenix, the Duenna Zoroennay, the young Virginia, orphaned in the overseas kingdom of the Langodots by the Valandian clan, if I could not separate the fiction from the truth, then was I not dreaming after all? But now the orchestra began to play somewhere and the ball careened like an avalanche of stones—how could one make oneself believe in a reality more real, in an awakening from this awakening?

I walked now in unpleasant confusion, watching my every step, for the dizziness had returned, which I named vertigo. But I did not give up my regal stride, not one whit, though the effort was tremendous, tremendous yet unseen, and given strength precisely for being unseen, until I felt help come from afar, it was the eyes of a man, he was seated in the low embrasure of a half-open window, its brocade curtain flung whimsically over his shoulder like a scarf and woven in red-grizzled lions, lions with crowns, frightfully old, holding orbs and scepters in their paws, the orbs like poisoned apples, apples from the Garden of Eden. This man, decked in lions, dressed in black, richly, and yet with a natural sort of carelessness which had nothing in common with artificial, lordly disarray, this stranger, no dandy or fop, not a courtier or sycophant, but not old either, looked at me from his seclusion in the general uproar—just as utterly alone as I. And all around were those who lit cigarillos with rolled-up banknotes in front of the eyes of their tarot partners, and threw gold ducats on green cloth, as if they were tossing nutmeg apples to swans in a pond, those for whom no action could be stupid or dishonorable, for the illustriousness of their persons ennobled everything they did. The man was altogether out of place in this hall, and the seemingly unintentional deference he paid to the stiff brocade in royal lions, permitting it to drape across his shoulder and bathe his face with the reflection of its imperial purple, that deference had the aspect of the most subtle mockery. No longer young, his entire youth was alive in his dark eyes, unevenly squinting, and he listened or perhaps was not listening to his interlocutor, a small, stout baldhead with the air of an overeaten, docile dog. When the seated one stood up, the curtain slid from his arm like false, cast-off trumpery, and our eyes met forcefully, but mine darted from his face in flight. I swear it. Still that face remained deep in my vision, as if I had gone suddenly blind, and my hearing dimmed, so that instead of the orchestra I heard—for a moment—only my own pulse. But I could be wrong.

The face, I assure you, was quite ordinary. Indeed its features had that fixed asymmetry of handsome homeliness so characteristic of intelligence, but he must have grown weary of his own bright mind, as too penetrating and also somewhat self-destructive, no doubt he ate away at himself nights, it was evident this was a burden on him, and that there were moments in which he would have been glad to rid himself of that intelligence, like a crippling thing, not a privilege or gift, for continual thought must have tormented him, particularly when he was by himself, and that for him was a frequent occurrence—everywhere, therefore here also. And his body, underneath the fine clothing, fashionably cut yet not clinging, as though he had cautioned and restrained the tailor, compelled me to think of his nakedness.

Rather pathetic it must have been, that nakedness, not magnificently male, athletic, muscular, sliding into itself in a snake's nest of swellings, knots, thick cords of sinews, to whet the appetite of old women still unresigned, still mad with the hope of mating. But only his head had this masculine beauty, with the curve of genius in his mouth, with the angry impatience of the brows, between the brows in a crease dividing both like a slash, and the sense of his own ridiculousness in that powerful, oily-shiny nose. Oh, this was not a good-looking man, nor in fact was even his ugliness seductive, he was merely different, and if I hadn't gone numb inside when our eyes collided, I certainly could have walked away.

True, had I done this, had I succeeded in escaping that zone of attraction, the merciful King with a twitch of his signet ring, with the corners of his faded eyes, pupils like pins, would have attended to me soon enough, and I would have gone back. But at that time and place I could hardly have known this, I did not realize that what passed then for a chance meeting of glances, that is, the brief intercrossing of the black holes in the irises of two beings, for they are—after all—holes, tiny holes in round organs that slither nimbly in openings of the skull—I did not realize that this, precisely this was foreordained, for how could I have known?

I was about to move on when he rose and, brushing from his sleeve the hanging fringe of the brocade, as if to indicate the comedy was over, came towards me. Two steps and he stopped, now overtaken by the awareness of how impertinent was that unequivocal action, how very scatterbrained it would appear, to go walking after an unknown beauty like some gaping idiot following a band, so he stood, and then I closed one hand and with the other let slip from my wrist the little loop of my fan. For it to fall. So he immediately . . .

We looked at each other, now up close, over the mother-of-pearl handle of the fan. A glorious and dreadful moment, a mortal stab of cold caught me in the throat, transfixing speech, therefore feeling that I would not bring forth my voice, only a croak, I nodded to him—and that gesture came out almost exactly as the one before, when I did not complete my bow to the King who wasn't looking.

He did not return the nod, being much too startled and amazed by what was taking place within him, for he had not expected this of himself. I know, because he told me later, but had he not, even so I would have known.

He wanted to say something, wanted not to cut the figure of the idiot he most certainly was at that moment, and I knew this.

"Madam," he said, clearing his throat like a hog. "Your fan . . ."

By now I had him once more in hand. And myself.

"Sir," I said, and my voice in timbre was a trifle husky, altered, but he could think it was my normal voice, indeed he had never heard it until now, "must I drop it again?"

And I smiled, oh, but not enticingly, seductively, not brightly. I smiled only because I felt that I was blushing. The blush did not belong to me, it spread on my cheeks, claimed my face, pinkened my ear lobes, which I could feel perfectly, yet I was not embarrassed, nor excited, nor did I marvel at this unfamiliar man, only one of many after all, lost among the courtiers—I'll say more: I had nothing whatever to do with that blush, it came from the same source as the knowledge that had entered me at the threshold of the hall, at my first step upon the mirror floor—the blush seemed part of the court etiquette, of that which was required, like the fan, the crinoline, the topazes and coiffures. So, to render the blush insignificant, to counteract it, to stave off any false conclusions, I smiled— not to him, but at him, exploiting the boundary between mirth and scorn, and he then broke into a quiet laugh, a voiceless laugh, as if directed inward, it was similar to the laughter of a child that knows it is absolutely forbidden to laugh and for that very reason cannot control itself. Through this he grew instantly younger.

"If you would but give me a moment," he said, suddenly serious, as if sobered by a new thought, "I might be able to find a reply worthy of your words, that is, something highly clever. But as a rule good ideas come to me only on the stairs."

"Are you so poor then in invention?" I asked, exerting my will in the direction of my face and ears, for this persistent blush had begun to anger me, it constituted an invasion of my freedom, being part—I realized—of that same purpose with which the King had consigned me to my fate.

"Possibly I ought to add, 'Is there no help for this?' And you would answer no, not in the face of a beauty whose perfection seems to confirm the existence of the Absolute. Then two beats of the orchestra, and we both become dignified and with great finesse put the conversation back on a more ordinary courtly footing. However, as you appear to be somewhat ill-at-ease on that ground, perhaps it would be best if we do not engage in repartee . . ."

He truly feared me now, hearing these words—and was truly at a loss for what to say. Such solemnity filled his eyes, it was as if we were standing in a storm, between church and forest—or where there was, finally, nothing.

"Who are you?" he asked stiffly. No trace of triviality in him now, no pretense, he was only afraid of me. I was not afraid of him at all, not in the least, though in truth I should have been alarmed, for I could feel his face, with its porous skin, the unruly, bristling brows, the large curves of his ears, all linking up inside me with my hitherto hidden expectation, as though I had been carrying within myself his undeveloped negative and he had just now filled it in. Yet even if he were my sentence, I had no fear of him. Neither of myself nor of him, but I shuddered from the internal, motionless force of that connection— shuddered not as a person, but as a clock, when with its assembled hands it moves to strike the hour—though still silent. No one could observe that shudder.

"I shall tell you by and by," I answered very calmly. I smiled, a light, faint smile, the kind one gives to cheer the sick and feeble, and opened up my fan.

"I would have a glass of wine. And you?"

He nodded, trying to pull onto himself the skin of this style, so foreign to him, poorly fitting, cumbersome, and from that place in the hall we walked along the parquet, which ran with pearly streams of wax that fell in drops from the chandelier, through the smoke of the candles, shoulder to shoulder, there where by a wall pearl-white servants were pouring drinks into goblets.

I did not tell him that night who I was, not wishing to lie to him and not knowing the truth myself. Truth cannot contradict itself, and I was a duenna, a countess and an orphan, all these genealogies revolved within me, each one could take on substance if I acknowledged it, I understood now that the truth would be determined by my choice and whim, that whichever I declared, the images unmentioned would be blown away, but I remained irresolute among these possibilities, for in them seemed to lurk some subterfuge of memory—could I have been just another unhinged amnesiac, who had escaped from the care of her duly worried relatives? While talking with him, I thought that if I were a madwoman, then everything would end well. From insanity, as from a dream, one could free onself—in both cases there was hope.

When in the late hours—and he never left my side—we passed by His Majesty for a moment, before he was pleased to retire to his chambers, I felt that the ruler did not even bother to look in our direction, and this was a terrible discovery. For he did not make sure of my behavior at the side of Arrhodes, *that* was apparently unnecessary, as though he knew beyond all doubt that he could trust me completely, the way one trusts—in full—dispatched assassins, who strive as long as they have breath, for their fate lies in the hands of the dispatcher. The King's indifference ought to have, instead, wiped away my suspicions; if he did not look in my direction, then I meant nothing to him, nevertheless my insistent sense of persecution tipped the scales in favor of insanity. So it was as a madwoman of angelic beauty that I laughed, drinking to Arrhodes, whom the King despised as no other, though he had sworn to his dying mother that if harm befell that wise man it would be of his own choosing. I do not know if someone told me this while dancing or whether I learned it from myself, for the night was long and clamorous, the huge crowd constantly separated us, yet we kept finding each other by accident, almost as if everyone there were party to the same conspiracy—an obvious illusion, we could hardly have been surrounded by a host of mechanically dancing mannequins. I spoke with old men, with young women envious of my beauty, discerning innumerable shades of stupidity, both good-natured and malicious, I cut and pierced those useless dodderers and those pouting misses with such ease, that I grew sorry for them. I was cleverness itself, keen and full of witticisms, my eyes took on fire from the dazzling quickness of my words—in my mounting anxiety I would have gladly played a featherbrain to save Arrhodes, but this alone I could not manage. My versatility did not extend that far, alas. Was then my intelligence (and intelligence signified integrity) subject to some lie? I devoted myself to such reflections in the dance, entering the turns of the minuet, while Arrhodes, who didn't dance, watched me from afar, black and slender against the purple brocade in crowned lions. The King left, and not long afterwards we parted, I did not allow him to say anything, to ask anything, he tried and paled, hearing me repeat, first with the lips, "No," then only with the folded fan. I went out, not having the least idea of where I lived, whence I had arrived, whither I would turn my eyes, I only knew that these things did not rest with me, I made efforts, but they were futile—how shall I explain it? Everyone knows it is impossible to turn the eyeball around, such that the pupil can peer inside the skull.

I allowed him to escort me to the palace gate, the castle park beyond the circle of continually burning pots of tar was as if hewn from coal, in the cold air distant, inhuman laughter, a pearly imitation from the fountains of the masters of the South—or else it was the talking statues like milky ghosts suspended above the flower beds, the royal nightingales sang also, though no one listened, near the hothouse one of them stood out against the disk of the moon, large and dark on its branch—a perfect pose! Gravel crunched beneath our steps, and the gilded spikes of the railing jutted up through wet foliage.

Ill-tempered and eager, he grabbed my hand, which I did not pull away immediately, the white straps on the jackets of His Majesty's grenadiers flashed, someone called my carriage, horses beat their hoofs, the door of a coach gleamed under violet lanterns, a step dropped open. This could not be a dream.

"When and where?" he asked.

"Better to say: never and nowhere," I said, speaking my

simple truth, and added quickly, helplessly: "I do not toy with you, my fine philosopher, look within and you will see that I advise you well."

But what I wished to add I could not utter. I was able to think anything, strange as it may seem, yet in no way find my voice, I could not reach those words. A catch in my throat, a muteness, like a key turned in a lock, as if a bolt had clicked shut between us.

"Too late," he said softly, with his head lowered. "Truly too late."

"The royal gardens are open from the morning till the midday bugle call," I said, my foot on the step. "There is a pond there, with swans, and near it a rotten oak. At exactly noon tomorrow or in the hollow of the tree you will find your answer. And now I wish that by some inconceivable miracle you could forget we ever met. If I knew how, I would pray for that."

Most unsuitable words, banal in these surroundings, but there was now no way for me to break free of this deadly banality, I realized that as the carriage began to move, he could—after all—interpret what I had said to mean that I feared the emotions he aroused in me. That was true enough: I did fear the emotions he aroused in me, however it had nothing to do with love, I had only said what I *had been able* to say, as when in the darkness, in a swamp, one extends a careful foot, lest the next step plunge one into deep water. So did I feel my way in words, testing with my breath what I would be able—and what I would not be permitted—to say.

But he could not know this. We parted breathlessly, in dismay, in a panic similar to passion, for thus had begun our undoing. But I, willowy and sweet, girl-like, understood more clearly that I was his fate, fate in that terrible sense of unavoidable doom.

The body of the carriage was empty—I looked for the sash that would be sewn to the sleeve of the coachman, but it was not there. The windows also were missing—black glass, perhaps? The darkness of the interior was complete, as if partaking not of night, but of nonexistence itself. This was no absence of light, it was a void. I ran my hands along the curved walls upholstered in plush, but found neither window frame nor handle, found nothing but those soft, padded surfaces before me and above me, the ceiling remarkably low, as though I had been shut up not inside a carriage, but in a quivering, slanted container; no sound of hoofs reached me, nor the usual clatter of wheels in motion. Blackness, silence, nothing. Then I turned to myself, for that self was to me a darker and more ominous enigma than anything that had taken place so far. My memory was intact. I think it had to be that way, that it would have been impossible to arrange things otherwise, therefore I recollected my first awakening, as yet deprived of gender, so completely alien, it was like remembering a dream of an evil metamorphosis. I recollected waking at the door of the palace hall, already in this present reality, I could even recall the faint creak with which those carved portals opened, and the mask of the servant's face, the servant who in his zeal to serve resembled a puppet filled with civilities—a living corpse of wax. All of this was a coherent whole now in my mind, and still I could reach back, there where I did not yet know what portals were, what a ball was and what—this thing that was I, was. And in particular I remembered—and it made me shiver, it was so perversely mysterious—that my first thoughts, already half-gathered into words, I had formulated in an impersonal, neuter mode. The it that was myself had stood, the I that was it had seen, I, it had entered—these were the forms used by me before the blaze of the hall, streaming through the open door, had struck my pupils and unlocked—it must have been the blaze, for what else?—and opened within me, I say, the bolts and latches from behind which there burst into my being, with the painful suddenness of a visitation, the humanity of words, courtly movements, the charm of the fair sex, and also the memory of faces, among which the face of that man was foremost—and not the royal grimace—and though no one would ever be able to explain this to me, I knew with unswerving certainty that I had stopped before the King by mistake—it had been an error, a confusion between what was destined for me and the instrument of that destiny. An error—but what sort of fate was it, that could make mistakes? No genuine fate. Then might I still save myself?

And now in this perfect isolation, which did not frighten me, on the contrary, I found it convenient, for in it I could think, could concentrate, when I made the wish to know myself, searching among my memories, now so accessible and neatly arranged, that I had them all in easy reach like long-familiar furniture in an old room, and when I put forth questions, I saw everything that had transpired that night—but it was sharp and clear only as far as the threshold of the court hall. Before that—yes, exactly. Where was I—was it!?—before that? Where did I come from? The reassuring, simplest thought said that I was not quite well, that I was recovering from an illness, like someone returning from an exotic voyage filled with the most incredible adventures, that, as a highly refined maiden, much given to books and romances, reveries and strange whims, a young thing too delicate for this savage world, I had suffered visions, perhaps in a hysterical delirium I imagined that passage through metallic hells, no doubt while on a bed with a canopy, on sheets trimmed with lace, yes, brain fever would even be somewhat becoming in the light of the candle illuminating the chamber enough so that, upon waking, I would not take fright again, and in the figures leaning over me recognize at once my loving guardians. What a pleasant lie! I had had hallucinations, had I not? And they, sinking into the clear stream of my single memory, had split it in two. A split memory . . . ? Because with that question I heard within me a chorus of answers, ready, waiting: Duenna, Tlenix, Angelita. Now what was this? I had all these phrases prepared, they were given to me and with each came corresponding images; if only there had been a single chain of them! But they coexisted the way the spreading roots of a tree coexist, so then I, by necessity one, by nature unique, could I once have been a plurality of branchings, which then merged in me as rivulets merge into the current of a river? But such a thing was impossible, I told myself. Impossible. I was certain of that. And I beheld my life to the present divided thus: until the threshold of the palace hall it seemed to be made up of different threads, while from the threshold on it was already one. Scenes from the first part of my life ran parallel and belied each other. The Duenna: a tower, dark granite boulders, a drawbridge, shouts in the night, blood on a copper dish, knights with the aspect of butchers, the rusted ax heads of halberds and my pale little face in the oval, half-blind looking glass between the frame of the window, misty, filmy, and the carven headboard—was that where I came from?

But as Angelita I had been raised in the sweltering heat of the South and, looking back in that direction, I saw white walls with their chalky backs to the sun, withered palms, wild dogs with scraggly fur by those palms, releasing frothy urine on the scaled roots, and baskets full of dates, dried up and with a sticky sweetness, and physicians in green robes, and steps, stone steps descending to the bay of the town, all the walls turned away from the heat, bunches of grapes strewn in piles, yellowing into raisins, resembling heaps of dung, and again my face in the water, not in the looking glass, and the water pouring from a silver jug—silver but dark with age. I even remembered how I used to carry that jug and how the water, moving heavily inside it, would pull at my hand.

And what of my neuter self and its journey on its back, and the kisses planted on my hands and feet, and forehead, by the flitting serpents of metal? That horror had faded now completely and even with the greatest effort I could scarce recall it, exactly like a bad dream one cannot put into words. No, it was impossible for me to have experienced, either all at once or in succession, lives so opposed to one another! What then was certain? I was beautiful. As much despair as triumph had welled up within me when I saw myself reflected in his face as in a living mirror, for so absolute was the perfection of my features, that no matter what madness I were to commit, whether I howled with the foam of frenzy at my mouth, or gnawed red meat, the beauty would not leave my face— but why did I think "my face," and not simply "me"? Was I a person at odds with, out of harmony with, her own face and body? A sorceress ready to cast spells, a Medea? To me that was utter nonsense, ridiculous. And even the fact that my mind worked like a well-worn blade in the hand of a rogue knight shorn of his nobility, that I cut asunder every subject without trying, this self-determined thinking of mine seemed in its correctness just a bit too cold, unduly calm, for fear remained beyond it—like a thing transcendent, omnipresent, yet separate—therefore my own thoughts too I held in suspicion. But if I could trust neither my face nor my mind, against what precisely could I harbor fear and suspicion, when outside of the soul and the body one had nothing? This was puzzling.

The scattered roots of my various pasts told me nothing of importance, inspection led to a sifting of bright-colored images, now as the Duenna of the North, now Angelita of the broiling sun, now Mignonne, I was each time another person with another name, station, descent, from under another sky, nothing had precedence here—the landscape of the South kept returning to my vision as if strained by a surfeit of sweetness and contrast, a color infused with azures too ostentatious, and if not for those mangy dogs, and the half-blind children with suppurating eyes and swollen bellies, silently expiring on the bony knees of their veiled mothers, I would have found that palmy coast overly facile, as slick as a lie. And the North of the Duenna, with her snow-capped towers, a sky churning leaden, the winters with tortuous shapes of snow invented by the wind, shapes which crept into the moat along the battlements and buttresses, emerged from the castle crenels with their white tongues across the stone, and the chains of the drawbridge as if in yellow tears, but it was only the rust coloring the icicles on the links, while in summer the water of the moat was covered by a sheepskin coat of mold: and all this, how well I remembered it!

But then my third existence; gardens, vast, cool, trimmed, gardeners with clippers, packs of greyhounds and the Great Dane of the harlequin that lay on the steps of the throne—a world-weary sculpture possessing the unerring grace of lethargy stirred only by breathing ribs— and in its yellowish, indifferent eyes gleamed, one might have thought, the reduced figures of the catabanks and grudgies. And these words, grudgies, catabanks, I did not know now what they meant, but surely I knew once, and when I delved thus into that past so well-remembered, remembered to the taste of chewed blades of grass, I felt that I should not go back to the bootees I outgrew, nor to my first long dress embroidered all in silver, as if even the child that I had been concealed treason. Therefore I summoned a memory inhumanly cruel—that of the lifeless journey face-up, of the numbing kisses of metal which, touching my naked body, produced a clanking sound, as if my nakedness had been a voiceless bell, a bell unable to ring out because it had not yet its heart, its tongue. Yes, it was to this implausibility that I appealed, no longer surprised that that raving nightmare held on in me with such tenacity, for it must have been a nightmare. To assure myself of this certainty I took my fingers and with the very tips of them touched my soft forearms, my breasts; an intrusion, without a doubt, and I submitted to it trembling, as if with my head thrown back I had stepped beneath an icy torrent of reviving rain.

Nowhere an answer to my questions, so I retreated from the abyss that was myself and not myself. And now back to that which was one, only one. The King, the evening ball, the court and that man. I had been made for him, he for me, I knew this, but again with fear, no, it was not fear, rather the iron presence of destiny, inevitable, impenetrable, and it was precisely that inevitability, like tidings of death, the knowledge that one would now no longer be able to refuse, evade, withdraw, escape, and one might perish, but perish *in no other way*—I sank into that chilling presence breathlessly. Unable to endure it, I mouthed the words "father, mother, brother and sister, girl friends, kith and kin"—how well I understood those words, willing figures appeared, figures known to me, I had to admit to them before myself, yes but one couldn't possibly have four mothers and as many fathers, so then this insanity again? So stupid and so stubborn?

I resorted to arithmetic: one and one are two, from a father and a mother comes a child, you were that child, you have a child's memories . . .

Either I had been mad, I told myself, or I was mad still, and being a mind, was a mind in total eclipse. There was no ball, no castle, no King, no emergence into a state of being stringently subject to the laws of everlasting harmony. I felt a stab of regret, a resistance at the thought that I must part with my beauty as well. Out of discrepant elements I could construct nothing of my own, unless I were to find in the design already existing some lopsidedness, chinks I might penetrate, thereby to rend open the structure and get to the core of it. Had everything truly happened in the way it was supposed to? If I was the property of the King, then how was I able to know this? Even to reflect on it at night ought to have been forbidden me. If he was behind everything, then why had I wished to make obeisance to him but had not done so at first? If the preparations had been flawless, then why did I recall things I should not have recalled? For, surely, with only the past of a girl and child to turn to, I would not have fallen into that agony of indecision which brought on despair, a prelude to rebellion against one's fate. And certainly they should at least have wiped out that sequence on my back, the animation of my nakedness, inert and mute, by the sparking kisses, but that too had taken place and now was with me. Could it be that some flaw lay in the design and execution? Careless errors, an oversight, hidden leaks, taken for riddles or a bad dream? But in that case I had reason to hope again. To wait. To wait, as things progressed, for further inconsistencies to accumulate, and make of them a sword to turn against the King, against myself, it did not matter against whom, as long as it ran counter to the fate imposed. So then, submit to the spell, endure it, go to the assignation the very first thing in the morning, and I knew, knew without knowing how or why, that nothing would hinder me from doing *that*, on the contrary, everything would steer me precisely in that direction. And my immediately surrounding here and now was so primitive, yes, walls, pliant upholstery, yielding softly at first to the fingers, and underneath that a barrier of steel or masonry, I didn't know, but could have pulled apart the cozy softness with my fingernails, I stood up, my head touched the concave curve of the ceiling. This, around me and above me, but inside—I, I alone?

I continued to examine and expose this villainous inability of mine to understand myself, and since levels upon levels of ideas sprang up at once, one on top of the other, I began to wonder if I ought to trust my own judgment, when, drowning madwoman that I was, like an insect in clear amber, imprisoned in my *obnubilatio lucida*, it was only natural that I would—

One moment. Where did it come from, my so elegantly parsed vocabulary, these learned terms, in Latin, logical phrases, syllogisms, this fluency out of place in a sweet young thing, the sight of whom was a flaming pyre for masculine hearts? And whence this feeling of terrible tedium in matters of sex, the cold contempt, the distance, oh yes, he probably loved me already, was maybe even mad about me, he had to see me, to hear my voice, touch my fingers, while I regarded his passion as one might regard a specimen on a slide. Was not this surprising, contradictory, asyncategorematic? Could it be that I was imagining everything, that the ultimate reality here was an old, unemotional brain, entangled in the experiences of countless years? Perhaps a sharpened intellect was my only true past, perhaps I had arisen from logic, and that logic constituted my one authentic genealogy . . .

I did not believe it. I was guiltless, yes, and at the same time full of guilt. Guiltless in all the tracks of time past-perfect merging towards my present, as the little girl, as the adolescent somber and silent through the gray-white winters and in the stifling must of the palaces, and guiltless too in that which had occurred today, with the King, for I could not be other than I was; my guilt—my hideous guilt—lay only in this, that I knew it all so well and considered it a sham, a lie, a bubble, and that wanting to get to the bottom of my mystery, I feared to make the descent and felt a shameful gratitude for the unseen walls that barred my way. So then I had a soul tainted and honest, what else did I have, what else was left, ah yes, there was something still, my body, and I began to touch it, I examined it in that black enclosure as a masterful detective might examine the scene of a crime. A curious investigation—for in searching by touch this naked body, I felt a faintly prickling numbness in my fingers, could this have been fear of my own self? Yet I was beautiful and my muscles were resilient, limber, and clasping the thighs in a way no one would hold them oneself, as though they had been foreign objects, I could feel in my tightening hands, beneath the smooth and fragrant skin, long bones, but the wrists and the inside of my forearms at the elbow for some reason I was afraid to touch.

I tried to overcome this reluctance, what could be there after all, my arms were swathed in lace, somewhat rough, being stiff, it was awkward going, so on to the neck. What they called a swan-neck—the head set on it with a stateliness not assumed but natural, inspiring respect, the ears below the braided hair—small, the lobes firm, without jewelry, unpierced—why?—I felt my forehead, cheeks, lips. Their expression, detected with the tips of my thin fingers, again disturbed me. A different expression from the one I had expected. Strange. But how could I have been strange to myself other than through sickness, madness?

With a furtive movement befitting the innocence of a small child prey to old wives' tales, I reached for my wrists after all, and for my elbows, there where the arm met the forearm, something incomprehensible was there. I lost all feeling in my fingertips, as if something had pressed against the nerves, the blood vessels, and once again my mind leaped from suspicion to suspicion: how did such information come to me, why did I study myself like some anatomist, this was hardly in the style of a maiden, neither Angelita nor the fair Duenna, nor the lyric Tlenix. But at the same time I felt a soothing compulsion: this is quite normal, don't be surprised at yourself, you eccentric, fanciful featherbrain, if you've been a bit unwell, don't return to that, think healthy thoughts, think of your rendezvous . . . But the elbows, the wrists? Beneath the skin—like a hard lump, was it swollen glands? Calcium deposits? Impossible, not in keeping with my beauty, with its absoluteness. And yet there was a hardening there, a tiny one, I could feel it only with a strong squeeze, above the hand, where the pulse left off, and also in the bend of the elbow.

And so my body had secrets too, its otherness corresponded to the otherness of my soul, to its fear in my self-musings, there was in this a pattern, a congruency, a symmetry: if here, then there too. If the mind, then the limbs also. If I, then you as well. I, you, riddles, I was tired, an overpowering weariness entered my blood, I was supposed to submit to it. To fall asleep, to drop into the oblivion of another, liberating darkness. And then spitefully the sudden decision not to give in to that urge, to resist the confining box of this stylish carriage (but not so stylish on the inside!), and this soul of a maid too wise, too quick of understanding! Defiance to the physical self-beauty with its hidden stigmata! Who was I? My opposition was now a rage, which made my soul burn in the darkness, so that it seemed actually to shine. *Sed tamen potest esse totaliter aliter*, where was that from? My soul? *Gratia? Dominus meus?*

No, I was alone and alone I jumped up, to sink my teeth into those soft, shrouded walls, I tore at the padding, dry, coarse material crackled in my teeth. I spat out threads with saliva, my fingernails were snapping, good, that was it, that was the way, I didn't know whether against myself or someone else, but no, no, no, no, no, no.

I saw a light, something budded out in front of me, like the small head of a snake, except that it was metal. A needle? I was pricked, above the knee, in the thigh, from outside, a tiny, barely noticeable pain, a prick and then nothing.

Nothing.

The garden was overcast. The royal park with its singing fountains, hedges clipped down all to one same level, the geometry of the trees, shrubs and steps, marble statues, scrolls, cupids. And the two of us. Cheap, ordinary, romantic, filled with despair. I smiled at him, and on my thigh was a mark. I had been punctured. So my soul, there where I had rebelled, and my body too, there where I had learned to hate it, they had had an ally. An ally of insufficient cunning. Now I did not dread him as much, now I played my role. Of course he had been cunning enough to impose the role on me, and from within, having forced his way into my stronghold. Cunning enough, but not enough—I observed the trap. The purpose I did not know yet, but the trap was visible, palpable, and one who sees is no longer so frightened as one who must live by conjecture alone.

I had so much trouble, this struggling with myself, even the light of day was a nuisance with its solemnity, the gardens for the greater glory and admiration of His Majesty—not of the vegetation—I truly would have preferred my night now to this day, but the day was here and so was the man, who knew nothing, understood nothing, absorbed in the burning pleasure of his sweet insanity, in the enchantment cast by me, not by any third party. Traps, snares, a lure with a fatal sting, and was I all this? And did the lashing fountains also serve this end, the royal gardens, the haze in the distance? But really, how stupid. Whose ruin, whose death was at stake? Would not false witnesses have sufficed, old men in wigs, a noose, poison? Perhaps something bigger was involved. Some vicious intrigue, as on the royal parquets.

The gardeners in high leather boots, intent upon the verdure of His Gracious Majesty, did not approach us. I remained silent, silence being more convenient, we sat on the step of an enormous stairway, as though built in preparation for a giant who would descend some day from his cloudy heights in order to make use of it. The emblems embossed in stone, the naked cupids, fauns, sileni, slippery marble dripping water, as dull and dismal as the gray sky. An idyllic scene, a Nicolette with her Aucassin, what utter bilge! I had come to my senses completely in these gardens, when the carriage drove off and I walked lightly, as if I had just stepped from a steaming, scented bath, and my dress was now different, vernal, with a misty pattern timidly reminiscent of flowers, it alluded to them, helping to inspire reverence, surrounding me with inviolability, Eos Rhododaktylos, but I walked between the dew-glistening hedges with a mark on my thigh, I did not need to touch it, I was unable to anyway, but the memory sufficed, they had not erased that from me. I was a mind imprisoned, chained at birth, born into bondage, but a mind still. And thus before he appeared, seeing that my time now was my own, that nearby was no needle nor sound detector, I began, like an actress readying herself for the performance, to say things in a whisper, the sort of things I did not know whether I would be able to utter in his presence, in other words I probed the limits of my freedom, in the light of day I searched for them blindly, by touch.

What things? Only the truth—first, the change of grammatical form, then the plurality of my past pluperfects, everything too that I had gone through and the prick that stilled rebellion. Was this out of sympathy for him, in order not to destroy him? No, since I did not love him, not at all. It was treachery: for no good purpose had we trespassed on one another. Then should I speak to him *thus*? That by sacrifice I wished to save him from myself as from a doom?

No—it was not that way at all. I had love, but elsewhere—I know how that sounds. Oh it was a passionate love, tender and altogether ordinary. I wanted to give myself to him body and soul, though not in reality, only in the manner of the fashion, according to custom, the etiquette of the court, for it would have to be not just any, but a marvelous, a courtly sinning.

My love was very great, it caused me to tremble, it quickened my pulse, I saw that his glance made me happy. And my love was very small, being limited in me, subject to the style, like a carefully composed sentence expressing the painful joy of a tête-à-tête. And so beyond the bounds of those feelings I had no particular interest in saving him from myself or another, for when I reached with my mind outside my love, he was nothing to me, yet I needed an ally in my struggle against whatever had pricked me that night with venomous metal. I had no one else, and he was devoted to me wholly: I could count on him. I knew, of course, that I could not count on him beyond the feeling he had for me. He would not rise to any *reservatio mentalis*. Therefore I could not reveal the entire truth to him: that my love and the venomous prick were from one and the same source. That for this reason I abhorred both, had hatred for both and wanted to trample both underfoot as one steps on a tarantula. This I could not tell him, since he would surely be conventional in his love, would not accept in me the kind of liberation I desired, the freedom that would cast him off. Therefore I could only act deceitfully, giving freedom the false name of love, and only in and through that lie show him to himself as the victim of an unknown someone. Of the King? Yes, but even were he to lay violent hands upon His Majesty, that would not set me free; the King, if the King was indeed behind this, was still so far removed that his death could not alter my fate in any way. So, in order to see if I would be able to proceed thus, I stopped by a statue of Venus, its naked buttocks a monument to the higher and lower passions of earthly love, so that in complete solitude I could prepare my monstrous explanation with its well-honed arguments, a diatribe, as if I were sharpening a knife.

It was extremely difficult. Repeatedly I found myself at an impassable boundary, not knowing where the spasm would seize my tongue, where the mind would stumble, for that mind was my enemy after all. Not to lie completely, but neither to get into the center of the truth, of the mystery. Only by gradual degrees then did I decrease its radius, working inwards as along a spiral. But when I caught sight of him in the distance, saw how he walked and began almost to run towards me, still a small silhouette in a dark cape, I realized that all this was for nothing, the style would not permit it. What sort of love scene is it, in which Nicolette confesses to Aucassin that she is his branding iron, his butcher? Not even a fairy-tale style, in removing me from the spell, if it could, could return me to the nothingness from which I had come. Its entire wisdom was useless here. The loveliest of maidens, if she considers herself to be the instrument of dark forces and speaks of pricks and branding irons, if she speaks *this* and *thus*, she is a madwoman. And does not bear witness to the truth, but instead to her own disordered mind, and therefore deserves not only love and devotion, but pity besides.

Out of a combination of such feelings he might pretend to believe my words, might look alarmed, assure me of steps taken to have me freed, in reality to have me examined, spread the news of my misfortune everywhere—it would be better to insult him. Besides, in this complex situation the more of an ally I had, the less of a lover filled with hopes of consummation—he would certainly not be willing to step far from the role of lover, his madness was normal, vigorous, solidly down-to-earth: to love, ah to love, scrupulously to chew the gravel on my path into soft sand, yes but not to toy with the chimeras of analysis concerning the origin of my soul!

And so it appeared that if I had been primed for his destruction, he must die. I did not know which part of me would strike him down, the forearms, the wrists in an embrace, surely that would have been too simple, but I knew now that it could not be otherwise.

I had to go with him, down alleys prettied by the skilled

artisans of horticulture; we removed ourselves quickly from the Venus Kallipygos, for the ostentation with which she displayed her charms was not in keeping with our early-romance stage of sublime emotions and shy references to happiness. We passed the fauns, also blunt, but differently, in a way that was more suitable, for the maleness of those shaggy things of stone could not impinge upon my purity, which was sufficiently chaste as to remain unoffended even close to them: I was allowed not to understand their marble-rigid lust.

He kissed my hand, there where the lump was, though unable to feel it with his lips. And where was my cunning one waiting? In the dark of the carriage? Or could it be that I was merely supposed to worm out of Arrhodes some unknown secrets: a beautiful stethoscope put to the breast of the doomed wise man?

I told him nothing.

In two days the love affair had progressed in due form. I was staying, with a handful of good servants, at a residence four furlongs removed from the royal estate; Phloebe, my factotum, had rented this chateau the first day following the meeting in the garden, saying nothing of the means which that step had required, and I, as the maiden with no head for financial matters, did not ask. I think that I both intimidated and annoyed him, possibly he was not let in on the secret, most likely he was not, he acted on the King's orders, was respectful to me in words, but in his eyes I saw an impertinent irony, probably he took me for a new favorite of the King, and my rides and meetings with Arrhodes did not surprise him greatly, for a servant who demands that his King treat a concubine in accordance with a pattern he can understand, is not a good servant. I think that had I bestowed my caresses on a crocodile, he would not have batted an eye. I was at liberty within the confines of the royal will, nor did the monarch once approach me. I knew by now that there were things which I would never tell my man, because my tongue stiffened at the very thought and the lips turned numb, like the fingers when I had touched myself that first night in the carriage. I forbade Arrhodes to call on me, he interpreted this conventionally, as the fear that he might compromise me, and the good fellow restrained himself. On the evening of the third day I finally set about discovering who I was. Dressed for bed, I stripped in front of the pier glass and stood naked in it like a statue, and the silver pins and steel lancets lay upon the dressing table, covered with a velvet shawl, for I feared their glitter, though not their cutting edge. The breasts, high-set, looked to the side and upwards with their pink nipples, all trace of the puncture on the thigh had disappeared; like an obstetrician or a surgeon preparing for an operation I closed both hands and pushed them into the white, smooth flesh, the ribs sank beneath the pressure, but my belly domed out like those of the women in Gothic paintings, and under the warm, soft outer layer I met with resistance, hard, unyielding, and moving my hands from top to bottom gradually made out an oval shape within. With six candles on either side, I picked up the smallest lancet, not out of fear but rather for esthetic reasons.

In the mirror it looked as if I intended to knife myself, a scene dramatically perfect, sustained in style to the last detail by the enormous fourposter and canopy, the two rows of tall candles, the glint in my hand and my paleness, because my body was deathly frightened, the knees buckled under me, only the hand with the blade had the necessary steadiness. There where the oval resistance was most distinct, not moving under pressure, right below the sternum, I thrust the lancet in deep, the pain was minimal and on the surface only, from the wound there flowed a single drop of blood. Incapable of showing the butcher's skill slowly and with anatomical deliberation, I cut the body in half practically to the groin, violently, clenching my teeth and shutting my eyes as tightly as I could. To look, no, I hadn't the strength. Yet I stood no longer trembling, only cold as ice, the room was filled with the sound, like something far from me and foreign, of my ragged, almost spastic breathing. The severed layers separated, like white leather, and in the mirror I saw a silver, nestled shape, as of an enormous fetus, a gleaming chrysalis hidden inside me, held in the parted folds of flesh, flesh not bleeding, only pink. What horror, terror, to look at oneself thus! I dared not touch the silvery surface, immaculate, virgin, the abdomen oblong like a small coffin and shining, reflecting the reduced images of the candle flames, I moved and then I saw its tucked-in limbs, fetal-fashion, thin as pincers, they went into my body and suddenly I understood that it was not *it*, a foreign thing, different and other, it was again myself. And so that was the reason I had made, when walking on the wet sand of the garden paths, such deep prints, that was the reason for my strength, it was I, still I, I was repeating to myself when he entered.

The door had remained unlocked—an oversight. He sneaked in, entered thus, intrigued with his own daring, holding out before him—as if in his justification and defense—a huge shield of red roses, so that, having encountered me, and I turned around with a cry of fright, he saw, but did not notice, did not yet understand, could not. It was not out of fear now, but only in a horrible, choking shame that I tried with both hands to cover back up inside of me the silver oval, it was however too large and I too opened by the knife for this to be done.

His face, his silent scream and flight. Let this part of the account be spared me. He'd been unable to wait for permission, for an invitation, so he came with his flowers, and the house was empty, I myself had sent out all the servants, that no one might disturb me in what I planned—by then there was no other way open to me, no other course. But perhaps the first suspicion had begun to grow in him back then. I recall how the preceding day we were crossing the bed of a dried-out stream, how he wanted to carry me in his arms and I refused, not out of modesty true or pretended, but because I had to. He noticed then in the soft, pliant silt my footprints, so small and so deep, and was going to say something, it was to have been a harmless joke, but he checked himself suddenly and with that now-familiar crease between his knitted brows went up the opposite slope, without even offering me, who was climbing behind him, a helping hand. So perhaps even then. And further, when at the very top of the rise I had stumbled and grasped—to regain my balance—a thick withe of hazel, I felt that I was pulling the entire bush out by its roots, so I dropped to my knees, ordered by reflex, releasing the broken branch, so as not to show the overpowering, incredible strength that was mine. He stood off to the side, was not looking, so I thought, but he could have seen everything out of the corner of his eye. Was it then suspicion that had sent him stealing in, or uncontrollable passion?

It didn't matter.

Using the thickest segments of my feelers I pressed against the edges of the wide-open body, in order to emerge from the chrysalis, and worked myself free nimbly, after which Tlenix, Duenna, Mignonne first sank to her knees, then tumbled face-down to the side and I crawled out of her, straightening all my legs, moving slowly backwards like a crab. The candles, their flames still fluttering in the draft raised by his escape through the open door, blazed in the mirror; the naked thing, her legs thrown apart immodestly, lay motionless; not wishing to touch her, my cocoon, my false skin, the she that was now I went around her and, rearing up like a mantis with the trunk bent in the middle, I looked at myself in the glass. This was I, I told myself wordlessly, I. Still I. The smooth sheaths, coleopterous, insectlike, the knobby joints, the abdomen in its cold sheen of silver, the oblong sides designed for speed, the darker, bulging head, this was I. I repeated it over and over, as if to commit those words to memory, and at the same time the manifold past of Duenna, Tlenix, Angelita dulled and died within me, like books read long ago, books out of a children's room, their content unimportant and now powerless, I could recall them, slowly turning my head in either direction, looking for my own eyes in the reflection, and also beginning to understand, though not yet accustomed to this shape that was my own, that the act of self-evisceration had not been altogether my rebellion, that it represented a foreseen part of the plan, designed for just such an eventuality, in order that my rebellion turn out to be, in the end, my total submission. Since still able to think with my former skill and ease, I yielded at the same time to this new body, its shining metal had written into it movements which I began to execute.

Love died. It will die in you as well, but over years or months, this same waning I experienced in a matter of moments, it was the third in my series of beginnings, and emitting a faint, shuffling hiss, I ran three times around the room, touching with outstretched, quivering feelers the bed on which it was denied me now to rest. I took in the smell of my unsuitor, unlover, so I could follow in his track, I known to him and yet unknown, in this newly begun—and likely the last—game. The trail of his wild flight was marked first by a succession of open doors and the roses strewn, their smell could be of help to me, in that it had become, at least for a while, a part of his smell. Seen from below, from the ground, therefore from a new perspective, the rooms through which I scuttled seemed to me to be primarily too big, full of cumbersome, useless articles of furniture, looming unfamiliarly in the semidarkness, then there was the light scrape of stone steps, stairs, beneath my claws and I ran out into a garden dark and damp—a nightingale was singing, I felt an inner amusement, for that was now a wholly unnecessary prop, others were called for by this succeeding scene, I poked about in the shrubbery a good while, aware of the gride of the gravel underfoot, I circled once and twice, then sped straight ahead, having caught the scent. For I could not have helped but catch it, composed as it was of a unique harmony of fleeting odors, of the tremors of the air parted by his passage, I found each particle not yet dispersed in the night wind, and thus hit upon the right course, which would be mine now until the end.

I do not know whose will it was that I let him get a good head start, for until dawn instead of pursuing him I roamed the royal gardens. To a certain extent this served a purpose, because I lingered in those places where we had strolled, holding hands, between the hedges, therefore I was able to imbibe his smell precisely, to make sure I would not mistake it later for any other. True, I could have gone straight after him and run him down in his utter helplessness of confusion and despair, but I did not do this. I realize that my actions on that night may also be explained in an altogether different way, by my grief and the King's pleasure, since I had lost a lover, acquiring only a prey, and for the monarch the sudden and swift demise of the man he hated might have seemed insufficient. Perhaps Arrhodes did not rush home, but went instead to one of his friends, and there, in a feverish monologue, he answering his own questions (the presence of another person needed only to reassure and sober him), arrived at the whole truth by himself. At any rate my behavior in the gardens in no way suggested the pain of separation. I know how unwelcome that will sound to sentimental souls, but having no hands to wring, no tears to shed, no knees on which I might fall, nor lips to press to the flowers gathered the day before, I did not surrender myself to prostration. What occupied me now was the extraordinary subtlety of distinction which I possessed, for while running up and down the paths not once did I take a waft of even the most deceptively similar trace for that which was my present destiny and the goad of my tireless efforts. I could feel how in my cold left lung each molecule of air threaded its way through the windings of countless scanning cells and how each suspicious particle was passed to my right lung, hot, where my faceted internal eye examined it with care, to verify its exact meaning or discard it as the wrong scent, and this took place more rapidly than the vibration of wings on the smallest insect, more rapidly than you can comprehend. At daybreak I left the royal gardens. The house of Arrhodes stood empty, stood open, not bothering then even to ascertain if he had taken with him any weapon, I found the fresh trail and went with it, no longer delaying. I did not believe I would be searching long. However the days became weeks, the weeks months, and still I tracked him.

To me this seemed no more abominable than the conduct of any other being that has written into it its own fate. I ran through rains and scorching suns, fields, ravines and thickets, dry reeds slid along my trunk, and the water of the puddles or flood plains that I cut across sprayed me and trickled in large drops down my oval back and down my head, in that place imitating tears, which had however no significance. I noticed, in my unceasing rush, how everyone who saw me from a distance turned away and clung to a wall, a tree, a fence or, if he had no such refuge, kneeled and covered his face with his hands, or fell face-down and lay there for as long as it took me to leave him far behind. I did not require sleep, thus in the night too I ran through villages, settlements, small towns, through marketplaces full of earthen pots and fruits drying on strings, where whole crowds scattered before me, and children went fleeing into side streets with screams and shouts, to which I paid no attention, but sped on my trail. His odor filled me completely, like a promise. By now I had forgotten the appearance of this man, and my mind, as if lacking the endurance of the body, particularly during the night runs, drew into itself till I did not know whom I was tracking, nor even if I was tracking anyone, I knew only that my will was to rush on, in order that the spoor of airborne motes singled out for me from the welling diversity of the world persist and intensify; for should it weaken, that would mean I was not heading in the right direction. I questioned no one, and too no one dared accost me, somehow I felt that the distance separating me from those who huddled by walls at my approach or fell to the earth, covering the backs of their heads with their arms, was filled with tension and I understood it as a dreadful homage rendered me, because I was on the King's hunt, which gave me inexhaustible strength. Only now and then a child, still quite small, whom the adults had not had time to snatch up and clasp

to their breasts at my silent, sudden appearance in full
career, would start to cry, but I took no heed of that,
because as I ran I had to maintain an intense, unbroken
concentration, directed both outwards, at the world of
sand and bricks, the green world, covered above with azure
blues, and inwards into my internal world, where from the
efficient play of both my lungs there came molecular
music, very lovely, since so magnificently unerring. I
crossed rivers and the coves of coastal bays, rapids, the
slimy basins of draining lakes, and every manner of beast
avoided me, withdrew in flight or frantically began to
burrow into the parched soil, surely a futile effort were I to
stalk it, for no one was so lightning-agile as I, but I
ignored those shaggy creatures scrambling on all fours,
slant-eared, with their husky whinnying, squeals and
wailing, they did not concern me, I had another purpose.

Several times I plowed through, like a missile, great ant
hills, and their tiny inhabitants, russet, black, speckled,
helplessly slid across my shining carapace, and once or
twice some animal of unusual size blocked my path, so
though I had no quarrel with it, in order not to waste
precious time on circlings and evasions, I tensed and
sprang, broke through in an instant, thus with a snap of
calcium and the gurgle of red spouts splashing my back
and head I hurried away so quickly, it was only later that I
thought of the death that had been dealt in this swift and
violent manner. I remember too that I stole across lines of
battle, covered with a scattered swarm of gray and green
surcoats, of which some moved, and in others there rested
bones, putrid or completely dried out and thereby white as
slightly grimy snow, but this also I ignored, because I had
a higher task, a task made for me and me alone. For the
trail would double back, loop around and cut across itself,
and all but vanish on the shores of salt lakes, there parched

by the sun into dust that bothered my lungs, or else washed away by rains; and gradually I began to realize that the thing eluding me was full of cunning, doing everything it could to baffle me and break the thread of molecules carrying the trace of its uniqueness. If the one whom I pursued had been an ordinary mortal, I would have overtaken him after a suitable time, that is, the time needed for his terror and despair to enhance duly the punishment in store, I would have surely overtaken him, what with my tireless speed and the unfailing operation of my tracking lungs—and would have killed him sooner than the thought that I was doing so. I had not followed at his heels at first, but waited for the scent to grow quite cold, so as to demonstrate my skill and in addition give the hunted one sufficient time, in keeping with the custom, a good custom as it allowed his fear to grow, and then sometimes I would let him put a considerable distance between us, for, feeling me constantly too near, he might in an access of despair have done some harm to himself and thus have escaped my decree. And therefore I did not intend to fall on him too quickly, nor so unexpectedly that he would have no time to realize what was awaiting him. So at nights I halted, concealed in the underbrush, not for rest, rest was unnecessary, but for intentional delay, and also to consider my next moves. No more did I think of the quarry as being Arrhodes, once my suitor, because that memory had closed itself off and I knew that it ought to be left in peace. My only regret was that I no longer possessed the ability to smile when I recalled to mind those ancient stratagems, like Angelita, Duenna, the sweet Mignonne, and a couple of times I looked at myself in a mirror of water, the full moon overhead, to convince myself that in no respect was I now similar to them, though I had remained beautiful, however my present beauty was a deadly thing, inspiring as great a horror as admiration. I also made use of these night bivouacs to scrape lumps of dried mud off my abdomen, down to the silver, and before setting out again I would move lightly the quill of my sting, holding it between my tarsi, testing its readiness, for I knew not the day nor the hour.

Sometimes I would noiselessly creep up to human habitations and listen to the voices, bending myself backwards, propping my gleaming feelers on a window sill, or I might crawl up on the roof in order to hang down freely from the eaves, for I was not (after all) a lifeless mechanism equipped with a pair of hunting lungs, I was a being that had a mind and used it. And the chase had already lasted long enough to become common knowledge. I heard old women frighten children with me, I also heard countless tales about Arrhodes, who was favored as much as I, the King's emissary, was feared. What sort of things did the simple folk say on their porches? That I was a machine set upon a wise man who had dared to raise his hand against the throne.

Yet I was supposed to have been no ordinary death machine, but a special device, one capable of assuming any form: a beggar, a child in a cradle, a lovely young lass, but also a metal reptile. These shapes were the larva in which the assassin emissary showed itself to its victim, in order to deceive him, but to everyone else it appeared as a scorpion made of silver, scurrying with such rapidity that no one yet had been able to count its legs. Here the story split into different versions. Some said that the wise man had sought to bestow freedom upon the people in opposition to the King's will, and therewith kindled the royal wrath; others—that he possessed the water of life and with it could raise up the martyrs, which was forbidden him by the highest authority, but he, while pretending to bow to the sovereign's will, in secret did marshal a battalion of hanged men, who had been cut down at the citadel after the great execution of the rebels. Still others knew nothing at all of Arrhodes and did not attribute to him any marvelous abilities, but only took him to be a condemned man, for that reason alone deserving their favor and support. Although it was unknown what had originally roused the King's fury, that he summoned his master craftsmen and commanded them to fashion him a hunting machine in their forge, everyone called it a wicked design and that command most sinful; for whatever the victim had done, it could not have been as awful as the fate the King had prepared for him. There was no end to these tall tales, in which the rustic imagination waxed audacious and unchecked, not changing in this one respect, that it conferred on me the most hideous qualities conceivable.

I heard, too, innumerable lies about the valiant ones hastening to relieve Arrhodes, men who supposedly barred my way, only to fall in uneven combat—lies, for not a living soul ever dared to do this. Nor was there any lack, in those fables, of traitors too, who pointed out to me Arrhodes's tracks when I was no longer able to find them—also an unmitigated lie. But as for who I was, who I might be, what occupied my mind, and whether or not I knew despair or doubt, no one said a thing, and this did not surprise me either.

And I heard not a little about the simple trailing machines known to the people, machines that carried out the King's will, which was the law. At times I did not hide myself at all from the occupants of the humble huts, but waited for the sun to rise, in order in its rays to leap like silver lightning on the grass and in a sparkling spray of dew connect the end of the previous day's journey with its new beginning. Running briskly, I was gratified when those I came upon prostrated themselves, when eyes turned glassy, and I delighted in the numb dread that surrounded me like an impervious aura. But the day came when my lower sense of smell went idle, in vain too did I circle the hilly vicinity seeking the scent with my upper smell, and I experienced a feeling of misfortune, of the uselessness of all my perfection, until, standing at the top of a knoll, my arms crossed as though in prayer to the windy sky, I realized, with the softest sound filling the bell of my abdomen, that not all was lost, and so in order that the idea be carried out I reached for that which long ago had been abandoned—the gift of speech. I did not need to learn it, I already possessed it, however I had to waken it within me, at first pronouncing words sharply and in a jangling way, but my voice soon grew humanlike, therefore I ran down the slope, to employ speech, since smell had failed me. I felt no hate whatever for my prey, though he had shown himself to be so clever and adept, I understood however that he was performing the part of the task that lay to him, just as I was performing mine. I found the crossroads where the scent had gradually disappeared, and stood quivering, but not moving from my place, for one pair of legs pulled blindly down the road covered with lime dust, while the other pair, convulsively clawing the rocks, drew me in the opposite direction, where the walls of a small monastery gleamed whitely, surrounded by ancient trees. Steadying myself, I crawled heavily, almost as if unwillingly, towards the monastery gate, under which stood a monk, his face upraised, possibly he gazed at the dawn on the horizon. I approached slowly, so as not to shock him with my sudden appearance, and greeted him, and when he fixed his eyes on me without a word I asked if he would permit me to confess to him a certain matter, which I had difficulty dealing with on my own. I thought at first that he was petrified with fright, for he neither moved nor made an answer, but he was only reflecting and at last indicated his consent. We went then to the monastery garden, he in the lead, I following, and it must have been a strange pair that we made, but at that early hour not a living soul was about, no one to marvel at the silver praying mantis and the white priest. I told him underneath the larch tree, when he sat, taking on unconsciously—out of habit—the posture of father confessor, that is, not looking at me but only inclining his head in my direction, I told him that first, before I ever set out on the trail, I had been a young woman destined by the King's will for Arrhodes, whom I met at the court ball, and that I had loved him, not knowing anything about him, and without thought embarked upon the love that I had wakened in him, till from the puncture in the night I realized what I might be for him, and seeing no other salvation for either of us I had stabbed myself with a knife, but instead of death a metamorphosis befell me. From then on the compulsion which previously I had only suspected set me on the heels of my beloved, and I became to him a persecuting Fury. However the chase had lasted, and lasted so long, that everything the people said of Arrhodes began to reach my ears, and while I did not know how much truth lay in it, I began once more to brood on our common fate and a liking for this man rose up in me, for I saw that I wanted desperately to kill him, for the reason that I could not any longer love him. Thus I beheld my own baseness, that is, my love turned inside-out, degraded, and craving vengeance on one whose only crime against me was his own misfortune. Therefore I wished now to discontinue the chase, and to cease arousing mortal fear around me, yes, I wished to remedy the evil, yet knew not how.

As far as I could tell, the monk by the end of this discourse had still not cast off his distrust, for he had straightway warned me, before I even began to speak, that whatever I might say would not bear the stamp of a confession, since in his judgment I represented a creature devoid of free will. And too, he might well have asked himself whether I had not been sent to him intentionally, indeed such spies existed, and in the most perfidious disguises, but his answer appeared to proceed from honest thought. He said: And what if you should find the one you seek? Do you know what you will do then?

I replied: Father, I only know what I do not wish to do, but I do not know what power slumbering in me might force its way out then, and therefore I cannot say that I would not be made to murder.

He said to me: What advice then can I give you? Do you wish that this task be taken from you?

Like a dog lying at his feet I lifted up my head and, seeing him squint in the glare of sunlight reflected off the silver of my skull, said: There is nothing I desire more, although I realize that my fate would then be cruel, as I would have no longer any goal before me. I did not plan the thing for which I was created, and will surely have to pay, and pay dearly, for transgressing against the royal will, because such transgression cannot be permitted to go unpunished, and so I shall in turn become the target of the armorers in the palace vaults and they will send a pack of metal hounds out into the world, to destroy me. And even should I escape, making use of the skills that have been placed in me, and go to the very ends of the world, in whatever spot I hide myself all things will shun me and I shall find nothing for which it would be worth continuing my existence. And too, a fate such as yours is closed to me, since each one in authority like yourself will tell me—as you have told me—that I am not spiritually free, therefore I cannot avail myself of the refuge of a cloister!

He grew thoughtful, then showed surprise and said: I am not versed in the construction of your kind, nevertheless I see and hear you and you seem to me, from what you say, to be an intelligent being, though possibly thrall to a limiting compulsion; yet if, as you indeed tell me, you struggle with this compulsion, O machine, and furthermore state that you would feel yourself delivered if the will to murder were to be taken from you, tell me then, just how does this will feel? How is it with you?

I replied: Father, maybe it is not well with me, but concerning how to hunt, track, detect, ferret out, lie in wait, stalk, sneak and lurk, and also smash obstacles standing in the way, cover traces, backtrack, double back and circle, concerning all of this I am extremely knowledgeable and to perform such operations with unfailing skill, turning myself into a sentence of relentless doom, gives me satisfaction, which no doubt was designedly inscribed by fire into my bowels.

"I ask you once again," he said, "tell me, what will you do when you see Arrhodes?"

"Father, I tell you once again that I do not know, for though I wish him no evil, that which is written within me may prove more powerful than what I wish."

Upon hearing this, he covered his eyes with his hand and said: "You are my sister."

"How am I to understand that?" I asked, astonished.

"Exactly as I say it," he said, "and it means I neither raise myself above you nor humble myself before you, for however much we may differ, your ignorance, which you have confessed to me and which I believe, makes us equals in the face of Providence. That being so, come with me and I shall show you something."

We went, one after the other, through the monastery garden, and came to an old woodshed, the monk pushed and the creaking door opened, in the dimness inside I made out a dark form lying on a bundle of straw, and a smell entered my lungs through my nostrils, a smell I had pursued incessantly, and so strong here, that I felt my sting stir of its own accord and emerge from its ventral sheath, but in the next instant my vision grew accustomed to the darkness and I perceived my error. On the straw lay only discarded clothes. The monk saw by my trembling that I was greatly agitated, and he said: Yes, Arrhodes was here. He hid in our monastery a month ago, when he had succeeded in throwing you off the scent. He regretted that he was unable to work as before, and so secretly notified his followers, who sometimes visited him at night, but two traitors sneaked in among them and carried him off five days ago.

"Do you mean to say 'agents of the King'?" I asked, still quivering and prayerfully pressing to my breast my crossed arms.

"No, I say 'traitors,' for they abducted him by a ruse and using force; the little deaf-mute boy whom we took in, he alone saw them leave at dawn, Arrhodes bound and with a knife held to his throat."

"Abducted him?" I asked, not understanding. "Who? To what place? For what reason?"

"In order, I think, to have use of his mind. We cannot appeal to the law for help, for the law is the King's. Therefore they will force him to serve them, and if he refuses they will kill him and go unpunished."

"Father," I said, "praised be the hour in which I made

so bold as to approach you and speak. I will go now on the trail of the abductors and free Arrhodes. I know how to hunt, how to track down, there is nothing I do better, only show me the right direction, known to you from the words of the mute!"

He replied: And yet you do not know whether you will be able to restrain yourself, you admitted as much to me!

To which I said: That is so, however I think that I will find a way. I have no clear idea as yet—perhaps I will seek out a skillful master craftsman, who will find in me the right circuit and change it, such that my desire becomes my destiny.

The monk said: Before you set out you may, if you like, consult with one of our brothers, because before he joined us he was, in the world, conversant with precisely such arts. He serves us now as a physician.

We were standing once more in the sunny garden, and though he gave no indication of it, I understood that still he did not trust me. The scent had dissipated in the course of five days, thus he could have given me the wrong as well as the right direction. I consented.

The physician examined me, maintaining the necessary caution, shining a dark lantern inside my body through the chinks of my interabdominal rims, and this with the utmost care and concentration. Then he stood, brushed the dust from his habit and said:

"It often happens that a machine sent out with these sort of instructions is waylaid by the condemned man's family or his friends, or by other persons who for reasons unknown to the authorities attempt to foil their plans. In order to prevent this, the prudent armorers of the King lock such contents hermetically and connect them with the core in such a way that any tampering whatever must prove fatal. After the placing of the final seal even they cannot remove the sting. Thus it is with you. It also often happens that the victim disguises himself in different clothing, alters his appearance, his behavior and odor, but his mind he cannot alter and hence the machine does not content itself with using the lower and upper senses of smell to hunt, but puts questions to the quarry, questions devised by the foremost experts on the individual characteristics of the human psyche. Thus it is with you also. In addition, I see in your interior a mechanism which none of your predecessors possessed, a multiple memory of things superfluous to a hunting machine, for these are recorded feminine histories, filled with names and turns of phrase that lure the mind, and a conductor runs from them down into the fatal core. Therefore you are a machine perfected in a way unknown to me, and perhaps even an ultimate machine. To remove your sting without at the same time producing the usual result is impossible."

"I will need my sting," I said, still lying on my back, "as I must rush to the aid of the abducted one."

"As for whether you will succeed, if making every effort, in restraining the releases that are poised above the core of which we speak, I cannot tell you yes or no," continued the physician, as though he hadn't heard my words. "I can do—if you wish—one thing only, namely, I can sprinkle the poles of the place in question with finely ground particles of iron using a tube. This would increase somewhat the bounds of your freedom. Yet even if I do this, you will not know up until the last moment whether, in rushing to the aid of someone, you are not still an obedient tool against him."

Seeing them both look at me, I agreed to submit to this operation, which did not take long, it caused me no pain but then neither did it produce in my mental state any

perceptible change. To gain their trust even more, I asked
if they would allow me to spend the night in the
monastery, the entire day having passed in talk,
deliberations and auscultations. They willingly agreed,
but I devoted that time to a thorough examination of the
woodshed, familiarizing myself with the smell of the
abductors. I was capable of this, because it sometimes
happens that a King's agent finds its way blocked not by
the victim himself, but by some other daredevil. Before
daybreak I lay down on the straw where for many nights
had slept the one allegedly abducted, and motionless I
breathed in his odor, waiting for the monks. For I
reasoned that if they had deceived me with some fabricated
story, then they would fear my vengeful return from the
false trail, therefore this darkest hour at early dawn would
suit their purpose best, if they meant to destroy me. I lay,
pretending to be deep in sleep, alert to the slightest sound
coming from the garden, for they could barricade the door
from the outside and set fire to the woodshed, in order that
the fruit of my womb tear me asunder in flames. They
would not even have to overcome their characteristic
repugnance for murder, inasmuch as they considered me
to be not a person but merely a machine of death; my
remains they could bury in the garden and nothing would
happen to them. I did not really know what I would do if I
heard them approach, and never learned, since that did
not come about. And so I remained alone with my
thoughts, in which recurred over and over the amazing
words spoken by the elder monk as he looked into my eyes,
You are my sister. I still could not understand them, but
when I bent over them something warm spread through
my being and transformed me, it was as if I had lost a
heavy fetus, with which I had been pregnant. In the
morning however I ran out through the half-open gate

and, steering clear of the monastery buildings according to the monk's directions, headed full speed for the mountains visible on the horizon—for there he had aimed my pursuit.

I hastened greatly and by noon more than one hundred miles separated me from the monastery. I tore like a shell between the white birches, and when I ran straight through the high grass of the foothill meadows, it fell on either side as if beneath the measured strokes of a scythe.

The track of both abductors I found in a deep valley, on a small bridge thrown across rapid water, but not a hint of Arrhodes's scent, so regardless of the effort they must have taken turns carrying him, which gave evidence of their cunning as well as knowledge, since they realized no one has the right to replace the King's machine in its mission, and that they were incurring the monarch's great displeasure by their deed. No doubt you would like to know what my true intentions were in that final run, and so I will tell you that I tricked the monks, and yet I did not trick them, for I truly desired to regain or rather gain my freedom, indeed I had never possessed it. However concerning what I intended to do with that freedom, I do not know what confession to make. This uncertainty was nothing new, while sinking the knife into my naked body I also did not know whether I wished to kill or only discover myself, even if one was to have meant the other. That step too had been foreseen, as all subsequent events revealed, and thus the hope of freedom could have been just an illusion, nor even my own illusion, but introduced in me in order that I move with more alacrity, urged on precisely by the application of that perfidious spur. But as for saying whether freedom would have amounted simply to renouncing Arrhodes, I do not know. Even being completely free, I could have killed him, for I was not so mad as to believe in the impossible miracle of reciprocated love now that I had ceased to be a woman, and if perchance I was yet a woman in some way, how was Arrhodes, who had seen the opened belly of his naked mistress, to believe this? And so the wisdom of my creators transcended the farthest limits of mechanical craftsmanship, for without a doubt in their calculations they had provided for this state also, in which I hurried to the aid of him who was lost to me forever. And had I been able to turn aside and go off wherever my steps led me, then too I would not be rendering him any great service, I big with death, having no one to whom to bear it. I think therefore that I was nobly base and by freedom compelled to do not that which was commanded me directly, but that which in my incarnation I myself desired. Thorny ruminations, and vexing in their uselessness, yet they would be settled at the goal. By killing the abductors and saving my beloved, in that way forcing him to exchange the disgust and fear he felt towards me for helpless admiration, I might regain— if not him, then at least myself.

Having forged through a dense thicket of hazels, beneath the first terraces I suddenly lost the scent. I searched for it in vain, here it was and there it vanished, as if the ones pursued had flown up into the sky. Returning to the copse, as prudence dictated, I found—not without difficulty—a shrub from which several of the thicker branches had been cut. So I sniffed the stumps oozing hazel sap and, going back to where the trail disappeared, discovered its continuation in the smell of hazel, because the ones fleeing had made use of stilts, aware that the trail of the upper scent would not last long in the air, swept away by the mountain wind. This sharpened my will; soon the hazel smell grew weak, but here again I saw through the ruse employed—the ends of the stilts they had wrapped in the shreds of a burlap sack.

By an overhanging rock lay the discarded stilts. The clearing here was strewn with giant boulders overgrown with moss on the north side and so piled up together that the only way to cross that field of rubble was by leaping from one rock to the other. This too the escapers had done, but not in a straight line, they had weaved and zigzagged, therefore I was obliged constantly to crawl down from the rocks, run around them in a circle and catch the particles of scent trembling in the air. Thus I reached the cliff up which they had climbed—so they must have freed the hands of their captive, but I was not surprised that he went with them of his own accord, for he could not have turned back. I climbed, following the clear spoor, the triple odor on the warm surface of the stone, though it became necessary to ascend vertically, by rocky ledges, troughs, clefts, and there was no clump of gray moss nestled in the crevice of a crag nor any tiny chink that could give a brief purchase to the feet which the fleeing ones had not used as a step, halting every now and then in the more difficult places to study the way ahead, which I could tell from the intensification of their odor there, but I myself raced up barely touching the rock and I felt my pulse strengthening within, felt it play and sing in magnificent pursuit, for these people were prey worthy of me and I felt admiration for them and also joy, because whatever they had accomplished in that perilous ascent, moving in threesome and securing themselves with a line whose jute smell remained on the sharp ledges, I accomplished alone and easily, and nothing was able to hurl me from that aerial path. At the summit I was met by a tremendous wind that whipped across the ridge like a knife, and I did not look back to see the green landscape spread out below, its horizons fading into the blue of the air, but instead, hurrying along the length of the ridge in either direction, I searched for further traces, and found them finally in a minute nick. Then suddenly a whitish scrape and a chipping marked the fall of one of the escapers, therefore leaning out over the brink of a rock I peered down and saw him, small, lying halfway down the mountain side, and the sharpness of my vision permitted me to make out even the dark spattering on the limestones, as if for a moment around the prone man there had fallen a rain of blood. The others however had gone on along the ridge, and at the thought that now I had only one opponent left guarding Arrhodes I felt disappointment, because never before had I had such a sense of the momentousness of my actions and experienced such an eagerness for battle, an eagerness that both sobered and intoxicated me. So I ran down a slope, for my prey had taken that direction, having left the dead man in the precipice, unquestionably they were in a hurry and his instantaneous death from the drop must have been obvious. I approached a craggy pass like the ruin of a giant cathedral, of which only the huge pillars of the broken gate remained, and the adjoining side buttresses, and one high window through which the sky shone, and silhouetted against it—a slender, sickly tree; in its unconscious heroism it had grown there from a seed, planted by the wind in a handful of dust. After the pass was another, higher mountain gorge, partly enveloped in mist, covered over by a trailing cloud out of which there fell a finely sparkling snow. In the shadow thrown by one turret of rock I heard a loose, pebbly sound, then thunder, and a landslide came rumbling down the slope. Stones pummeled me, till sparks and smoke issued from my sides, but then I drew all my legs under me and dropped into a shallow recess beneath a boulder, where in safety I waited for the last rocks to descend. The thought came to me that the hunted one guarding Arrhodes had chosen by design a place of avalanches he knew, on the chance that I, being unfamiliar with mountains, might set off an avalanche and be crushed—and though this was only a slight possibility, it raised my spirits, for if my opponent did not merely flee and evade but also could attack, then the contest grew more worthy.

At the bottom of the next gorge, which was white with snow, stood a building, not a house, not a castle, erected with such massive stones that not even a giant could have moved one single-handed—and I realized it had to be the enemy's retreat, for where else in this wilderness? And so, no longer bothering to find the scent, I began to lower myself, digging my back legs into the shifting rubble, with my front legs practically skimming over the powdered fragments, and the middle pair I used to brake this downward slide, in order that it not become a headlong plunge, until I reached the first snow and noiselessly now proceeded across it, testing every step so as not to drop into some bottomless crevice. I had to be cautious, for that one expected my appearance precisely from the pass, therefore I did not draw too near, lest I become visible from the walls of the fortress, and then, squeezing myself under a mushroom-shaped stone, I patiently waited for night to fall.

It grew dark quickly, but the snow still sifted down and whitened the gloom; because of this I didn't dare approach the building, but only rested my head on my crossed legs in such a way as to keep the building within view. After midnight the snow stopped, but I did not shake it from myself, for it made me resemble my surroundings, and from the sliver of moon between the clouds it shone like the bridal gown that I had never worn. Slowly I began to crawl towards the misty outline of the stronghold, not taking my eyes off the window on the second floor, in which a yellowish light was glimmering, but I lowered my heavy lids, for the moon dazzled and I was accustomed to the dark. It seemed to me that something moved in that dimly lit window, as if a large shadow had swept across a wall, so I crawled faster, till I came to the foundation. Meter by meter I began to scale the battlement, and this was not difficult, as the stones had no mortar joints and were held in place only by their enormous weight. Thus I reached the lower windows, which loomed black like parapet loopholes intended for the mouths of cannons. They all gaped dark and empty. And inside too such silence reigned, it was as though death had been the only occupant here for ages. To see better, I activated my night vision and, putting my head inside the stone chamber, opened the luminous eyes of my antennae, from which issued forth a phosphorescent glow. I found myself facing a grimy fireplace made of rough flagging, in which a few split logs and slightly charred twigs had grown cold long ago. I saw also a bench and rusted utensils by the wall, a crumpled bed and some sort of stone-hard rolls of bread in the corner. It struck me odd that nothing here was preventing my entrance, I didn't trust this beckoning emptiness, and though at the other end of the room the door stood open, perhaps for that very reason sensing a trap, I withdrew as I had entered, without a sound, to resume my climb to the top floor. The window from which the faint light came—I did not even consider approaching it. Finally I scrambled up onto the roof and, finding myself on its snow-covered surface, lay down like a dog keeping watch, to wait for day. I heard two voices, but could not tell what they were saying. I lay motionless, both longing for and fearing the moment when I would leap upon my opponent to free

Arrhodes, and tensed like a taut coil, wordlessly picturing the course of the struggle that would be ended by a sting; at the same time I looked within myself, now no longer seeking there a source of will, but trying to find some small indication, even the smallest, as to whether I would kill only one man. I cannot say at what point this fear left me. I lay, still uncertain, for not knowing myself, yet that very ignorance of whether I had come as a rescuer or as a murderess—it became for me something hitherto unknown, inexplicably new, investing my every tremor with a mysterious and girlish innocence, it filled me with an overwhelming joy. This joy surprised me not a little and I wondered if it might not be another manifestation of the wisdom of my inventors, who had seen to it that I find limitless power in the bringing of both succor and destruction, however I was not certain of this either. A sudden, short noise, followed by a babbling voice, reached me from below—one more sound, a hollow thud, as of a heavy object falling, then silence. I started to crawl down from the roof, nearly bending my abdomen in two, such that with the chest-half of the body I clung to the wall, while my back pair of legs and the tube of the sting still rested on the edge of the roof, until with my head shaking from the strain I approached, hanging, the open window.

The candle, thrown to the floor, had gone out, but its wick still glowed red, and by exerting my nocturnal vision I saw beneath the table a body, recumbent, streaming blood—black in that light—and although everything within me yearned to spring, I first sniffed the air redolent of blood and stearin: this man was a stranger to me, therefore a struggle had taken place and Arrhodes slew him before me. The how, why and when of it never crossed my mind, for the fact that I was alone with him, and he alive, in this empty house, that there were now only the two of us, hit me like a thunderbolt. I trembled—bride and butcher—noting at the same time with an unblinking eye the rhythmic twitches of that large body as it breathed its last. If I could only leave now, steal softly away into the world of snow and mountains, anything rather than remain with him face to face—face to feeler, that is—I added, doomed to the monstrous and the comic no matter what I did, and the sense of being mocked and jeered at tipped the scale, pushed me so that I slid down, still suspended headfirst like a wary spider and, no longer caring about the screech of my ventral plates across the sill, in a nimble arc leaped over the corpse, and was at the door.

I don't know how or when I broke it down. Across the threshold were winding stairs and on them, on his back, Arrhodes, the head twisted back and propped against worn stone, they must have fought on these stairs, that was the reason almost nothing of it had reached me, so here at my feet he lay, his ribs were moving, I saw—yes—his nakedness, the nakedness I had not known, but imagined only, that first night at the ballroom.

He gave a rattle, I watched as he tried to lift his lids, they opened, first the whites, and I, rearing, with a bent abdomen, I gazed down into his upturned face, not daring to touch him nor retreat, for while he lived I could not be certain of myself, though the blood was leaving him with every breath, yet I clearly saw that my duty extended up until the very last, because the King's sentence must be executed even in the throes of death, therefore I could not take the risk, inasmuch as he was still alive, nor indeed did I know if I truly desired him to wake. Had he opened his eyes and been conscious, and—in an inverted view— taken me in entirely, exactly as I stood over him, stood now powerlessly carrying death, in a gesture of supplication, pregnant but not from him, would that have been a wedding—or its unmercifully arranged parody?

But he did not open his eyes in consciousness and when dawn entered between us in puffs of finely sparkling snow from the windows, through which the whole house howled with the mountain blizzard, he groaned once more and ceased to breathe, and only then, my mind at rest, did I lie down beside him, and wrapped him tightly in my arms, and I lay thus in the light and in the darkness through two days of snowstorm, which covered our bed with a sheet that did not melt. And on the third day the sun came up.

Books by Stanislaw Lem
available in Harvest/HBJ paperback editions from
Harcourt Brace Jovanovich, Publishers

The Chain of Chance

The Cyberiad: Fables for the Cybernetic Age

Eden

Fiasco

The Futurological Congress

His Master's Voice

Hospital of the Transfiguration

Imaginary Magnitude

The Investigation

Memoirs Found in a Bathtub

Memoirs of a Space Traveler: Further Reminiscences of Ijon Tichy

Microworlds: Writings on Science Fiction and Fantasy

More Tales of Pirx the Pilot

Mortal Engines

One Human Minute

A Perfect Vacuum

Return from the Stars

Solaris

The Star Diaries

Tales of Pirx the Pilot